Hot Nights

"I missed you so much, Michael!" she cried, standing on tiptoe to plant a welcoming kiss on his cheek.

"Me, too!" he said, hugging her tightly and bending his head toward hers. Before Phoebe knew what was happening, Michael's lips met hers in the dark and his greeting turned into a long kiss. For a dizzying moment she responded with her whole self. In the next second her body tensed. She turned her head away in confusion and curled her toes in the dirt.

Suddenly Phoebe saw as clear as day that Michael had been biding his time for three whole months now, waiting patiently for her broken heart to heal. Ever since May he had been so careful not to touch her — not that way. Phoebe closed her eyes. In spite of the August heat, she shivered. Michael had waited long enough, and in her heart Phoebe knew their kiss hadn't been a mistake.

Books from Scholastic
in the **Couples** series:

Coming Soon . . .

SUMMER HEAT!

M. E. Cooper

SCHOLASTIC INC.
New York Toronto London Auckland Sydney

The lyrics from "Summertime" by Dubose Heyward & George Gershwin are reprinted by permission of Chappell/Intersong Music Group USA. Copyright © 1935 by Gershwin Publishing Corp. Copyright renewed, assigned to Chappell & Co., Inc., International Copyright Secured. ALL RIGHTS RESERVED.

ISBN 0-590-40236-6

Copyright © 1986 by Cloverdale Press. All rights reserved. Published by Scholastic Inc.

12 11 10 9 8 7 6 5 4 3 2 1   7   6 7 8 9/8 0 1/9

SUMMER HEAT!

Chapter 1

Phoebe Hall knelt in the grass looking for her barrette. The sun had already set and the last batch of burgers sizzled on the grill. Her friend Chris Austin sat beside her, her back propped against the picnic table, dreamily running her fingers through Ted Mason's hair. Chris surveyed the crowded backyard of the Halls' mountain cabin and said with a contented sigh, "This party's the best one yet, Pheeb!"

Ted opened his eyes, groaned, and began fanning himself dramatically with his hand. "It's certainly your hottest party yet — "

Phoebe sat back on her heels and looked from Chris to Ted. "Oh, I don't know, Ted," Phoebe said slowly, a wicked gleam lighting up her big green eyes. "Remember last year's barbecue — when Woody came stomping and growling through the woods?"

Ted lifted his head from Chris's lap and hooted. "Remember?" Chris and Phoebe doubled over with laughter.

"I almost died!" Chris gasped, wiping tears from her eyes. "There we were in the pines and for a minute I thought it was Phoebe's dad pouncing on us."

"Webster has the nerve to pride himself on his timing!" Ted snorted. Chris blushed scarlet and Phoebe giggled as Ted affectionately ruffled Chris's silky blonde hair and pulled her down beside him on the grass. Chris wound her arms around his neck. Phoebe smiled. A year ago Chris never would have let Ted kiss her like that, not in front of so many people.

Phoebe turned away and groped under the table for her barrette. Yes, this year's party was almost perfect, she thought. Phoebe gave a little sigh. Ted and Chris were so much in love. Watching couples in love was beginning to make her feel left out and very alone.

A car door slammed and Phoebe scrambled to her feet. She pushed her thick red hair out of her eyes and peered into the dusk beyond the circle of light cast by her mother's old paper lanterns. At the end of a long line of cars parked along the dirt road, headlights went off on a van. A tall figure started up the grass toward her. "Michael! You're here," Phoebe shouted, "just like you promised." She whooped and ran barefoot across the lawn straight into Michael Rifkin's arms.

"I missed you so much, Michael!" she cried, standing on tiptoe to plant a welcoming kiss on

2

his cheek.

"Me, too!" he said, hugging her tightly and bending his head toward hers. Before Phoebe knew what was happening, Michael's lips met hers in the dark and his greeting turned into a long kiss. For a dizzying moment she responded with her whole self. In the next second her body tensed. She turned her head away in confusion and curled her toes in the dirt.

"Rifkin — " Peter Lacey yelled from across the yard. Michael's hands abruptly fell from Phoebe's shoulders and she quickly stepped away from his side as Peter approached. Michael's old friend Wanda Davis and her date, Charlie Walker, followed close on his heels. "The barbecue started at four. I mean I've heard of late entrances. You've practically missed all the food!" Peter affectionately whacked Michael on the back.

"Left that much more for us, didn't it?" Charlie said, patting his stomach. He slung his guitar over his shoulder and heartily pumped Michael's hand.

Wanda linked her arm in Michael's as they all headed up the driveway. "Boy, have I missed you — and your music. Rehearsals have been pretty tough the two weeks you've been gone. Charlie's been doing his best to help me out but it's not the same. But tell me, wasn't the festival great, just like I predicted? What were the kids like this year? Is Ned Fenwick still there fiddling square dance tunes on his Stradivarius?"

Michael sank back dramatically against the mailbox. "Give me a break," he groaned. "I just got here. I'm hot and starving. . . . Not that I

3

don't appreciate this warm welcome." He grinned and smoothed his unruly hair off his forehead. He shot a glance at Phoebe. The smile faded from his face. She had fallen a few steps behind them and was intently watching her feet as she walked.

"This place isn't *that* far from Rose Hill — unless you came by way of Alaska," Peter joked.

Michael turned away from Phoebe and forced himself to smile. "Not quite via Alaska, but just about. I've been driving nine hours straight from Massachusetts. There're a lotta miles between here and there! And I have to admit I made a couple of wrong turns," he added sheepishly. "There's a very interesting cow pasture a few miles back. I thought it was 'the dirt road on the left' Phoebe described in her invitation. But it was the cow path on the left. Anyway, it took me longer than I thought it would and I'm absolutely famished."

"Did I hear the word famished?" Chris walked over from the grill carrying a plate heaped with food. "Welcome to the Third Annual Hail Barbecue," she said warmly. "It's your first time up to the cabin, isn't it?" She handed Michael the plate and a soda. He nodded and sat down on the edge of the picnic table.

The barbecue was in full swing. Michael hadn't expected the party to be so big. He knew about half the kids. A slow bluesy tune drifted across the yard and he could see a couple dancing very close on the screened-in porch. A child's metal swing set glinted in the lantern lights, and beyond that a lopsided wire fence enclosed what Michael

4

supposed was Phoebe's garden. She had written him about it. He smiled when he spied the droopy silhouettes of the sunflowers Phoebe had described as nearly twice as tall as herself. Where the forest began, tall pines veiled all but the top of the rising full moon. Michael gazed at the moon, then looked around for Phoebe but she was nowhere in sight. With a sigh, he set down his plate and began answering Wanda's questions about his stint at a summer music festival in Massachusetts.

Phoebe had slipped to the outskirts of the group gathered around Michael. She hid in the shadows of the old apple tree, her fingers resting lightly on her lips. Michael's kiss had taken her completely off guard. So had her own response. She hadn't wanted it to stop, even wished she were still kissing him now. She leaned against the tree and pressed her hands to her temples, not sure if she was about to shout for joy or burst into tears. Phoebe hugged the thick gnarled trunk, and pressing her cheek against the scratchy bark, looked up. Touching the tree seemed to ground her. If there hadn't been a party going on she would have climbed up into its familiar branches just to be by herself and think. When she was ten years old, climbing a tree and just sitting there thinking used to solve all her problems, even the humiliation the time her fifth grade best friend Carrie Alson told her all the boys at day camp hated her because she was fat and had red hair and was afraid to jump in the deep part of the lake.

5

But life at almost seventeen was far more complicated than life at ten, and Phoebe wasn't afraid of jumping into lakes anymore — only of jumping into another relationship. She couldn't bear being hurt again. Didn't Michael realize that? What could he have been thinking when he kissed her? Maybe it was just some crazy mistake. Phoebe glanced toward Michael, searching for an answer.

His back was turned toward her and he was gesturing as he talked. Every so often he'd run his fingers through his tangled dark hair. Phoebe had a crazy impulse to run up to him, throw her arms around his neck, and kiss him — right in front of everyone. But she couldn't. No matter how lonely she felt, she was afraid of falling in love again. So she hugged her arms to herself and kicked forlornly at a clump of dandelions, trying to stop the quivering in the pit of her stomach. But the more she watched Michael, the more quivery she felt. And then she had another very scary feeling — as scary as falling in love: How much longer would a great looking, incredibly popular guy like Michael Rifkin be available? If she could ever face love again, would he still be there waiting for her? Suddenly Phoebe saw as clear as day that Michael had been biding his time for three whole months now, waiting patiently for her broken heart to heal. Ever since May he had been so careful not to touch her — not that way. Phoebe closed her eyes. In spite of the August heat, she shivered. Michael had waited long

6

enough, and in her heart Phoebe knew their kiss hadn't been a mistake.

The last time they had kissed that way was the night of the prom. They had been alone in the deserted bleachers of the school stadium when Phoebe had burst into tears over her breakup with her boyfriend Griffin Neill. Michael had talked to her a long time, soothing her, calming her, but she couldn't stop crying. Finally he had taken her in his arms. When he began kissing her, she had kissed him back, wishing, hoping, pretending that she would open her eyes and the tall, tuxedoed guy she was holding would be not Michael Rifkin, her singing teacher's son, but Griffin, whom she still loved.

Phoebe felt awful about that night, as if in some weird way she had been using Michael. She had pulled away from him and apologized and tried to explain how mixed up she felt. He looked hurt but seemed to understand. Still, the next morning Phoebe woke up feeling so embarrassed and confused that she never wanted to see him again.

But two days later Michael turned up again. And the next day and the next: at her house, at school, at her singing lessons. And he just kept smiling his big, warm smile as if nothing bad had happened between them. He never mentioned the prom again. Neither did she. Their relationship had weathered the awkwardness and blossomed into a warm, comfortable friendship; now he was as close to Phoebe as Chris, or Sasha or Woody, her oldest, dearest friends. Except for a friendly peck on the cheek or casual hug, Michael had hardly touched her. And she had liked it that way, because as she had patiently explained to Chris all summer, Michael was just a friend. Phoebe had believed that with all her heart, just like she had really believed she would never fall in love again, not after Griffin.

"Pheeberooni!"

"Woody! You scared me!" Phoebe jumped. A blush worked its way up her neck and covered her face.

"Sorry!" Woody Webster slapped his hand over his heart and bowed, doffing his Orioles baseball cap. "So, what's up? I mean, the party's there and you're here." He gestured toward Michael and a group of kids listening to Ted.

"Uh, nothing, Woody. I just needed to be alone." Phoebe rubbed her temples again. "A little headache — the heat — you know."

Woody solemnly shook his head no, then wriggled his ears and stared bug-eyed at Phoebe.

"Stop that, Woody." Phoebe laughed in spite of herself. She wasn't exactly in the mood for Woody's clowning, but at least laughing made the blush die down.

"Okay, I'll stop," Woody said obediently and dropped to the ground. He folded his long legs into a lopsided lotus position and patted the ground next to him. "If you'll sit beside me on my cozy sofa here, I'll control myself, on one condition."

Phoebe didn't take up the offer to join him on

the grass, and eyed him skeptically. She was having a hard time following Woody's mental gymnastics. She just wanted to be alone and figure out what was happening between Michael and her. But to be polite she asked, "What's that?" She lifted her hair up off her neck and fanned her face with her hand. She wished she had found her barrette before Michael had come. She was feeling terribly sticky and probably looked a mess.

"That we have a heart-to-heart. Here and now. Just you and me. Webster and Hall."

Phoebe stopped fanning herself. "A heart-to-heart?" she repeated and looked down at Woody's face. In the shadows she couldn't make out his expression, but his voice sounded serious. Maybe something had happened between Kim and him. They hadn't been together much all afternoon. But as disloyal as it made her feel, Phoebe couldn't talk to Woody now. Tomorrow maybe. It probably wasn't serious at all. No doubt Woody Webster was about to pull this year's Barbecue Prank. He probably needed Phoebe's help for whatever he had up his sleeve. "Webster, your timing is horrendous."

"What a vile accusation!" Woody grabbed a dandelion, stretched himself out, and with a mighty sigh, kicked his feet in the air and played dead.

Phoebe laughed. "Look, Woody, I'm sorry. You can be alive again. Your timing is fine, really. It's just mine that's off. Can't we talk later or Monday when I get back to Rose Hill?"

Woody sprang to his feet. "Um — I guess so.

I mean if you really can't now. Except Phoebe —
I don't mean to sound so mysterious — it's just
really important. That's all." Woody hooked his
thumbs in his red suspenders and regarded
Phoebe intently. "Yeah, later's okay, but we've
gotta talk tonight." He sounded to Phoebe as if
he were trying to convince himself of something.
"It's important."

"Uh-oh — so's this!" Phoebe suddenly motioned toward the picnic table and Ted.

Kennedy High's star quarterback vaulted up
onto the table. He reached down beside him and
tried to pull Chris up by his side. She laughingly
backed off. He straightened up and clapped his
hands for attention. "Hey, Lacey, turn down the
sound. I've got an announcement." When shouting didn't work he stomped his foot a couple of
times on the weathered pine boards. Finally Chris
and Wanda took up the cry. "Pipe down, everyone, Ted has an announcement."

"Now — *team* — " Ted started, and was
greeted with a chorus of groans.

"Watch out, Mason," Brad yelled from the
porch steps where he was sitting with Brenda on
his lap. "Not everyone's on your team here."

"Speak for yourself, Davidson," Ted countered
good-naturedly, then continued. "Listen, we're
all having a great time at this party. Right?"

"Right!" everyone except Phoebe shouted.

"In spite of the fact it's nine P.M. And it's
ninety-five degrees. And everyone's melting," Ted
said.

"That's because Phoeberooni throws the best,

10

happiest, craziest parties in town!" Woody shouted from under the tree.

"Right on — and out of town, too, I might add!" Ted cheered. "Three cheers for Phoebe — " After the cheers, he looked around the yard, a puzzled expression crossing his face. "Speaking of Phoebe, where is she?"

"Here." Phoebe stepped out of the shadows, giving a silly three-fingered wave. She knew Michael had turned around and was looking at her. She tried to avoid his gaze and focused her attention on Ted's little speech. She was feeling rather grateful for Ted's theatrics — his timing had been perfect. He had rescued her from Woody and whatever that heart-to-heart was about. Phoebe just wasn't in the mood for confidences right now — about practical jokes or relationships. Still she had a funny feeling that wherever Ted's performance was leading, Chris wasn't going to like it. Ted had that crazy, impulsive look about him that meant he was about to do something Chris would no doubt think was out-of-bounds.

"So, Mason, we all know we love Phoebe and Phoebe's parties," Kim Barrie broke in impatiently. "Now can we get back to dancing and having fun? We've all got to start heading back soon."

"Party pooper!" Ted scooped some popcorn off the table and fired it at Kim. "As far as I'm concerned, the evening's just begun." He turned and winked at Chris, who blushed furiously. "Now look, everyone — over there behind the

11

garden, above those tall trees, what do you see?"

All heads turned. "A full moon!" Janie Barstow cried excitedly. "Oh, Henry, isn't it beautiful," she said, turning to her boyfriend.

"Looks like cheese to me," Kim blurted out. "A big wheel of beautiful imported camembert."

"Leave it to Kim to be romantic," Woody groaned, snapping his suspenders against his tanned bare chest, and pulling Kim over to his side. Phoebe breathed a sigh of relief. At least whatever was ailing Woody had nothing to do with Kim. They looked pretty lovey-dovey to her. She stole a glance at Michael. He was standing only a few feet away. Charlie was between them, so she couldn't quite see his face. But she could tell he wasn't looking at her anymore. She didn't know if she felt relieved or disappointed.

"Well, we're all — or rather most of us — agreed that is a moon. A big full moon and we're all dying of the heat. Right?" Ted eyed the crowd wickedly.

"Right!" everyone answered.

"Hey, he's got brains as well as brawn — this guy can really reason!" Brad taunted.

Ted ignored Brad's comment. He ticked off points on his fingers. "So — number one, it's hot. Number two — it's August. Number three — there's a big, fat full moon hanging in the sky. And what that all adds up to is — " Ted paused for effect " — *a moonlight swim!*"

"Brilliant, Mason!" Brad applauded.

Everyone else cheered except Chris.

"A what?" Chris frowned. But no one heard

12

her. "Hey, wait a minute." She raised her voice. "Ted Mason, you're nuts. Where are we going to go swimming? In Phoebe's bathtub?"

"Good idea!" Woody quipped. "We'll be packed in like a bunch of sardines in cool well water — just like Sasha Jenkins' favorite treat from the health food store."

"Come off it, Woody," Sasha punched him in the arm.

Ted grinned affectionately at Chris. "No, silly. How can president of the student body and head of the honor society act so dumb?" Ted scolded, then he playfully tousled Chris's hair. "Right down the road is the Fillmore Nature Preserve and Lost Lake. It's got a great beach and — "

"You know as well as I do, state parks close at sundown." Chris's voice rose slightly and her frown deepened.

"Oh boy," Woody murmured. "Here we go again."

Kim cleared her throat and raised her eyebrows. "You said it."

Phoebe silently agreed. Arguments between Ted and Chris were becoming more and more frequent. A little while ago they looked so happy together. Now they were about to really lock horns.

"Of course it's past sundown, Chris." Ted jumped off the table and reasoned patiently. "That's why it's a moonlight swim. And it's more romantic to swim in the dark, isn't it?" he added softly, reaching for her hand.

Chris folded her arms across her chest. "Ted,

13

it's against the law. Besides, someone could get hurt. Accidents do happen, and there's no lifeguard," she pointed out. Her clear blue eyes met Ted's, and her expression softened. "Let's not fight about this. I just don't feel it's right. Besides, if Phoebe's parents were around they wouldn't let us." She looked imploringly at Phoebe, and gently touched Ted's arm.

Phoebe gaped at Chris and muttered, "I don't believe this!" Chris had just cast Phoebe in the role of referee and Phoebe didn't like it. What did Chris expect her to do? Before Phoebe could say a word, Ted pulled his arm away from Chris and complained, "Come off it, Chris, I'm not talking about swimming the English Channel — I'm talking about a dip in Lost Lake before we head back to Rose Hill."

Phoebe knew she should do something, say something. Everyone was beginning to look uncomfortable. "Uh — Chris, I don't think it's the law part that would bother my folks," Phoebe improvised. "I mean Dad and Shawn and I have gone swimming at sundown lots of times." She was stretching the truth a bit; they usually did manage to be out of the water by sundown. Still, a white lie to keep the peace here would be forgivable.

Michael gave a dry little laugh and cleared his throat. "I think what Phoebe's saying is they'd only mind the moonlight part." Phoebe caught his eye and he winked at her. She flashed a hesitant smile, as first Sasha, then Kim started giggling. Then everyone but Chris was laughing and the tension was broken.

14

Chris gave Phoebe a disgusted look. Phoebe just pursed her lips. This was her party and Chris had no right to start putting a damper on things. Sometimes Chris's prissiness made her sick.

Michael waited for the laughter to die down, then continued, "Anyway, everyone doesn't have to go swimming, Chris. Just whoever wants to — though I for one am going to find Lost Lake or Lost Lagoon or whatever you call it, and jump right in!"

As everyone started laughing again, Chris grumbled, "That's not the point." She marched across the lawn and flopped down in the hammock.

"Ever the diplomat, Rifkin!" Peter chuckled, slinging one arm around Michael's shoulder. "If you don't make it in music, you've got a great career ahead of you in the State Department."

"I'll second that!" Ted exclaimed, casting a grateful glance at Michael. Avoiding Chris, he strode toward his car to grab his bathing trunks.

But Phoebe didn't think Michael was being the least bit diplomatic. When he said he was going to the lake he had looked directly at her. His whole expression said he wanted her there with him. And Chris or no Chris, and no matter what her parents felt about moonlight, Phoebe knew she was going swimming.

Chapter 2

The group made its way down to the lake in one big, noisy crowd. Phoebe was becoming more and more frustrated as they walked and she found herself fighting back tears. She just wanted a few minutes alone with Michael, to find out what — if anything — was happening between them. But Michael kept walking with Peter — talking about music and about Peter's girl friend Monica Ford and her cousin Jeremy, who was due in at Dulles airport that night from London.

Ted finally jogged on ahead of everyone else — to "try the water on for size," he had shouted, then vanished around a bend in the road. Phoebe suspected Ted was hurting really badly about Chris staying behind and was just running off to lick his wounds — and Phoebe didn't blame him. All this empty moonlight made you feel

16

pretty miserable when you weren't part of a couple.

The first couple to split off from the group was Sasha and her new boyfriend, Rob. They heard a screech owl deep in the pines, and tiptoed off to try to find its perch. Then Janie and Henry and Brad and Brenda quietly dropped out along the way, leaving Phoebe alone with Michael and Peter. Michael fell silent and Phoebe couldn't think of anything to say. Not with Peter there. Finally Peter put on his headphones and headed toward the closed boat rental concession. Then Michael jogged off behind him, yelling something Phoebe couldn't quite hear.

She stood there a second, leaning against a trash can, fiddling with her flipflops and wondering if she should bother going down to the lake at all, or if she should just head back to the house alone. Either way she'd feel pretty dumb, and she certainly didn't want to face Chris, who was probably still fuming about Phoebe's irresponsible behavior. She took a deep breath. No. She'd stay here. Being alone was probably exactly what she needed. And it was cooler down by the lake. After one last glance at Michael and Peter, she kicked a stone across the parking lot and headed down to the waterfront.

She tossed her flowered chintz overalls behind her, and walked down the dock in her one-piece suit, ready for a solitary swim. How could she have possibly imagined Michael had come swimming just to spend time with her? She almost had to laugh as she stood there all alone hanging off

17

the ladder, testing the dark water with her toe. She felt lonely, left out, and foolish.

From her solitary lookout on the pier, Phoebe watched Brenda climb aboard the raft anchored in the middle of the lake. Brad hoisted himself up beside her. Brenda's white bikini glistened beneath the full moon. Next to Brad, Brenda looked very fragile in the eerie light. They stood close on the rocking wooden platform, then Brad pulled Brenda down by his side. It looked so romantic out there, Phoebe thought wistfully as she tied her hair up with a scarf.

"Don't. Don't do that." Michael's soft, musical voice startled Phoebe. He had come up behind her, and gently pushed her hand away from her head. He had changed into a pair of cutoffs. His old white jeans and blue shirt were bunched up in his hand. He took the scarf from her hand and tossed it down with her other stuff. Phoebe's hair fell down her back.

"But my hair," Phoebe said. "It — it'll get all wet." She backed away slightly. The quivering in her stomach had started up again.

Michael shook his head. "It's just . . . I've never seen your hair like that, all free and loose. It suits you, Phoebe."

The way he said it took Phoebe's breath away. She put one hand on the top of the ladder, to steady herself. "Oh, thanks," she said quietly. Her free hand strayed up to her hair, while her eyes focused on the weathered planks at her feet.

She couldn't look up at Michael but she felt him leaning toward her. Phoebe's heart started

18

pounding and her mouth went dry. She took another small step backwards, right off the edge of the dock.

"Oooooh — " she screamed before her back hit the water hard and she went under.

Michael plunged in after her, and even before she surfaced, his arm was firmly around her. She came up sputtering and coughing, her back stinging and feeling bruised. "Pheeb," Michael gasped. He sounded really frightened. "Are you okay? Can you swim? Just hang on to me." Phoebe sneezed and pushed her dripping hair off her face. She tread water trying to catch her breath, and glared at Michael, suddenly feeling very angry and embarrassed. At the look of concern in his dark eyes, Phoebe's anger began to melt away, and a goofy smile started across her face.

"Of course I can swim!" Phoebe started coughing and giggling all at once. Michael looked at her hard, as if he didn't quite believe her, then slicked his hair back and smiled. His smile quickly turned into a hearty laugh. "I guess you can." But he kept his arm around her, guiding her toward the ladder as they kicked their way through the water.

Phoebe tried to cover her embarrassment by talking very fast. "I just hate jumping right in, you know. I'm the type who puts one toe in at a time — very, very slowly — and then a foot, just one foot."

They had reached the ladder, and Phoebe's toes brushed against the mossy first rung. She started to climb up, but turned as Michael laughed behind her. The moonlight reflected off his wet skin.

"Jumping in all at once is better," Michael insisted, kicking his feet occasionally to keep himself afloat. "You get wet all at once, and not as cold. Besides," he added with a wink, "no one teases you as much about being chicken."

"But I'm always so afraid I'll freeze. Or that the water will be too deep. Or I'll dive in and hit my head — you know, all the stuff they scare you with when you're five years old in tadpole swim class at the pool." Phoebe was talking even faster now, suddenly aware of Michael's arms on either side of her as she faced him, half in, half out of the water. His hands were only inches away from her shoulders as he held on to the slick sides of the ladder.

"You shouldn't be so afraid." Michael wasn't smiling now. And Phoebe could no longer pretend they were talking about jumping into lakes. The wooden ladder scraped her back. But she couldn't move away. With one hand Michael tilted Phoebe's chin toward the light. Shadows flickered across the pale skin of her face and arms. The pattern of her suit seemed to dance across his chest in the moonlight.

"Oh, Michael," Phoebe suddenly burst out. "I can't help it. I can't help being this scared." She lowered her voice to a whisper and cast her eyes down toward the water. "I don't want to be afraid. But I am. I really am. I — I don't want to get hurt again," she added, so softly that Michael

20

could hardly make out the words. "I couldn't bear it. And I don't — " Phoebe faltered. "I don't want to hurt you, not again, not like at the prom."

Then Michael's finger was on her lips. Phoebe forced herself to meet his eyes. Then his hand was caressing first her hair, then her shoulder, lingering over the thin strap of her suit. He slowly traced the outline of her throat, her ear, her jaw. This time she didn't move away. The rungs of the ladder pressed hard against her spine as Michael leaned his body into hers. Just before their lips met he whispered, "Phoebe, you'll never have to be afraid — not that way — again."

> *One of these mornin's*
> *You goin' to rise up singin',*
> *then you'll spread yo' wings*
> *an' you'll take the sky.*
> *But till that mornin'*
> *there's a nothin' can harm you*
> *with Daddy and Mammy standin' by.*

As the last few bars of "Summertime" rang out over the yard, Wanda leaned back against a tree, an intense expression on her face. The closing chords of Charlie's mellow accompaniment died down, then faded out.

Woody shook his head in admiration, then led the little burst of applause. "Wanda, you've just gotta do *Porgy and Bess* someday. No one sings like you."

Wanda accepted Woody's compliment graciously, but turned to Charlie. "I don't think Mr. Walker's so bad, either. He's already booked in some Georgetown clubs this winter, and when they find out he sings as good as he looks, they're not going to let him go. I wish I could persuade him to change colleges and head up to New York, though."

"Yeah, Charlie. You'd better clue me to when you've got those bookings. I'll announce them on WKND. Everyone is really dying to hear you strum up a storm. And Wanda, there's no reason we can't do a taped special of a Kennedy High alumni — " Peter suggested enthusiastically, then glanced across the lawn. "Hey, Ted, Brad, you can call off the search party, the lost sheep have found their way home."

Woody turned and the smile left his face. Michael and Phoebe were walking arm-in-arm up the driveway. From the expressions on their faces, Woody knew they weren't just friends anymore.

"Hey, Rifkin, we thought you drowned!" Ted bellowed, striding toward the couple.

Brad placed a restraining hand on Ted's arm. "Leave them alone," he said.

Ted watched Phoebe and Michael, then turned to Woody. "Hey Webster, Phoebe always confides in you. How long's this been going on?"

Woody gave Ted a long hard look and shifted uncomfortably. Ted was obviously still smarting from his argument with Chris and was startled by this new romance in their midst. Woody finally answered Ted with a shrug. "Beats me."

"I think since about an hour ago," Peter said

softly to the other guys. "And it's about time. Phoebe hasn't been herself since Griffin. And Michael hasn't been himself since Phoebe and whatever didn't happen at the prom."

"You guys are worse gossips than girls!" Kim scolded, giving Woody's arm a shake. "Hey Woody, you look like you've seen a ghost. You know it's not the first time friends have fallen in love." She looked lovingly into Woody's eyes, then frowned. She pulled him away from the other kids and asked, "Is something wrong?"

Woody shook his head. "No — not really." He bent down and fiddled with the yellow laces on his red high-topped sneaker.

"Are you upset about Phoebe and Michael?" Kim's voice grew small. Woody straightened his shoulders. He drew her close and kissed her softly on the mouth. He stood like that a minute, not moving, and then said, "Don't be ridiculous, Kim. Since you, I haven't given Phoebe — or any other girl — a second thought. You know that." He poked her glasses further up on her nose, and looked intently into her eyes.

Kim smiled and sighed a contented sigh. "Yes, of course. I know." After an instant, she said, "But something's wrong. All night I've felt it. Do you want to talk about it?"

Woody shook his head no. He gave his suspenders a weak snap and shrugged. "Something is wrong, but it has nothing to do with you or me. Trust me on that."

Kim studied Woody's face. "I trust you," she said.

23

Woody watched Kim go back into the kitchen, then looked around the yard. He needed a couple of minutes alone. He started toward the hammock, then spied Chris walking in the same general direction. Ted was standing alone by the volleyball net, spinning a severely deflated ball on one finger. Chris touched Ted's arm and shyly handed him a soda. Ted took the can, set it down near the net, and pulled Chris over toward the hammock.

"Woody?"

Woody jumped and gulped. "Phoebe." He looked down at her. Her pale cheeks were as pink as the splashy flowers on her overalls, her huge eyes were shining, and for the first time in months she looked alive again. "Phoebe, you look great," Woody said in an affectionate voice.

Phoebe's blush deepened. "Yeah — " She dug at the grass with her bare toe. "I have a couple of minutes now. If you want to talk, that is. I mean before, I couldn't. . . . I — "

"Don't try to explain," Woody interrupted. "How long — I mean, I thought you were just friends," he said, a nervous edge creeping into his voice.

Phoebe giggled. "Me, too — until just now." She grabbed Woody's hand and pulled him over toward Shawn's swing set. "I guess I want to talk to you, too." Phoebe started swinging lazily on a swing, trailing her toes in the dirt. As she talked to Woody, she watched Michael help Peter load sound equipment into Charlie's truck.

24

"Uh, Pheeb — " Woody scraped some rust off the seesaw with his nail. "I think maybe you were right. I — I don't know what got into me earlier. What I had to say — it's not *that* big a deal. I mean, it can wait until next week. When you're back in Rose Hill, just call me. We'll meet after I get off work." Woody jumped on one side of the little seesaw. He balanced his lanky body precariously, as he walked across to the other end, then leapt off. "Look, I promised Kim I'd help inside," he said, hitching up his baggy white pants and hurrying toward the house.

"Sure, Woody!" Phoebe called after him, letting the swing twirl around on its chain. "I'll phone next week, as soon as I get back."

Woody walked quickly toward the porch, keeping his head down. He let the screen door slam behind him, and went to the far, dark end where he flopped down in a sagging wicker chair. Through the screen he watched Michael walk up to Phoebe. His dark head was bent over Phoebe's red one as he began pushing the swing. Higher and higher he pushed her until Phoebe was screeching for him to stop, her shrieks and laughter rippling across the yard.

"Oh, Phoebe!" Woody mumbled morosely. She looked so in love and so happy and so right with Michael. How could he tell her now: Griffin Neill was back in town. And Woody had been so dumb. This morning at the Arena Stage, Griffin had asked him about Phoebe: Did she have a new guy yet? "No, Griffin, not yet. But maybe I'd better talk to her first, before you call. She's had a rough summer, you know." At Woody's reply, Griffin's face had said it all. Griffin Neill was still in love with Phoebe Hall.

Chapter
3

It was the third straight week in a row of record-breaking temperatures. And the third straight Sunday the Rose Hill Community Pool was mobbed. Phoebe stood outside the locker room, her turquoise plastic beach bag in one hand. With the other hand, she shaded her eyes and tried to pick out Chris in the crowd.

It was Chris who spotted Phoebe first. Chris had just climbed out of the pool, and was standing to the left of the diving platform, shaking water out of her ear. "Phoebe Hall!" she shouted, beckoning. She smoothed back the wet strands of hair that had escaped from her braid and smiled as Phoebe approached. "What are you doing here?"

"Hi!" Phoebe said, walking up and handing her a towel. "I decided to drive down with my dad and Shawn this morning — they had tickets

27

for the Orioles game. Your mom said you were over here. I sort of felt like talking." There was a moment of awkward silence between the girls. The smile faded from Chris's face as she fiddled with the straps of her royal blue tank suit, then met Phoebe's eyes.

"I guess I owe you an apology. I didn't get a chance at your party," she said a bit stiffly. "I was wrong. I shouldn't have expected you to take my side about going off to the lake."

Phoebe interrupted and said warmly, "Oh, Chris, come off it. It's not such a big deal." She stared directly at her friend and remembered how just a year ago Chris would have been lecturing her for ages about water safety and breaking the law and being honorable. Chris had loosened up a lot since then. Phoebe grinned and stuck out her hand. "But thanks anyway. Apology's accepted."

Chris giggled and pumped Phoebe's hand ceremoniously. "Of course," she added, a wicked gleam lighting up her eyes, "I had no idea there was a romantic rendezvous in the works!"

"Chris!" Phoebe wailed. "Lower your voice — what will people think?"

"You sound like me! Since when do you care what people think, Ms. Hall!" Chris laughed. She threw herself down on the white plastic lounge chair.

While Phoebe dug out her sunscreen from her bag, Chris popped on her sunglasses and studied her friend. "Hey, that's your new suit, isn't it?"

28

"Do you like it?" Phoebe asked, smoothing out the turquoise and black geometric print fabric.

"Mmm-hmmm. Love it! But before you put on that sunscreen, aren't you going to christen it?" Chris motioned toward the pool.

Phoebe colored slightly. "I sort of did already — in the lake. Oh Chris, I think I'm really in love with Michael," she blurted out.

"So what else is new?" Chris teased. "I've been telling you for months that you two were made for each other. In fact, no one was at all surprised — except Woody, for some reason," Chris added with a shrug.

"I know," Phoebe admitted in a small voice. She handed Chris the sunscreen and kept talking as Chris smoothed the lotion on her back. "But I *am* surprised — and that's the truth!" she said almost fiercely, as if trying to convince herself.

Chris stopped rubbing Phoebe's freckled shoulders and asked gently, "You mean you really had no idea how much Michael has liked you all along? It was so obvious. Every time you were together."

Phoebe inhaled deeply. She took the bottle from Chris and silently began smoothing the lotion on her legs. She debated inwardly about telling Chris about Michael and how happy and scared she was. Sure, Chris was her best friend and had been ever since junior high. But Chris was also a bit straight-laced and more reserved than anyone else Phoebe'd ever met. Worse yet, Chris lived by a whole set of rules and regulations Phoebe didn't exactly agree with. Now and then Phoebe would run headlong into one of Chris's rules as if into a brick wall, and they'd have a fight, like the time Phoebe fell in love with Griffin and hadn't broken up with Brad yet. Or the time Chris refused to lie for her when Phoebe was about to go to New York for a weekend alone with Griffin. Phoebe had gotten in the habit of playing it safe with Chris, and not telling Chris *everything* she was feeling. Besides, some things were too private to talk about, even with your best friend. So she had never told Chris about prom night — in fact, Phoebe had never told anyone.

Phoebe screwed the top on the bottle and sat with her cheek pillowed on her knee, eyes closed. For a second she relived Michael's kisses down by the lake, then the sound of his laugh as he swung her higher and higher on Shawn's swing, and finally the way he had kissed her good-night. They had been standing at the bottom of the driveway. She had just promised to come home to Rose Hill the next night so they could see each other. He had taken her hand between both his and asked her to listen to the crickets, the wonderful music they made on their fiddles. He laughed his crazy laugh and told Phoebe the cricket's music would always be their special song. He had touched her hair gently and didn't seem to mind that it had dried all tangled and wild. His good-night kiss was sweet and fleeting. Her parents were back at the cabin and Michael was the only guest still there. Her father had made sure they knew he was on the porch, noisily puttering around with a blown flood light. Then Michael took off in his van.

Phoebe had walked back to the house and yelled good-night to her parents upstairs, then pulled Shawn's He-Man sleeping bag out onto the porch. She lay there watching the moon set behind the mountain while the crickets fiddled Michael's tune. It seemed only a few seconds later when she opened her eyes and the sound of crickets had turned into the song of birds.

The next minute Phoebe had sat bolt upright on the porch floor, drawing the sleeping bag over her thin nightgown. The morning air was chilly and Phoebe had just remembered the night's terrible dream.

"Pheeb?" Chris hesitantly touched her arm. Phoebe jumped slightly. Her attention turned back to reality and the Rose Hill pool. When she turned toward Chris, her face was pale and her eyes had a frightened look.

"Sorry. I guess I'm a bit spaced-out," she managed.

"So you want to talk about it?" Chris asked. "I mean, you seemed so happy Saturday night, and now you look — "

"Oh, Chris!" Phoebe cried. "I'm so confused. You see — " She faltered only an instant. "You see, I wasn't *really* surprised about Michael. I mean, I *was* surprised last night. But it's happened before and what if he doesn't believe me this time?"

"Phoebe Hall!" Chris admonished with a

31

puzzled smile. "You must be in love. You're making absolutely no sense."

"Stop making fun of me," Phoebe declared hotly.

"I'm not making fun of you," Chris said, giving Phoebe's shoulder a gentle shake. "But I don't understand. You mean you and Michael have been more than friends all along — after what you told me?"

"No, Chris. Everything I said was true, believe me. I haven't been lying all summer. We've just been friends. But I never told you about prom night. It was — " Phoebe floundered. "It wasn't just friendly that night, not at all," she lamented woefully.

"Hmmm — I always wondered what happened that night. It was sort of strange, your showing up with him just two nights after breaking up with Griffin. In fact," Chris shifted uncomfortably in her chair, "I guess everyone thought it was a bit strange — "

"I can imagine!" Phoebe said with a brittle little laugh. "The grapevine must have been sizzling."

"He's so gorgeous, Phoebe, and most of the crowd never noticed him before. And he looked so in love with you — even then."

Phoebe bit her lip and toyed with her earrings. "He did?"

Chris just nodded.

"I didn't realize that then. I didn't realize much of anything," Phoebe continued in a wistful voice. "I was just hurting so much. And

Michael had been so nice to me, he tried so hard to cheer me up when I ran into him the day after Griffin and I split up. He made me laugh when I thought I'd never laugh again — not after Griffin." Phoebe's voice trembled slightly. She took a deep breath and continued more steadily. "So when he asked me to do him a favor and go to the prom — just as a pal — I agreed, but I sure didn't feel like it. We kind of had fun. It's all a blur, really. But it was afterwards that everything got crazy." Phoebe lowered her voice. She kept her eyes averted from Chris when she told her about kissing Michael, and how intense it all got before she realized it wasn't Griffin in her arms at all. By the time she finished her story, tears were falling from beneath her sunglasses.

Chris silently handed Phoebe some tissues. Her deep blue eyes were full of sympathy as she regarded her friend. Chris sighed and said, "I think it makes perfect sense. I just wish you had told me sooner. You've been worried about this all summer — and, I know," Chris's face clouded over, "I know sometimes I'm a bit critical of people, but you can really talk to me. Even if I do disagree with you, I'll always listen." Then she frowned. "But what are you afraid of now?"

Phoebe hadn't meant to tell Chris about her dream, but it all came spilling out. How she had dreamed she was in the water kissing Michael, and then his deep dark eyes had turned into familiar gray-blue ones. Suddenly Phoebe had found herself in Griffin's arms and he was swimming toward the center of the lake, taking her with him. Phoebe had tried to scream and warn him; the lake was deep and the water was dangerous. But no sound came out of her mouth. Then they both went under. She opened her eyes and it was dawn.

"Oh, Chris, it was so crazy. What does it mean? What if Michael thinks about us last night and gets scared? How can he possibly trust me after what happened at the prom? What if he thinks I'll look at him tonight and say, 'No, I don't want you. I want Griffin.'"

"Well, do you?" Chris said evenly.

"Do I what?" Suddenly Phoebe understood and turned pale. "Chris, how can you possibly ask me that? No. No, I don't want Griffin. That's all past; this is now." She slapped the plastic armrest of the beach chair hard. "I'm over Griffin. I am."

Chris nodded. "I believe you. And I know Michael will. Just tell him the truth, like you told me now. But tell him soon — tonight, Phoebe. Because if I were in his shoes I'd be at least a little worried." Chris considered her next few words. "You really loved Griffin Neill — " Her voice trailed off. "Let me put it this way. If Ted and I broke up, it would be a long time before I could really love someone else — even though Ted and I have certainly had our ups and downs. There'd always be a sort of secret place in my heart that would love him."

Phoebe silently considered Chris's advice. Phoebe was over Griffin. She knew that. But

Michael had no way of knowing for sure until she spelled it out plain and clear. Yes, Griffin still lived in that secret place in her heart. He always would. And as much as her heart still ached sometimes, she wouldn't have wanted it any other way. She just wished he would stay out of her dreams.

Phoebe glanced gratefully at Chris. "Thanks, Chris. I'll do that. I'll talk to him tonight. It really helps talking to you like this."

Chris nodded, leaned back on the beach chair, and lifted her face toward the sun. She looked every bit the All-American Golden Girl she was. Still, something about Chris looked out of whack. Cool, confident Chris Austin actually looked wistful — even sad. Phoebe hadn't noticed until now, she'd been so caught up in her fears about Michael and the excitement of really being in love again. "Chris," she finally ventured, "I feel so selfish. What happened between you and Ted the other night . . . I mean, after the swim?" She held her breath, waiting for Chris's answer.

Chris threw back her head and laughed. "What always happens between me and Ted, of course. We both felt stupid. After the swim he came back looking sad and lonely and I realized I had pulled a real creepo number on him. We had the most wonderful time making up."

"Great!" Phoebe grinned. The wistful look was gone and Chris looked herself again. Maybe it had just been a trick of the light. "After all, Austin, I want next year's Hall barbecue to find you two still hogging that hammock."

A shadow of a frown crossed Chris's face. She quickly bent over and began rummaging in her bag.

Phoebe stretched and patted her stomach. "By the way, I'm starved. Want to grab something before I head home?"

"Sure," Chris said, not meeting Phoebe's eye.

Phoebe began folding her towel. "Do you realize that in exactly four and one-half hours I get to go on my first official date with the love of my life, Michael Rifkin? We're going to a concert on the mall. Imagine, music under the stars. I'll wear my new dress, the pink one." Phoebe swirled once in front of an imaginary mirror, and looked over her shoulder for Chris, but Chris was already heading for the locker room.

Chris closed the locker room door firmly behind her, and discreetly wiped away a tear that had strayed halfway down her cheek. She had no idea why she felt like crying. Ted and she had made up last night, and everything was back to normal between them. Maybe Phoebe's story about Michael and the prom and Griffin had really gotten to her. Yes, that was it. Poor Phoebe, she thought. What a crazy summer she had had — what a crazy year. Maybe now with Michael, Phoebe would be really happy again.

Chris peeled off her suit, pulled the elastic band out of her braid, and climbed into the shower. She turned on the faucet full-force and poured shampoo into her palm. As the warm water beat down on her shoulders she burst into tears. She leaned her head against the gray metal stall, her whole body wracked with sobs. Why was it so hard to picture herself with Ted at next year's Hall barbecue?

Chapter
4

Sunday night Chris was rather restless, bored, and very out of sorts. She prowled the downstairs of the deserted Austin house trying to find something to do, something to get her mind off Ted. She tried TV, the Sunday paper, and her stepsister's two-thousand-piece jigsaw puzzle. Nothing worked. Nothing took away the crazy feeling she had inside.

Phoebe's poolside comment about next year's barbecue had rattled her terribly. Worse yet, her overreaction made no sense. Chris Austin wasn't used to things not making sense. She hadn't lied to Phoebe; her relationship with Ted was fine, just fine. Sure, they had had a pretty heavy discussion Saturday night in the car. In fact, when Ted accused her of being inhumanly cool, calm, and collected, and always in control, Chris had totally fallen apart. Ted had instantly reached toward her, held her, and whispered he was sorry, that he loved her. Then he kissed her like he meant it, first her hair and her forehead, then her eyes and her cheeks, until finally his lips met hers in a silent reassurance that all was right between them.

Chris flopped face down on the blue damask sofa. She leaned her head out over the edge, her hair falling in front of her face. She shook her head and traced the pattern of the Persian carpet with her finger. "Calm, cool, collected — no one ever gets through to you, Chris." That was it. That was what Ted had said. And that was what bothered her, that he could still say that even though he was the one person besides Phoebe to whom Chris had ever totally bared her soul. It must be true. No one really knew her. She didn't let them. Chris suddenly sat up and shivered in the air-conditioned room. She hugged her arms to her chest and stared woefully at the big old grandfather clock. Not even nine yet. Time sure was creeping. She felt like a ghost in the big empty room.

The clock had struck ten when the phone finally rang. "Oh, Ted!" Chris cried aloud, and practically tripped on the ironing board trying to pick up the receiver on the second ring. Hearing the voice on the other end, her face fell.

"Hi, Chris. It's me, Brenda."

"Oh, hi!" Chris said, trying not to sound too disappointed.

There was silence on the other end of the phone. "Chris, is everything all right there?" Brenda's voice sounded worried.

Chris shook her head. "Sure, Bren, everything's fine. . . . Really." She forced a cheery note into her voice. Her stepsister had an uncanny way of knowing when Chris was upset.

"Listen, are Mom and Dad back from Georgetown yet?"

"No." Chris twiddled the cord. She didn't feel very talkative.

"Uh — will you be awake when they get back?"

"Brenda — they're going to blow up if you aren't home by eleven tonight. You heard Dad this morning," Chris warned, sensing that Brenda wanted her to run interference on the home front about yet one more missed curfew. Brenda had been seeing Brad every night and not coming home until one or two. Her father had hit the roof over breakfast, and laid down some new laws. "You'll be grounded. Then you won't be able to see Brad at all," Chris reminded her gently.

"Oh, Chris. Doesn't anyone understand? He'll be gone in a couple of weeks — I want to spend all the time I can with him." Brenda's voice trembled, then she paused. A subtle note of defiance entered her voice. "Besides, tonight's different. The meeting here just broke up and Tony planned a kind of summer doldrums party for the Garfield House staff."

Chris sighed. At least their father's attitude toward the local halfway house and Brenda's

40

work there had changed. He approved of his stepdaughter's summer job and of Tony. Only a year ago he'd tried to keep her away from her old crowd of "creepy friends," as he used to put it. "Oh, Bren. I understand — who wouldn't? Except parents. But you'd better be careful. I'll tell them about the party."

"Thanks, Chris," Brenda said warmly. After a second she added, "Hey, are you sure you don't want to talk about something? I've got a minute."

Chris could picture Brenda at the pay phone in the back hall of the old Georgetown house, rock music blaring in the community room. Brenda would have one hip against the wall, and one hand over her ear. She would look so serious, so caring. Chris swallowed hard and considered confiding in her stepsister. But how could she? She wasn't even sure what she was feeling. And Chris wasn't used to talking about anything until she had it completely figured out for herself. So she just said, "Brenda, really, nothing's wrong."

The next morning Chris's fears about Ted had vanished with the heat. She had fallen asleep to a terrible storm, with the sheet pulled over her head and the air conditioner turned on high so she wouldn't hear the thunder. She woke up clear-headed and light-hearted and blamed Sunday's strange mood on the weather. She jogged an extra mile, argued politics over breakfast in the kitchen with her dad, showered in the downstairs bathroom so as not to wake Brenda, and backed the Chevette out of the driveway, whistling the Kennedy High Fight Song — not minding for once that she couldn't carry a tune. She walked into the congressional district office half an hour early for work, feeling she didn't have a problem in the world.

Before noon she had written letters in response to three angry constituents, fielded several desperate calls about lost Social Security checks, and gone through a record number of service academy transcripts. The stack of academy applications in her in-box dwindled to a handful, and she was determined to clear them up before breaking for lunch. The phone rang three times before Chris looked up from her work and remembered that she was covering the switchboard. "Congressman Barnes's office, may I help you?"

"Yes. I've sent in my application to the congressman to sponsor me at Annapolis next year. I just wanted to be sure all the supporting material had come in. My name's Lewis, Wesley Lewis, that is."

"Wesley!" Chris shrieked, then looked guiltily around the office. The other interns were already out to lunch, and Mrs. Dean, the office manager, was still holed up with the congressman and his staff in the conference room. "It's me, Chris — Chris Austin. How are you?" Chris couldn't believe it. Sasha Jenkins's old boyfriend was calling just at the time she was covering the phones.

"Chris?" Wesley's smooth voice tightened on

the other end of the phone. "Are you working for the congressman now?"

"Yes," Chris replied. "For the summer. I'm an intern. You know, I have my sights set on the White House some day. I want to get some first-hand government experience," Chris added a little too brightly. Wesley hadn't sounded overjoyed to hear her voice.

"Oh, yes, I see. Uh, Chris, you know about me and Sasha — breaking up — don't you?"

Chris took a deep breath. Wesley sounded so embarrassed. "Yes, Wes, I know. These things happen sometimes," she said lamely.

"She's okay, isn't she?" Wesley asked. Chris cringed at the hopeful note in his voice. He wanted Sasha not to be all right, not to still be with her new guy, Rob. It was so obvious that Wes still loved her. Chris's heart ached for him.

Chris didn't mention Rob. She said simply, "Yes, she's fine." She didn't know what else to say. An awkward silence followed.

Finally, Wesley said, "Good. I'm glad to hear that. And give her my regards." Before Chris could respond, Wesley continued. "About my application. Can you check on it? I can call back if you're busy now."

"No need. I've got a stack of applications right in front of me." Chris riffled through the papers as she spoke. "Here you are, Wesley C. Lewis. Let's see. Everything's in order, Wes. And I must say you've got a pretty impressive record. I think you've got a good chance at Annapolis. I really do," Chris added warmly.

"Thanks, Chris," he said. "And — and it's good talking to you. Good luck en route to the White House."

Chris laughed. "It's a long way from student body president of Kennedy High to the White House, Wes. But thanks anyway." Wesley didn't hear her. He had already hung up.

Chris stared down at the neatly typed letter in her hand. Wesley's signature was firm, clear, and precise. That would impress the congressman as much as Wesley's superior record. Three straight years on the honor roll at Leesburg was about as impressive as a kid could be academically. She fingered the letter absently. Too bad in a way about Wesley and Sasha. Being head-over-heels in love with each other hadn't seemed to matter in the end. It was as if they had come from two different planets. Chris bit the inside of her lip. Well, as different as she and Ted were, they weren't about to split up. They'd gotten pretty good about working out their differences. Sure they fought a lot, but time after time Ted would come round to her side or she to his. Things between them always ended up being good as new — no, *better* than ever.

"Chris? Chris Austin?" A pleasant, resonant voice interrupted Chris's thoughts.

Chris nervously shuffled some papers on her desk and turned guiltily, expecting to meet the face of her boss, Congressman Barnes. Instead she looked up into a pair of unfamiliar but very friendly blue-green eyes. They belonged to a guy she'd never seen before. He was leaning on

44

her desk and Chris got a feeling he had been watching her a long time.

"Did I interrupt something?" he asked smoothly. His long fingers tapped Wesley's application. "You seemed to be making quite a study of this applicant's transcript."

Chris frowned. Who did this guy think he was, walking into the district office, acting as if he belonged there? She briskly shoved Wesley's file under a stack of papers. Information on applicants' transcripts were supposed to be confidential. Chris looked directly into the guy's eyes and said in a cool, efficient voice, "Can I help you?" Her frown deepened slightly as she asked, "How did you know my name?"

The stranger straightened up and tightened the knot in his tie. He was tall, much taller than he had seemed at first, with the lean, easy posture of a track-and-field star. Chris figured he'd spent most of the summer outdoors: His tan was deep and his neatly groomed sandy hair was sunstreaked. His features were even, his expression open, and his chin strong and determined. His roundish cheeks were ruddy.

He gave Chris a long, wide-eyed look, and said simply, "I *should* know your name. After all, I voted for you." And suddenly he was smiling a deeply dimpled smile. Chris couldn't help smiling back.

"You what? You mean *you* go to Kennedy High?" she asked, amazed that someone in her class — someone so cute and self-confident — could be a total stranger. She prided herself on knowing — at least by sight — most of the upperclassmen in the school. Besides, he looked older; she had taken him for a college sophomore.

"I do." He wagged a warning finger in Chris's startled face. "And you can make believe you don't know me, but you do. In fact, from what I can see, you're obviously one of my biggest fans."

"Fans? I'm *your* fan?" Chris's eyes narrowed slightly and she sat back in her seat. Who was he, anyway? Maybe some kind of crazy. He looked proper enough in his pale yellow shirt and conservative preppy tie, but you never knew. She gave a nervous glance around the office. No one was back from lunch yet, and the congressman was still in the conference room with Mrs. Dean and some aides. Chris quickly gathered some file folders in her arms. She pushed back her creaky swivel chair. "I can't talk now. Congressman Barnes needs these right away." A few steps across the cluttered office would bring her to the safety of the conference room, the congressman, and Mrs. Dean.

Before she could get up the stranger had moved to her side of the desk. He spun her chair around and placed one hand on each of the worn wooden arms, effectively blocking her escape route. Chris's eyes widened with apprehension. The blood drained from her face. She took a quick, sharp breath and forced herself to meet those intensely blue-green eyes. She kept up eye contact and tried to remember the other safety tips she had learned in her Women's Self-Defense course at the Y last year. Don't panic. Move slowly. Talk in a slow, reasonable, calm tone with your captor. Then yell for help at the top of your lungs. But don't yell "help." Yell "FIRE."

The word "Fire" was already on her lips when the conference room door burst open and the congressman and his senior staff noisily filed into the main office.

"Montgomery, you sure work fast!" Larry Eagleton, a legislative aide, shouted across the room.

Before Chris could react to the fact that the aide knew this guy, the congressman himself strode over, and extended his hand. "Greg! Welcome at last to the district office. I think you'll like it here." He smiled genially at Chris and winked.

Chris's mouth fell open. "*You* work for Congressman Barnes?"

Greg Montgomery just grinned. "I have, all summer. I'm an intern — just like you, but down at the Capitol Hill office. In case you hadn't noticed, we're wearing the same rising-young-executive uniforms!"

"Uniform?" Chris repeated blankly, then glanced down at her outfit: a yellow tailored striped shirt, and a narrow cream-colored cotton scarf, which matched her slim-cut skirt — and Greg's trousers.

"I don't believe this!" she exclaimed and burst out laughing. "What a coincidence!"

"Coincidence!" Greg scoffed and said in a

47

mockingly dramatic tone. "People don't just accidentally dress alike. Take butterflies for example: They dart around looking for someone who matches them, scale for scale, color for color, dot for dot, pinstripe for pinstripe! That's how they find the perfect mate!"

"What *are* you talking about?" Chris dismissed Greg's statement with an impatient wave of her hand, and busied herself with some papers. She was painfully aware that she was blushing. Talking about the mating habits of butterflies with a guy she'd just met was unexpectedly unnerving. He was obviously flirting with her, and Chris was annoyed and a little bit flattered. He said he knew her from school. Well, if he did, he should already know about Ted. The Austin/Mason duo was big news on the Kennedy campus.

As if Greg had read her mind, he said, "Of course there are other things that make people perfect matching couples. Like being star quarterback and dating the homecoming queen!"

Chris detected a note of mockery in Greg's voice. She looked up at him quickly, but his expression was friendly, open, and sincere. He was sitting on the edge of her desk, making a chain of paper clips. He met her eyes and held her glance. She was the first to look away.

"Well, I'm glad you two already met!" Mrs. Dean walked in. "Chris, I forgot to tell you Greg was starting with us today. He's going to be a floater between the Capitol Hill office and this one. Mondays and Wednesdays here. The rest

48

of the week down on the Hill. Try to make him feel at home, show him the ropes. He can help you finish those applications." Mrs. Dean started toward her desk, and turned abruptly. "Oh, why not break for lunch now, and take Greg with you. I'll cover the phones until the rest of the crew gets back. Jeff and René are due any minute."

Chris barely nodded agreement. Since Mrs. Dean had told her to go to lunch with Greg she would, but she had a hunch an hour alone with this guy was going to be unsettling. Was he making fun of her? Flirting with her? Just being friendly? Talking to him felt like driving down a perfectly straight stretch of interstate, that suddenly, without warning, turned into a twisty dirt road someone forgot to mark on the map.

"So are we going to brownbag it or not?" Greg interrupted her thoughts.

"Oh, sorry. I was just trying to work that out," Chris improvised, reaching into her desk drawer for her bag. Then she made the connection. Suddenly she knew why Greg's goofy repartée seemed familiar. "Montgomery, your last name is Montgomery. That's Monty for short, isn't it?" Her tone was almost accusing.

Greg arched his eyebrows and grinned.

"It's you!" she gasped, tapping a pink inter-office memo taped to the glass surface of her desk. A dozen or so more pink slips were taped to the wall, the top of the computer monitor, and the margins of the bulletin board. Each one was signed "Monty" in a bold scrawl. They were

49

mostly drawings, caricatures of various well-known figures around the Washington scene. "I get it now," Chris said excitedly, "the bit about me being your fan. *You're* the mysterious Monty who sends these far-out memos." Chris slapped her forehead. "How dumb can I be? No, no, don't answer that!" She glared at Greg, who seemed about to say something. "But I have to admit," she enthused, "I love those cartoons. They're great! I can't draw at all!" she concluded wistfully. She looked at Greg with new appreciation in her eyes. Then she sank back down in her chair. "I thought you were some kind of nut coming in here to hassle me or bother the congressman," she confessed, laughing in embarrassment and pushing a stray strand of hair back in her ponytail. "Do you believe it?"

Greg shrugged sheepishly. "Really, I didn't mean to scare you, though I can't say anyone's ever reacted to good old clean-cut me as if I were some sort of madman before. It is —" he archly dusted off an imaginary speck from his jacket, then continued " — I must admit, flattering!"

Twenty minutes later, Chris was trying to figure out how she ever survived her summer lunch hours without Greg. She had met him less than an hour earlier, and she felt as comfortable with him as with Phoebe. She felt like she'd known him her whole life. After leaving the office, they had raided the 7-Eleven for the makings of a picnic and headed toward the town park with enough junk food to feed an army.

50

"I'm stuffed!" Chris finally said, licking potato chip crumbs from her fingers. "You finish these!" She shoved the nearly empty bag toward Greg's side of the park bench. She looked up at him and was startled to find him studying her face.

"You know," he said thoughtfully, as he dug out the last few chips, "you're different than you seem." He leaned back on the bench and stretched his long legs straight out in front of him. A pigeon pecked at the grass near his feet and Greg generously dumped the potato chip crumbs in front of the bird.

"Why? How do I seem?" Chris asked tentatively.

"Cool, calm — "

" — and collected," Chris interrupted with a bitter laugh. "I know, also totally in control and sure of myself. That's about it, isn't it?"

Greg looked at her intently, then said, "Maybe that's not what I was going to say at all."

"Come off it, Greg." Chris dug the pointy toe of her shoe into the grass. "I know how I seem, how I am. I know what people think about me." Her voice came out all tight and sharp and brittle as glass. She bit her lip and stared out across the park. She hadn't meant to snap at Greg. What was wrong with her, anyway? She was getting too thin-skinned for her own good.

Chris watched a little blonde girl of about ten or eleven taking a tennis lesson on the public courts. Chris had started learning tennis at about that age. Out of habit she focused her attention on the game. The girl was good, Chris thought,

51

leaning forward to watch her ace the first serve.

Suddenly the ball went flying off the court, bouncing down the walk. Greg leaped off the bench and grabbed it in midair. "Here!" he yelled, and tossed it back. The girl expertly fielded it, and shyly waved her racket in thanks.

Chris smiled. "Good play," she said, wanting to somehow apologize for her little outburst.

"Do you like tennis?" Greg asked. His voice was calm and steady. He didn't sound upset.

"You bet!" Chris grinned and ventured a glance at him. He wasn't looking at her, but at the game.

"So let's play sometime," he suggested. "Maybe Wednesday, a quick game after work, here on the public courts."

Chris mentally went over Ted's schedule with the Ramblers. "Okay. That would be fun, Greg. I could use some work on my serve. Besides Ted's got a game in Ocean City that day, so I'm free."

"So it's a date?" Greg asked, gathering up the sandwich wrappings from the bench.

Chris laughed. "It's a date. But we'd better get back to the office or we won't have jobs to go to on Wednesday." Chris started for the trash can near the courts.

"I won, I won!" The high, childish voice floated across the lawn. Chris grinned and looked over toward the courts. A tall, slender woman had walked up to the net. Her pale blonde hair was pulled back low on her neck and tied with a silky blue scarf. She was wearing a dark blue sundress, and as the little girl ran up she bent

52

to kiss her, smiling a wonderfully radiant smile.

Chris's eyes blurred over, and a tear slipped down her cheek.

"Chris?" Greg was by her side. He didn't touch her, but he stood very close.

"I'm sorry," she whispered, turning her face away. "It's just — it's just that woman. She reminds me of my mother. She died a few years ago," Chris said haltingly, motioning toward the courts.

Greg didn't say any of the usual things, the kinds of things she had hated to hear when her mother died. Like how sorry he felt. Or he knew how she was feeling. Or how sad it all was. All those polite, well-meant phrases that sounded like people said them from a script, not from their hearts. He simply handed Chris his handkerchief. "Thanks," Chris mumbled, and blew her nose. In a second she had regained some composure. "I'm sorry about that. This doesn't happen to me often. She just looked so much like my mom." Her voice was almost steady now.

They walked silently back through the park. Greg opened the office door for Chris. "Thanks," she said, avoiding his eyes. She had never cried in front of a stranger before.

She hurried down the hall to the ladies' room, where she dabbed cold water on her eyes and tried to figure out what had come over her. It was so unlike her to break down that way, in the middle of a public park with a guy she barely knew. She hugged her arms to herself and leaned back against the sink.

Going back into the office suddenly felt like more than Chris could bear. She'd have to sit at a desk across from Greg and act like nothing out of the ordinary had happened at lunch, wondering while they sorted transcripts what he was thinking. She felt dumb and terribly embarrassed.

She stared down at her feet and fought an impulse to run out the back door. A deep sigh escaped her lips. No, Chris Austin never ran away. Her father had taught her to face the consequences of her actions no matter what. She squared her shoulders and started for the door. She's get through the afternoon with Greg, and she'd make up some excuse to get out of playing tennis on Wednesday.

Halfway down the hall an odd thought crossed her mind. Greg was different, different from Phoebe or Sasha or Woody or even Ted. Greg Montgomery had known not to touch her. He had recognized immediately that she had needed a private place to be alone inside, to nurse a hurt too deep for hugs to take away.

And he didn't make her feel like something was wrong with her for not wanting, just then, to be touched. Even though she had just made his acquaintance, Chris knew there was something very special about Greg Montgomery.

Chapter
5

Jeremy Stone squinted through the viewfinder of his camera. He focused the zoom lens center stage on a brightly dressed, brown-haired figure: his cousin, Monica Ford. Her shoulder-length hair obscured her face as she bent to disengage the microphone from its stand. As she lifted the mike to her mouth, Jeremy zoomed in for a closeup. She raised a slender hand to quiet the screaming audience. Whatever she said at first was drowned out by the cheers and hoots and whistles. She looked every inch the WRRK D.J. in her black and yellow knit tube skirt and hand-painted sneakers. She pushed her bangs out of her eyes and peered into the dimly lit room of Rockers, Georgetown's newest rock club. She grinned at the audience before making her announcement. Jeremy zoomed the lens in even closer, until only Monica's hands and face filled the frame: the big pink bracelet sliding down her arm as she held her hand against one ear, her sparkling brown eyes, the lone long plastic earring brushing her bare shoulder. She seemed to be looking clear to the back of the room, right into the camera and Jeremy's eyes. As she began to speak, he snapped a quick succession of pictures.

"Rockers — and our red-hot warm-up band, The Uncolas — thank you all for that kind welcome. Some opening set, wasn't it?" The audience broke out in a renewed bout of applause. "And you ain't seen nothing yet, folks. Coming up next set on our night of Monday Madness is Seventh Sister, Baltimore's top local band who have hit the big time with their album 'Broken Peaces.' " More applause, more cheers. "But while their sound crew is setting up, we've got fifteen minutes of your WRRK all-time favorite summer dance tunes. So hit the floor, folks, and strut your stuff!"

Jeremy kept the camera trained on Monica as she leapt off the stage into Peter Lacey's arms. Through the lens, he followed their progress toward him across the crowded dance floor, snapping their pictures until he lost them in the confusion of strobe lights and dancing bodies. He let his camera drop back down to his neck and jumped down off the chair. Just before he sat down a blur of color by the ticket taker's table caught his eye. His picked up his camera again, and aimed it toward the door.

She wasn't a slender girl. She wasn't fat,

56

either. Just round and soft-looking and not very tall. Her clothes were a crazy mixture of styles: femininely boyish. She was wearing a pink-flowered jumpsuit beneath an old blue scouting shirt. Jeremy focused in closer until her gloriously thick red hair filled the frame. He began snapping picture after picture. She had a pretty face — not beautiful, but expressive. The kind of face he could photograph for hours. Every emotion would show on it. Tonight it was radiant. He had never seen anyone look so completely happy in his life. Suddenly the face dropped out of his picture, then came up again. He pulled back the zoom and watched the girl fasten a big purple butterfly clip on one side of her hair. She looked slightly out of breath, and Jeremy smiled as he watched. There were blades of grass stuck in her hair and clinging to the shoulder of her shirt.

A hand reached into the picture and began gently brushing the grass out of the girl's hair. Jeremy adjusted his lens to a wider angle. "Darn!" he murmured. She was with a guy, a tall guy with unruly dark hair and a very big smile. Jeremy found himself smiling back at him through the camera ."Oh, well," he muttered to himself, then he tried to focus on his subjects. The guy was wearing a grass-stained "I love Beethoven" T-shirt. They weren't holding hands. They weren't even touching, but Jeremy could feel a strong current of electricity running between them. Just as Jeremy snapped his final picture, the girl leaned fleetingly against the

57

guy and looked up into his eyes. A second later they were standing a few inches apart. But Jeremy put away his camera. He was out of film now. Anyway he felt a bit odd, as if he had been spying on two people very much in love.

Phoebe walked into Rockers and practically choked. The heat was suffocating, and the air smelled stale.

The noise jarred Phoebe terribly, and she fumbled with her hairclip. It fell to the floor right in front of the ticket taker's table. While Michael paid their admission, Phoebe rested one hand on the table and stooped to pick up the clip. The floor was vibrating like crazy. She felt like she had walked into an earthquake in progress. The crowd was stomping and dancing and screaming along with the music. Phoebe took a deep breath and fastened the clip on one side of her hair.

For a second she wondered if she were dressed right; most of the girls had on short, tight skirts or stirrup pants and skimpy halters. At least the club was dark enough that no one would notice the grass stains on her jumpsuit. She leaned ever so slightly against Michael. The gentle pressure of his arm as he tucked his wallet back into his jeans pocket reassured her.

In the middle of all the noise and commotion of the club it was hard to believe that a few minutes earlier she had been in Michael's arms listening to the crickets in Rose Hill Park. Phoebe closed her eyes and tried to block out the din. She drifted back to the moment when the sun dropped behind the horizon, sending up strange streamers of color.

They had laughed at the weirdly beautiful sunset. Michael had said it looked a lot like the Northern Lights and the Alaskan sky at Christmas. Still laughing, he had taken her into his arms and drawn her down to the grass beside him. The lawn was freshly mown and cool against her bare arms. Phoebe lay with her cheek pressed against Michael's chest, absently tracing the picture of Beethoven on his T-shirt with her finger. They were supposed to be listening to crickets, but all Phoebe wanted to hear was the strong, steady beat of Michael's heart.

She hadn't wanted to leave that place, but Michael had promised Peter they'd come to see Monica's debut stint as a club D.J. And Michael never broke promises. Phoebe opened her eyes and tried to let the rhythm of the music move her. There would be lots of time later to be alone with Michael.

"Pheeb, there they are!" Michael had spotted Peter, waving frantically in their direction.

As they approached the table, Monica greeted Phoebe with a knowing smile. "You look great! I love your hair like that!"

Phoebe bit her lip shyly. She was happy to see the crowd easily accepting her new relationship with Michael, but she still felt awkward in public about the change.

"Thanks, Monica," she murmured, stuffing her hands in her pockets. "Actually, *you're* the one

59

who looks outrageous!" Phoebe gazed with admiration at Monica's bright but tastefully crazy outfit. She glanced quickly at Peter. He was grinning at Monica. "She makes some D.J., doesn't she? I'd better watch my step at WKND next month or I might have to share the spotlight." The way Peter said it, Phoebe knew he wouldn't mind sharing his post as the high school's top D.J. Not now. Earlier in the summer, Monica's landing the D.J. job at WRRK had almost broken them up. Peter had really wanted the job. But they had managed to work things out, and now he even loved his job at Variety Records, the record store at the mall. Monica and he seemed to have come through their troubles happier with each other than ever before.

Monica's eyes were shining with excitement. "Isn't this great?" She stood behind Peter's chair, beating time to an old sixties version of "Heatwave." "Oh, I almost forgot." She motioned toward a boy sitting at the table, a camera dangling around his neck. "This is my cousin from London, Jeremy Stone. Jeremy, Phoebe Hall and Michael Rifkin."

"Hi!" Phoebe giggled self-consciously. It was the first time someone had run her name together with Michael's like that. It sounded good. The right words with the right tune, she thought.

Jeremy stuck out his hand toward Phoebe and grinned. In a clipped British accent, he said, "I feel as if we've already met." He laughed at the bewildered expression on Michael's face.

60

"You, too. I was taking pictures of the crowd when you walked in, and I got a few of you. If they work out, I'll give them to you."

For a second his eyes met Phoebe's, and in that second her world tilted out of balance. His eyes were a familiar blue-gray, exactly the color of Griffin's.

Phoebe quickly looked away and lay her hand on Michael's knee, under the table. It took a couple of minutes before she could focus her attention back on the slightly built, brown-haired Jeremy Stone. As Michael asked him questions, she studied Jeremy's face. It was thin and pointed with very sharp, angular features. He was handsome and had an air of nervous energy that Phoebe knew a lot of girls would find appealing. He only resembled Griffin about the eyes, but his were smaller and brighter — yet not as intense and magnetic as Griffin Neill's.

Phoebe was glad. She had decided instantly she liked Monica's cousin, but being around someone even remotely like her old boyfriend for any length of time would definitely make her uncomfortable.

"How long are you here for?" she finally asked.

"I don't actually know." He shrugged. "I hope forever, but if I'm lucky, at least the school year. My father got assigned to the British Embassy here — it's quite a feather in the old man's cap — but it's hard on the family. My sister, Fiona, is in a ballet school, and she might get an apprenticeship with a professional company. If she does, she won't be able to come here. Mother's staying behind until Fiona hears about her standings in the last batch of exams. Tough on them both, really. For me, it's a dream come true," he said. "Ever since I was a kid I wanted to be a cowboy and to come to America. Don't care much about being a cowboy now, but I'd rather like to go to Hollywood."

Phoebe paled slightly. Did this guy even have the same dreams as Griffin? She flinched when Michael asked, "You want to be an actor?" Michael knew Griffin was an actor. Then she remembered Michael wouldn't see the resemblance between Jeremy and her old boyfriend. He'd never met Griffin.

Phoebe resisted an impulse to cover her ears. She didn't want to hear Jeremy's answer.

"What? Me, an actor?" Jeremy shook his head vehemently and laughed. "Never. I couldn't stand people telling me what to do. Anyway, I can't act for beans. I want to direct films. Or at least be a cameraman."

The rest of the conversation rolled by Phoebe. Her reaction to Jeremy was unnerving. She didn't feel attracted to him, although he was good looking enough. He wasn't quite her type. Still, the faint resemblance to Griffin caught her off guard. How could she possibly be thinking of Griffin now, after holding Michael so close in the park? She rubbed her hands against her temples. Just because a guy's eyes matched Griffin Neill's or he had dreams of making it big in Tinseltown, Phoebe's first thoughts shouldn't be of Griffin.

She loved Michael now. The ghost of Sunday morning's dream flitted across her mind. She willed herself to block it out. Again, under the table, she squeezed Michael's hand. He squeezed back, and looked at her lovingly with shining eyes.

Phoebe smiled weakly and tried to get herself into focus with the scene around her. Monica was over at the tape deck, talking to a member of the sound crew. Peter had left the table.

"You okay, Pheeb?" Michael leaned over and asked softly.

"Sure. Sure I am," she said firmly, as if to convince herself.

"Do you want to get out of here?" Michael whispered. Phoebe glanced quickly at Jeremy. He was reloading his camera. Yes, getting out of here would make the memories fade away.

Michael mistook the meaning of her glance. "Right. We'll wait 'til Peter is back. I don't want to leave Jeremy alone." He nuzzled her hair. "Sweet Phoebe. Always thinking of other people."

Phoebe looked uneasily at Michael as Peter came flying up to the table. "You won't believe this!"

Peter could hardly stand still and his face was wreathed in smiles. He had totally lost his usual cool. "I just ran into the manager of the record store. He has five front row tickets to — "

Peter paused for effect. His dark eyes rested briefly on Jeremy, Phoebe, and Michael in turn. Then he said, slowly emphasizing each word

63

" — next week's Springsteen concert."

"What!" Phoebe shrieked.

"Fabulous!" Jeremy slammed his hand down on the table. "What I wouldn't give to photograph that!"

"Peter, you really have all the luck," Michael said with admiration.

"No, *we* have all the luck. We can all go. Monica, me and the three of you." Peter heaved a mock sigh. "This'll be the second Springsteen concert I go to this summer — how lucky can you get?" Peter gave a loud whoop and slapped his hands to the rhythm of the music, then motioned wildly for Monica to join them.

"Peter." Michael lay a hand on Peter's arm. "Let me call you tomorrow at the record store, okay? We'll talk about the concert then, Phoebe's not feeling well."

Peter put his arm around Phoebe. "Headache?"

Phoebe nodded. "It's *so* hot in here! I thought air conditioning was supposed to cool things off." Jeremy grimaced in sympathy and tugged at the collar of his loose cotton shirt.

Michael took Phoebe's hand as they got up from the table. Phoebe smiled wanly and mumbled, "I'll be okay. Once we're outside. It's just the noise and this air." She slung her bag over her shoulder and turned toward Jeremy. "Uh, nice meeting you." She mustered up the courage to look him in the eye; the shadowy resemblance to Griffin had vanished. Strobe lights do funny

64

things sometimes, she thought, suddenly feeling very foolish.

"Michael, this is crazy! What if a patrol car comes by?" Phoebe warned in a whisper, as Michael stealthily drove across the deserted Kennedy High parking lot. She nervously peered through the back window of the van. Not a car was in sight. She relaxed slightly and smiled at Michael across the front seat. He looked as if he were about to burst with some exciting piece of news. He must be as bad as Shawn at keeping secrets, Phoebe thought, and reached across the seat for his hand.

"No one will see us. I promise. I come here lots at night, when I need to be alone." Michael's tone was reassuring. "No one's caught me yet, and I've been doing this all summer. Anyway, I have a key."

"A key?" Phoebe didn't understand. They had left Rockers and headed down some back roads to Rose Hill. But the last place she expected to end up was on the grounds of the school. Michael steered the van to the north end of the faculty lot and pulled up onto the grass. He parked behind a clump of pines surrounding the old colonial chapel that served as the school theater. Phoebe's heart seemed to catch in her throat. Michael had a key to the building — the same building where she had first met Griffin.

Michael jumped out of the van and opened up the back. He noisily rummaged for something in the dark. Phoebe just sat in the passenger seat, one hand on the door, the other pressed over her eyes. She tried to still her whirling thoughts. What was the matter with her, anyway? She was in love with Michael, yet all night no matter where they went or what they did. Griffin's ghost seemed to rise up between them, as it had in Phoebe's terrible dream. Did she really want Griffin back? Phoebe's heart responded for her: No. She was sure she didn't. It had been all wrong — the craziness, the impetuousness of their relationship. It had been a wonderful romance while it lasted, but Griffin was the wrong kind of guy for Phoebe. She knew that now. She was too loyal, and she could only love one guy at a time. And Griffin wasn't loyal that way. Michael was.

"Come on, Pheeb," Michael urged, opening the passenger door. Phoebe leapt down to the ground, but didn't take Michael's outstretched hand.

"We're going in there?" she asked in a trembling voice, looking toward the auditorium. She fiddled with her hair and slipped on her scout shirt even though she was warm. She needed a few minutes to pull herself together.

"Of course. Like I said, I've got the key — and a surprise," he added, a bit shyly. He looked down at Phoebe. "Hey, I'm serious. We won't get in trouble here — even if someone does turn up. I'm supposed to be here."

"I — I don't understand," Phoebe stammered. Not that she was terribly afraid of being caught with Michael here, even though she was already out past her curfew. She was afraid of what she'd feel when Michael opened the door.

"*That's* part of the surprise." Michael grabbed her hand.

Phoebe took a deep breath. A second later they were darting across a moonlit stretch of lawn to the back door of the little theater.

The key turned easily in the lock and the thick wood door opened with a creak. It was August, but summer hadn't yet worked its way into the old stone building. Phoebe braced herself as a blast of damp, musty air hit her in the face. All her memories of Griffin seemed to rush out at her. But they quickly rushed past her into the night, as Michael slipped his arm around her shoulder and whispered in her ear, "Are you really that afraid of the dark?"

Phoebe leaned into Michael's arm. His touch brought her back into the present and her feelings about Griffin vanished like a bad dream.

"Of the dark?" Phoebe repeated, then shook her head and declared vehemently, "Oh, Michael. No, not when I'm with you." She let him lead her down the hall, past the stage, and to one side of the auditorium. The safety lights were lit over both exit doors, and moonlight poured through the old stained glass windows. Phoebe had never seen the chapel look so beautiful.

Michael flipped on a wall switch. A small overhead light came on, and Phoebe found herself standing in front of the pipe organ. The magnificent old instrument smelled moldy and hadn't worked for years: The school board never found a way to budget its repair. "The organ," she gasped. "I forgot all about it. It looks different — like it's been polished. Oh, Michael, have you fixed it? That's your surprise, isn't it?" She clapped her hands in delight.

By way of an answer, Michael plopped himself down on the red cushioned bench and toggled a few switches on the side of the organ. Flashing Phoebe a wicked smile, he launched into the crashing theme to a TV horror show. Phoebe clapped her hands over her ears and groaned.

"Oh, stop it. I hate that music."

"Hate Bach's toccata and fugue in D minor? How could you!" Michael feigned disdain and switched to another Bach air, this time from a cantata that Phoebe was studying with Michael's mother. Phoebe loved the piece and began singing the soprano solo, while Michael played the choral counterpoint. Subtly he shifted the bass rhythm into a strong rock beat, Phoebe couldn't keep the tempo or a straight face, and finally collapsed beside him on the bench.

"Bach would kill you!" she said as soon as she recovered.

"Don't kid yourself. He'd love it. I bet he'd love synthesizer and computer music — even old washtubs. Pull out this stop." He gestured to a stop on the left of the keyboard. Phoebe instantly tugged the wooden knob. A flutelike sound filled the auditorium. At the same time, Michael switched the melody to a Talking Heads tune. The effect was electric, and Phoebe loved it.

Suddenly something banged overhead. "Michael," Phoebe shrieked, pulling his hands off the keyboard. She lowered her voice to a hoarse whisper. "What was that? Someone's coming." She looked around in panic for some place to hide.

Michael laughed. "Hardly. Probably just a bat up in the bell tower."

"Bats?" Phoebe shrieked and grabbed at her hair. She had heard somewhere that bats loved a woman's long hair — especially if it was red.

Michael tousled Phoebe's hair and flipped the off-switch on the side of the organ. The pipes seemed to shut down with a sigh. Phoebe glanced around nervously. The moonlit theater suddenly looked spooky, not romantic.

"Bats aren't going to get in your hair. They didn't bother Charlie and me all summer. We were here almost every night before I went off to the music festival. Charlie has a grant from the State Arts Council to fix the organ. Kennedy's powers-that-be were only too happy to give us a key. I got lots of practice time in, too. It's nice here at night. Quiet. No one bothers you if you make lots of noise. It's really pretty, too, up there." Michael waved toward a little door Phoebe had never remembered seeing before.

"Up where?" she wondered aloud.

"Come on." He took her hand again. "I'll show you."

A few minutes later they stood at the top of the bell tower looking out over the flat expanse of Rose Hill. "I can't believe I never knew you could come up here," Phoebe exclaimed, lifting her hair off her neck and letting the breeze cool her shoulders. She had draped her shirt over the stone casement and was leaning out the window trying to pick out Rose Hill's landmarks.

"Fat chance the school administration would let kids come up here." Michael chuckled. "Look." He pointed toward the northern border of the town. "There's my house."

Phoebe studied the view and easily spotted the towering Washington Monument in Washington, the brightly lit Rose Hill Mall, and the factory chimney behind the abandoned railroad station — the place where she'd kissed Griffin for the very first time. She closed her eyes and willed away the image of Griffin standing by the edge of the platform, his old soft shirt billowing out behind him in the rush of air from a passing freight. She squeezed Michael's hand and glanced up at him. He was looking into the distance, humming a catchy tune, a wonderful smile dancing across his face.

"And there's your house, Phoebe." He pointed just west of the school. Phoebe stood on tiptoe and tried to spot the modest ranch-style house down on Elm. She thought she saw the roof but she wasn't sure. "Which one?" She laughed. "The houses in our part of town sort of look alike, not like your neighborhood."

"Look, there!" He took her hand and pointed her finger. Phoebe still couldn't tell exactly. Suddenly she realized Michael must have spent a lot of time up here at night, looking out at the trees and stars and houses, taking the time to figure out which one was hers.

She said softly, "Michael, you must come up here lots."

Michael tugged at his hair and looked down at her. "Yes. I spent a lot of time here this summer, once I figured out which key unlocked the tower door. While Charlie worked, I took lots of breaks." He laughed, then put his hands on Phoebe's shoulders and rested his chin on her head. Phoebe leaned back against his chest and closed her eyes. Leaning against him felt natural and safe, even though his heart was beating very fast. It was a few seconds before he spoke.

"I'm glad you're here with me now. It sure beats looking at a rooftop, imagining what you might be doing — who you might be with."

"Oh, Michael. I wasn't with anyone else. You know that!" Phoebe cried, turning around in his arms, she looked up into his eyes. "I'm sorry. I'm sorry you had to wait so long. I should have known sooner — how I felt." Phoebe's voice faltered.

"It's okay — now," Michael said with a funny catch in his voice. He looked out over Phoebe's head at the stars.

Until he left for Massachusetts, he *had* waited. Then he gave up. He was convinced Phoebe would never want him, not the way he wanted her. She'd probably never want another guy to be anything but just a friend after the way Griffin had hurt her. Michael's hand tightened around Phoebe's waist. He felt like killing Griffin for that.

But Griffin was part of the past now, Michael was sure of it. He had been sure since the night of the barbecue when Phoebe came running down the hill toward him, her hair wild in the moonlight and her smile welcoming. His feelings for her had overwhelmed him. He probably should have told her then, about Leah. He hadn't really meant to wait. But he couldn't bring himself to tell her. Besides, what happened to him at the music festival was a summer thing that didn't matter now. All that mattered now was Phoebe, in his arms where she belonged, where she had *always* belonged.

"It's more than okay, Phoebe, isn't it?" he asked finally, his voice deep.

Phoebe threw her arms around his neck. "How can you ask that?" she whispered fiercely. Then she drew his head down toward hers. He held her so tight as they kissed that she could hardly breathe, and the floor seemed to tilt beneath her feet.

Eventually she pulled away, her cheeks damp with tears. She held Michael's face between her hands and fervently exclaimed, "Oh how I love you, Michael Rifkin. I love you so very much." There in the bell tower in the moonlight was the first time she had said that.

Michael couldn't reply. But he didn't have to. He simply smiled joyously and held Phoebe tightly in his arms.

Chapter
6

Phoebe kicked off her sandals and propped her bare feet on the seat across from her. She glared at Woody across the booth.

"Webster! You're the one who dragged me all the way down here to Sticky Fingers and you've hardly said a word all afternoon — " she looked at the dish before him " — or barely touched that boringly predictable hot-fudge sundae." Phoebe disconsolately stirred the soupy remains of her own Sticky Fingers Tutti-Fruity Bubble-Gum Delight and eyed Woody's half-eaten treat greedily. "I mean, you let me win hands-down!" Phoebe complained, referring to her ongoing contest with Woody. For nearly four years now they had made the rounds of local ice-cream parlors, trying to outdo each other on the weirdest, stickiest, grossest combinations of sundae ingredients. Whoever won got treated to the next pig-out. Phoebe was paying today — as usual. No one ever out-weirded Woody Webster — except for today.

"Sorry," Woody mumbled, not even looking up at Phoebe. He slumped down further in his chair, and continued chaining together plastic straws from the table dispenser. "Not that you should be complaining. I have to pay next time," he grumbled.

Phoebe cocked her head at the uncharacteristically sharp edge to Woody's voice. "Hummpf—is that why you're so grumpy? Who'd ever have thought Woody Webster was such a rotten loser?" Phoebe teased. She pulled Woody's sundae bowl to her side of the table, and dipped her finger into the hot fudge. It was hard and cold. She pushed the bowl away. Not worth the calories.

"Oh, Pheeberooni, lay off it, will you? I'm not in the mood." Woody crumbled the long chain of straws in his hand and tossed it into his soda glass.

Phoebe sat back in her seat and stared at Woody in disbelief. "Woody?" she said in a hurt voice. "Have I done something — said something?" Suddenly she reached across the table and shook his arm gently. "Is something wrong — I mean really wrong — like at home or with Kim?"

Woody pressed his hands against his forehead and stared down at the table. After a long moment he raked his fingers through his hair, looked up, and met Phoebe's eyes. She had never seen him look so woebegone. He looked like a teddy

74

bear with all the stuffing taken out.

"I — I didn't know about you and Michael," Woody started. "Oh, Phoebe, you've got to believe me. I really didn't. I thought he was just a friend — like we've always been. You know."

Phoebe frowned. "Woody, what are you talking about?"

Woody gave a disgusted snort. "Sorry, that didn't make sense." Woody suddenly leaned across the booth toward Phoebe and asked earnestly, "This thing between you and Michael — it makes you happy, doesn't it? I mean, you really like him, don't you?"

Phoebe didn't know how to respond. She colored and looked down. "Oh, Woody. How can you ask that? Can't you tell?" A silly smile crossed her face. "Oh, I like him — a whole, whole lot." When she met Woody's glance her eyes were shining. She reached across the table and squeezed his hand. "I'm in love again, Woody. I never, ever thought it would happen. Not again." Slowly the smile faded from Phoebe's face. "But I don't get it, Woody. What's me being in love have to do with you looking so miserable — and ordering that dumb hot-fudge sundae?" Phoebe was afraid to hear his answer. Ordering that sundae was like someone throwing in his towel before the end of a race. "I mean, you and Kim, you're still together — you didn't hope that I — "

Woody shook his head quickly. "No, Phoebe. I know I used to hope you'd be my girl. But it wasn't meant to be — and then I found Kim. No, Phoebe, that's not it." Under his breath, he added, "I wish it were.

"Listen," Woody continued, looking more uncomfortable with every word. "I can't believe I have to be the one to tell you this. And I feel like such an idiot, Phoebe. But I promised . . . I promised to tell you." Then he blurted out very quickly, "It's Griffin. He's back, Phoebe. In Rose Hill. He's not with Sara any more."

Phoebe's whole world skidded to a halt.

She was staring straight at Woody, but looking right through him. Griffin was back. No, that was impossible. She didn't believe it. She had heard wrong. She blinked her eyes, and then she saw Woody's anguished face. The raucous din of the ice-cream parlor broke into her thoughts, and for a second she thought she was going to faint: Her heart was beating so fast, her temples pounded, her bare arms felt all clammy and cold. Her stomach hurt as if someone had punched her, real hard.

"Pheeberooni?" Woody whispered. "Pheeb?" He squeezed her hand.

Phoebe pulled her hand away and regarded Woody intently. "Who told you? Who told you that — about Griffin being back and all?" Her voice was amazingly calm and steady.

Woody glanced down at his hands. "Griffin. He came to the Arena Stage Saturday, looking for you. He didn't know your summer job was finished, I guess. He asked me — he asked me to tell you he would like to see you." Woody's last few words were barely audible.

Phoebe sat up very straight and clasped her hands in front of her on the table. She squeezed them together so tightly her knuckles turned white. "I don't believe this," she started in a cold, tense voice. "I don't believe this at all. All summer, not one word. Not even a crummy postcard from the Guthrie Theater — nothing. Woody, he was the one who wanted to stay friends. Remember, remember how I told you that." She began speaking faster, her voice shaking. "Now that Sara's dumped him — I bet, I just bet that's what happened — " Phoebe suddenly didn't care that she sounded so mean and cold. "He wants me to come running at the snap of his fingers. Oh, Woody, how could he? How could he?" Tears welled up in Phoebe's eyes. She buried her face in her arms, and sat sobbing at the table.

Woody came around to her side of the booth. "Oh, Phoebe, don't cry. He's not worth it."

"I thought he was your friend," Phoebe mumbled morosely.

"He is," Woody said quietly, smoothing his hand over Phoebe's back. "He is. But I — well it's none of my business, is it? I just don't want you to be hurt again. That's all."

"Hurt again?" Phoebe looked up quickly, her face tear-stained but her eyes flashing fire. "I wouldn't worry about that if I were you. I wouldn't give him the time of day," she declared vehemently.

Woody fell silent. Phoebe pulled some napkins

77

out of the dispenser and noisily blew her nose. She took a couple of deep breaths and tried to pull herself together. Slowly she began to feel more normal. She was still angry inside, but less shaky, less as if her world had skidded off its track.

"So, then," Woody finally ventured, "I'll tell him not to call. I'll do that for you, Phoebe. If I had known about Michael, I would have told Griffin you had another guy. Then he wouldn't have asked me to tell you he was back. I'll just tell him you're not interested. Okay?"

Phoebe started to nod yes, but something stopped her. She knew she should tell Woody to let Griffin know she didn't ever want to see him again. Never, ever again. But suddenly the word "never" sounded so final, so cold, like something far off at the edge of the earth. But if she saw Griffin — even if she heard his voice on the phone — what would happen? What would happen between her and Michael? Even before she knew Griffin was back in town, he was like a ghost haunting her new romance. She was getting better at pushing down the memories, setting them aside, making room for the new, stronger feelings she had when Michael held her. If she saw Griffin face-to-face, and looked up into his eyes, what would she feel then?

She looked up at Woody. "I don't know. I don't know what you should do. I have to think about it," she said in a low, flat voice. "Yes, that's it, Woody. Give me a little time. I'll call you and let you know what to do. Just don't say anything yet if you see him. Okay?"

A faint frown crossed Woody's face. "Okay," he agreed with a worried sigh. He picked up the check, but Phoebe took it from his hand. "Next time you pay. Remember, this is for our last pig-out," she reminded him with a feeble laugh. Her hand was shaking as she reached into her bag for her wallet. She took out a ten-dollar bill and a little antique compact.

Phoebe checked her makeup in the tiny mirror. Woody felt miserable watching her quickly wipe off the mascara from under her eyes. If only he hadn't told her Griffin was back. But he had promised Griffin, and a promise was a promise. And like Phoebe had said, Griffin had become one of Woody's really good friends. Woody sighed and studied his hand. He wished somehow Griffin and Phoebe had never met. But that was all history now. At least he hadn't told Phoebe *everything* Griffin had said. He clenched his fists and vowed silently: Phoebe would never, ever know that Griffin felt he couldn't live without her. Even under pain of death Woody wouldn't tell her that.

"Who's that — with Chris?" Phoebe said suddenly, peering at a reflection in her mirror. She snapped the compact shut and quickly turned around in her seat. Chris was standing just inside the door, looking crisp and cool in her tennis whites. Beside her was a guy Phoebe'd never seen before. He had two rackets in his hand and a gym bag slung over his shoulders. Phoebe had heard of people looking larger than life, but she had never quite known what it meant until that moment. Chris's companion was broad-shouldered and slim, yet he seemed to fill the whole door. The spacious ice-cream parlor didn't seem big enough for him. Phoebe's next thought was: Where's Ted?

Woody whistled under his breath. "Amazing. If I didn't know Chris was our Chris Austin, I'd say an ad walked in right off the pages of *Sports Illustrated*."

At that moment Chris spotted them and waved energetically in their direction.

"Oh, Woody!" Phoebe muttered in a panicky voice. "They aren't coming over here, are they? Do — do I look all right?" she stammered. Why did Chris have to turn up now? Later she'd probably want to talk to Chris, tell her the whole thing. But she wasn't ready yet. She needed time to sort out her feelings.

Woody gave Phoebe's arm a reassuring squeeze. "Pheeberooni, you look fine." After a second, he added softly, "I won't say a thing. To anyone. You know that."

Phoebe heaved a sigh of relief. "I know, Woody. I know I can trust you." But trusting Woody wasn't the problem. Trusting Chris was. Chris knew Phoebe too well not to notice something was wrong. She crossed her fingers under the table. Putting on an act in front of Chris was almost impossible. She forced a smile as Chris bounced over to the table.

"Hi — " Chris greeted Phoebe and Woody with a grin. Her cheeks were faintly flushed, her eyes wide and sparkling. But when she saw the money in Phoebe's hand, her face fell. "Oh, you're leaving already?"

Phoebe and Woody exchanged glances. "Uh — well, we *were* leaving — but we can hang out a few minutes more," Phoebe said, seeing the disappointment register on Chris's face.

"Great!" Chris beamed, then motioned toward the guy. "This is Greg — the friend I told you about from work. Woody Webster, Phoebe Hall." Chris made the introductions and flopped down across from them in the booth.

Greg slipped in beside Chris, angling his long legs into the aisle. When Chris had mentioned her upcoming tennis game with her new friend, Phoebe had thought it was a girl, especially since Chris had sounded so totally confident about trouncing her opponent. Phoebe was no expert at tennis, but Greg looked like he'd be pretty tough competition across the net. Though there was plenty of room between them, Phoebe squashed herself into the corner of the booth. Again she had that overwhelming feeling that Greg took up more space than he actually did. She smiled shyly at him and passed the menu. She glanced quickly at Chris who was studying the list of flavors posted on the wall. Fortunately she hadn't seemed to notice Phoebe's shaky hands or red-rimmed eyes.

"So, Greg — how does it feel to play the unbeatable Chris Austin?" Woody said jovially.

"You mean formerly unbeatable Chris Austin," Chris groaned and buried her head in her arms. She looked up all smiles and giggled. "So guess who pays today? I made a bet I'd win in straight sets."

"You lost?" Phoebe and Woody gasped in unison and met each other's eyes. No one ever beat Chris, not even Ted. Phoebe squinted at Chris. If Chris lost, how come she looked like such a winner? Phoebe wondered. Chris didn't take defeat easily — not even over something so silly as losing out to Janie Barstow for prom queen.

"She lost!" Greg said a trifle smugly, and Phoebe couldn't help but grin watching his finger move down the list of the ice-cream parlor's most lavish — and expensive — concoctions. Chris glared over at him, but she couldn't manage to look angry. She started laughing. "Pheeb, would you believe it? Greg is practically a pro! And he didn't tell me — the creep!" Chris stuck her tongue out at him.

He was unmoved. He simply shrugged and said, "Why should I tell you I'm a pro? It's not the truth. I can't help it if I play tennis with my sister — "

"His sister," Chris broke in excitedly, "is Carrie Montgomery! You know, the girl who was on the cover of *Newsweek* last May."

"Really?" Woody eyed Greg with new interest. "I don't know the first thing about tennis, but I remember seeing that photo and reading about that hot new eighteen-year-old giving all the old pros trouble at some big match."

Phoebe tried to look interested, but keeping track of a conversation was almost impossible. Besides, she didn't have much patience for professional tennis players after what had gone on between Kim and tennis superstar Chan Lawrence earlier that summer. She sat scrunched in the corner of the booth folding and unfolding her ten-dollar bill, a blank smile pasted on her face. Her mind was on Griffin — and Michael — and the knot forming in her stomach. Saturday night's dream had come back to her in a flash. Maybe it had been some sort of premonition.

"Tell them, Phoebe, tell them I don't *always* order butter pecan!" Chris was tugging Phoebe's arm. Phoebe stared blankly at her friend.

"Butter pecan what?" she asked in confusion.

Woody came to her rescue. "Aw, what would she know. She's too spaced out — too much sugar. Just before you guys came in Phoebe demolished the biggest, grossest sundae you've ever seen — and half of mine!"

Phoebe shrugged and mentally scrambled to piece together whatever conversation she had missed. Chris must have been defending her predictable taste again.

"Hey, Greg," Woody piped up, "how long have you been at Kennedy? I mean, I've never seen you around."

"Spare us," Chris pleaded. "Who wants to talk about school when we've got three whole weeks of vacation left!"

"Hey, the student body president is supposed to *love* school. You're supposed to be a model student. I'm supposed to look up to you. I'm supposed to want to be exactly like you — to match!" Greg wagged a finger in Chris's face. His tone was light and teasing, but Phoebe sensed some deeper meaning behind his words. Chris must have, too. She blushed slightly and looked down at her ice cream. Phoebe frowned. For the second time that afternoon she thought about Ted. Then she remembered Chris had mentioned Ted had a game out in Ocean City today.

"Don't change the subject — we were talking about ice cream, not school." Chris sniffed. "Besides, being elected president doesn't mean I don't like having fun."

"Good!" Greg said. "Glad to hear that." He rubbed his hands together and pretended to leer at Chris.

Chris avoided Greg's eyes and looked around the room. "Hey, look! There's Brenda!" she cried, beckoning to her stepsister and Brad, who had just walked in the door.

"Actually I've been at Kennedy exactly one year," Greg said to Woody as Brad walked up.

"Hi, guys — what brings you here? Our excuse is a broken down air conditioner and no popcorn at Cinema 9. I'm hot and starved." Brad greedily eyed a colorful sundae the waitress had set in front of Greg. Then he noticed Greg.

"Hey, if it isn't the old sea captain himself." Brad reached out and pumped Greg's hand.

"You know each other?" Chris sounded amazed.

"Know each other!" Greg groaned. "Brad and

I locked horns weekly for an entire two semesters last year — "

"Not with each other, though — with the whole student council!" Brenda laughed and settled down next to Chris. "Good to see you, Greg. Having a good summer?" she added with a welcoming smile.

"You bet!" he mumbled through a mouthful of strawberry ice cream.

Brad pulled a chair up to the end of the table and punched Greg's shoulder. "This kid here's the most persistent creature I've ever met. He drove me nuts. Every week he came to us with a new proposal. He wanted to start — in this order — a freshman crew team, a freshman yachting club, a freshman rowboat squad, an intramural windsurfing meet, and finally an all-school sailboat race. Eventually — just to get rid of him — we gave in. Kennedy High's going to have a crew team next year."

"Freshman crew team?" Chris asked.

"You're a freshman?" Phoebe gasped, looking directly at the tall boy sitting across from her. He looked as old as Brad, or Michael — or Griffin.

"No." Greg looked directly at Chris. "A sophomore. Freshman was last year."

Phoebe watched Chris sit back in her seat and study Greg. Maybe she imagined it, but some subtle tension in Chris's shoulders seemed to dissolve.

Chris finally responded. "That's great — I mean — " she added quickly, "about finally getting a crew team going. Ted'll love it. He's crazy about boats but almost never gets a chance to sail them." Phoebe noticed it was the first time Chris had mentioned Ted.

"Captain Montgomery to the rescue." Greg pounded the table to get everyone's attention. "I've got a great idea. How about we all go sailing next weekend? My folks have a big place on the Eastern Shore. There's lots of space — and a couple of boats, not counting our little dinghy." He laughed. "Come on — I'd love to have you all — and Ted," he added, looking at Chris. "I've heard so much about him. I could say 'Kennedy's star quarterback slept here.' " There was a lightly mocking edge in his voice.

Chris didn't seem to notice. She was too excited about the prospect of a weekend at the beach. "A weekend sailing on Chesapeake Bay!" she nearly shouted, her eyes widening. "Oh, Greg, that would be wonderful! I've only sailed on lakes, up in the mountains. Never on the ocean." Almost as an afterthought, she added, "I'll check with Ted tonight — and Dad. I'm not sure he'll let us go."

"Oh, I bet he will," Brenda said. "After all, Greg's father is his broker."

"I forgot about that. Greg told me, our fathers *do* know each other." Chris laughed.

"Of course, we'll need some very official looking document saying we'll be well-chaperoned," Brad commented.

Greg turned to Woody and Phoebe, and said warmly, "Hey, what about you two?"

86

"Me — " Woody gulped. "I'm afraid the only sailing I've ever done is in my bathtub. I had a supposedly unsinkable red plastic toy tug that went the way of the *Titanic* when I was about five. Killed a whole crew's worth of Legos. I've been a landlubber ever since." He groaned. "Just hearing the word sea makes me turn green."

Greg flashed Phoebe a questioning smile. She tried to smile back. All she could manage was a silly grimace. She couldn't even begin to think of the weekend. By then she'd have made her decision about Griffin. "Uh, thanks, Greg. That's really nice, but I don't think my parents would let me go."

"Not with Michael, they wouldn't!" Brenda teased.

Phoebe paled slightly, and forced a laugh. "With any male, really — under the age of thirty and over the age of ten."

Woody cracked up — a little too loudly Phoebe thought, but no one noticed. Everyone began talking about the weekend: how to get there, what to bring.

Phoebe tried to meet Woody's eye, but he kept looking away, talking very fast, cracking dumb jokes about bathtubs and sailboats. The more he clowned around, the more annoyed Phoebe began to feel. She knew it was unfair, being angry at her old friend. But Woody had just given her the worst news of her life, and he sat there laughing with the crowd as if nothing had happened.

Phoebe shrank back further in her seat and tried to tune out Woody's voice. She shouldn't be feeling this way. Just because Griffin was somewhere nearby, she shouldn't feel so hollow and scared and cold inside. She knew she was over Griffin. She loved Michael now. But if that was true, why was she so terribly afraid to even hear his voice again?

Chapter
7

"Hey, Mason, on the way back, pick up some sodas — but don't drop 'em!" Tommy Lofredo, the Ramblers' first baseman, yelled down the beach.

Ted lengthened his stride and pretended not to hear over the sound of the waves. As soon as he was really out of earshot, he stuffed his Ramblers' T-shirt into the back of his bathing trunks and relaxed his pace to a comfortable jog. He was sick of Lofredo's jokes about his poor fielding, just like he was sick of everyone on the Ramblers' team — especially himself. Not that the Ramblers had lost today; they'd shut-out the Ocean City Sharks for the third time this season. But no thanks to Ted. He had struck out three times, hit into a double-play, and practically blown the game by spacing out over a fly ball hit to center. Fortunately "Fats" Grossman had appeared somewhere out of left field, making a terrific play and saving the game. Now the Ramblers' beach party victory celebration was in full swing and Ted wanted to get away from the horseplay, the noise, and endless rehashing of the day's play-by-play. Personally, he didn't feel like he had very much to celebrate. Besides, he needed some time alone. Coach Beely's post-game man-to-man talk with Ted had left a funny taste in his mouth and a knot in his stomach.

Not that Beely had been so tough. Ted would have felt chastened but all right about a real dressing-down. Instead the coach had asked if he was having problems at home, or with his girl friend. Ted was taken aback. "Problems?" He glared suspiciously at the coach. "No problems. My playing just stank, that's all." And he had slammed off to the showers angry that the beefy-faced coach was more concerned with psychological problems than just helping a guy play better ball. What Ted needed to know was how to time his swing better, improve his stance, to spot trick pitches. Ted *knew* that a guy's attitude could affect how he played a game — but he wasn't sure he agreed with the current fashion of blaming every mistake a player made on some kind of head hang-up. He and Chris had had a couple of heavy arguments on that topic. Chris was big on psychology these days, and she had refuted point-by-point Ted's theory that how well you played had much more to do with how much you *loved* to play football, or baseball, or whatever, and much less to do with problems, in

90

school, at home, with your girl friend. Ted loved football best so he played it best. He loved the feel of the cold autumn wind blowing down the grandstands across the field and through his hair; the roar of the crowd, the chant of the cheer-leaders; the locker room hijinks, the parties, even the occasional rowdy fights that broke out when you knew the officials had somehow given your team a bum deal. Ted loved putting his muscle to the whole game, shoulder to shoulder with every other guy on the team, and knowing that even if you lost somehow you won.

Chris never understood that feeling. Just like she never understood when you played a game the most important thing was having fun.

Thinking of Chris made Ted's stomach flip-flop. His fists clenched up, his shoulders tightened. He hadn't called her since Phoebe's party. He hadn't wanted to hear her apologize for something she couldn't help doing. Or for being someone she couldn't help being.

Ted took a deep gulp of air, shook out his hands, and tried to loosen up. A silvery gull wheeled above the whitecaps, plunged into the water, and soared up again with a harsh, joyous cry. It looked so free and strong and wild. Ted watched it and spread out his arms. He jogged into the breaking waves and kicked his feet up high as he ran. He zig-zagged down the beach through the breakers, flapping his arms and imitating the gull's hoarse, keening sounds. The sea spray spattered his face and hair, and the late afternoon sun beat down on his bare shoulders.

Ted gave a wild whoop and smiled. Knots of late afternoon bathers still dotted the sands, but Ted was oblivious to their stares. He didn't notice the startled bunch of kids watching in horror as he leapt gracefully over their sandcastle, pretending to fly.

The scream came from somewhere off to his right. Ted whirled around. A woman in a black and red bathing suit came tearing across the sand from the boardwalk. Two ice-cream cones fell from her hand as she ran. Behind her trailed a toddler hugging a dirty blanket and wailing.

Ted looked in the direction they were running. A lone figure was struggling through the breakers toward something bobbing in the rough waves. Ted glanced over his shoulder. He remembered passing a lifeguard station but it was the end of the day and lifeguard hours were over. The station tower was down on the sand, the rowboats pulled up above the tideline.

Ted broke into a run. In seconds he reached the water's edge and pushed his way through the quickly growing crowd. He couldn't see the woman but he noticed that someone had picked up the howling toddler. Then he heard the woman screaming: "My baby, my baby — " Her high-pitched voice cut through Ted like a knife. He fought his way toward the center of the crowd. A couple of guys were holding the woman back. On the sand lay the limp body of a nine- or ten-year-old boy.

A girl wearing a park service tank suit was bent over the pale form. She was so small, at first Ted thought she was a child. But he knew lifeguards had to be at least sixteen to work at this beach. She looked very strong and with her well-defined muscles, Ted pegged her for some kind of athlete. She scarcely looked winded as she pressed her head against the boy's thin chest and listened intently for his heartbeat.

"Come on, you dumb kid!" she muttered. "Breathe. Breathe." She pinched the boy's nose, cupped her hand beneath his chin, and yanked open his mouth. Sealing her lips on his, she forced four short, quick breaths into his lungs, then turned her head away. She repeated the procedure again. A kind of cough came out of the boy. She turned his head to the side.

"Help him! Do something for him!" the hysterical mother cried as she broke away from the restraining hands and threw herself on top of the lifeguard. Ted sprang into action. He grabbed the woman and pulled her to her feet. "Stop it!" Ted shouted in a firm voice. "Stop it or your boy will die. Can't you see she's a lifeguard?" He turned and addressed the crowd. "Someone go get help. Call the rescue squad. The kid's going to need medical attention — fast." The lifeguard seemed oblivious to the commotion as she hovered over the prone figure of the child, rhythmically forcing her breath in and out of his mouth.

A stifled groan rose up from the sand. The boy was stirring. His arms were weakly fighting off the lifeguard. He began coughing and was sick all over the sand. Ted let go of his grip on the mother's arm, and she ran, weeping, to her son.

Ted stood by the lifeguard's side as the medical attendants led the shivering boy away. The crowd broke up and scattered in different directions along the beach. Ted watched the departing figures and frowned. "The mother didn't even say thank you."

"That's okay. It's all in a day's work. People get really upset and forget the thank you's. I understand." She didn't sound like she was from the East Coast. Ted couldn't place her accent, but her voice was expressive as she added, "Still, I wish these people would take better care of their kids. It's a miracle I was walking by when some guy spotted him out there and yelled for help."

He turned toward the girl and really looked at her for the first time. She had walked over to the water and was washing off the sand from her arms and legs. She was barely five feet tall, and the ocean looked big and fierce behind her. She splashed the seawater on her head and neck, slicked back her short black curly hair, and glanced up at Ted. Her huge blue eyes were fringed with jet black lashes. She had a dark tan and a dusting of freckles on her upturned nose. She wasn't beautiful like Chris, but she was attractive in an earthy way. Her face had a frank, straight-forward expression Ted didn't quite know how to respond to.

"By the way, I'm Molly — Molly Ramirez." She poked out her hand. Ted took it. It was a ridiculously small hand to have just saved a life, he thought. He held it a second longer than he meant to. Then he hooked his thumbs in the pockets of his trunks and laughed awkwardly. "Uh — I'm Ted Mason."

Molly's face opened into a smile. "Hi, Ted Mason. Nice meeting you."

It sounded like some kind of parting line and Ted expected her to go somewhere. But she just stood there with her hands on her hips, looking past him out to sea, then back at the boardwalk, as if she were waiting for something to happen. As he watched her, he thought he had never seen anyone look so good in a regulation park service tank suit.

"Ted?" Molly's voice held a question. Ted brought her face into focus. He hadn't heard a word she had said. "That's your name, isn't it?" He got the feeling she was laughing at him. "I said, how about walking to the boardwalk for something to eat? I'm starved. I'd just closed down the station and was heading for some food when that kid went under. Oh drat! Where's my bag?" She looked around in confusion, then spotted a red canvas carryall on the sand. "Everything I own's in here!" she said and started toward the boardwalk. She looked over her shoulder and met his eye and said, "Aren't you coming?" She touched his arm. Ted felt as if he'd just been touched by a high voltage wire, and he was powerless to resist.

Molly stopped at the first aid station on the boardwalk and filed her report. "The kid's okay," one of the medics said. "Good work, Ramirez, as usual!"

Molly grinned, and pointed at Ted. "Thank him, too. The mother went berserk, almost killed me. Could have killed the kid, too. Ted's got a sure hand with a crazy crowd."

"It's all in a day's work!" he said, echoing Molly's words.

"What do you do?" Molly started. "Wait, let me guess." She pushed up her sunglasses and peered hard at him. Ted squirmed slightly under her glance. It was so piercing, so direct. Her big blue eyes seemed to look right through him to the depths of his soul. He looked away quickly. He wasn't used to someone looking at him like that — at least not a girl he'd just met.

An impish grin crossed Molly's face. "I know. You're a jock. I should have known by that!" She pointed to his Ramblers shirt. It was all wet now, and dangling like a red and white flag out of the back of his trunks. "You still in school?" she asked.

"Yeah, but not around here," Ted answered. "Back in Rose Hill. I'll be a senior at Kennedy High — you've probably heard of it."

Molly shrugged. "There are a lot of schools named after the Kennedys. One in my town, too. But I go to Pacific Point. I'm going into junior year — "

"Pacific Point?" Ted asked, confused. They were standing in front of a candy concession. Molly was poking in her bag for some change.

"Pacific Point, California." Molly raised her eyebrows. "Everyone around here spotted my accent on my first day. It's like, narly, dude," she said with a laugh, faking a stereotypical California voice.

"You're from California?" Ted asked, feeling strangely disappointed that she lived so far away. "What are you doing here working as a lifeguard?" It was hard to imagine a California girl coming to the East Coast just to work at Ocean City for the summer.

"I work for the Park Service. There was a job here, so I applied. I love to travel — meet new people, see new places." Then she added in a low voice, "It's been a rough year. My father died a few months ago and Mom felt a change of scene would do me good. I have an aunt who lives near here and I've been staying with her all summer."

Molly's hand, clenching a five-dollar bill, rested on the counter. She was looking longingly at the cotton candy. At that moment she looked so young and frail that Ted instinctively laid a protective hand on hers. Her tiny hand vanished beneath his. "I'm sorry about that. About your father," he said. He pulled some money out of his pocket and paid for the candy.

Molly's eyes met his. She studied his face. "Thanks." She didn't pull her hand away. They walked toward the railing of the boardwalk. Ted liked the feel of her hand in his. He was still carrying her candy. She leaned out over the railing, and began talking. "I thought it wouldn't hurt so much. He'd been dying a long time. I thought we'd all be used to it. But I was so angry I ran away from home, sort of lost control for a while, and had to see a counselor."

97

She broke off suddenly. Her voice trembled and she sounded like she was going to cry. She pulled her hand out of Ted's and rubbed her arm across her eyes. But she didn't turn her face away and she didn't apologize.

"I'm doing much better now. It was just really hard at first. I loved my dad so much." She reached for her candy, then hoisted herself up on the rail. She straddled the weathered wood, one bare leg dangling over the side of the boardwalk. Ted watched her pick the fluffy pink stuff off the stick. She unwound it bit by bit and licked it off her fingers. She offered a handful to Ted. As she sat there with her candy she looked just like a child. It was hard to imagine she'd been through so much.

"I'd be angry like that, too," Ted said softly, looking out over the ocean. "No one I know has died, but other things get to me. Sometimes everything seems so wrong, so unfair, I feel like breaking out. That's why it feels so good to play football, I guess. Get those feelings out." He thought of Chris. Chris had lost her mother a few years ago. But Ted and she had been going together for months before she ever talked about it. Everyone in school knew, of course, especially because her father had recently married Brenda's mother. Still, Ted had felt hurt that Chris hadn't shared her feelings with him for such a long time. He could still remember the first time she had cried in front of him. It was in the dark, at the revival house during *Gone with the Wind*. That was the night she finally talked about her mom, and how hard it had been ever since to tell anyone she loved them. Sitting with Molly, thinking of Chris, Ted suddenly felt uncomfortable. He remembered how long it had been since he'd last *really* talked to Chris.

He looked up guiltily into Molly's eyes. Her face was calmer now. Her eyes had a farsighted look about them that seemed to delve right to the bottom of his soul. She gazed directly at him over the top of her cotton candy. "You know, Ted Mason, I like you. Even if you are a football hero."

Ted was taken aback. Molly said "football hero" like it was some kind of insult. "What do you mean?" he said.

Molly touched his arm. "Hey, don't look so hurt. I just said I liked you. It's just back home I'm not supposed to like jocks. Believe me, we have plenty of them. You should see some of those surfers. Cute, too, like you. But — my crowd, we're different. I've spent two years of high school making fun of anyone who fits into a category: football heroes, jocks, bikers, druggies, cheerleaders. Let's say me and my friends have made a specialty of not fitting in."

"I'm scarcely the druggy-cheerleader type." Ted laughed. Thinking of Chris, he added, "And there are some people who think I'm pretty crummy at fitting into whatever scene football heroes are supposed to fit into." His voice came out tight and bitter.

Molly regarded Ted silently a second. "Whoever told you that is nuts!" Molly declared

99

staunchly. "I mean that. I don't think you could be crummy at anything you do — that's not what I meant about fitting in. That's what's wrong with words." Molly stood up, and tossed the remains of her candy into a trash can. She leapt lightly onto the railing and began walking toward the stairs leading down to the beach. Ted watched her a minute, then jumped up and followed her, walking toe-to-toe along the narrow trail. Keeping his balance was hard, but when he leapt down beside her on the sandy stairs, they were both laughing.

"See, there's an advantage to being short, and not being built like a football player. It makes tightrope walking easier," Molly stated, looking out over the water. A sad look flitted across her expressive face. "My crowd prides itself on not fitting in," she began, "because fitting in is like being put inside a cage. Someone says, Hey, you're this or that and they fence in your life. I hate fences, Ted Mason. I hate those categories. They're wrong. They stop you. I'm sixteen and I want to try everything on for size. I want to see everything, do everything, be anything I want to be. I don't want someone's idea of me to stop me. That's what I meant. And it was unfair. Because I was thinking that I like you — whatever and whoever you are — and back home I might not even have talked to you, because you're probably the center of the kind of crowd my crowd makes fun of. So I hate cages and labels and fences and then I go and make them, too," Molly concluded in a tone of self-disgust.

She stooped down and scooped up some smooth white stones and angrily hurled them one at a time across the beach. The first few arched up high and fell short of the water. The next one sailed straight out — like a bullet — into the dark waves.

"You've got some arm," Ted said in a shaky voice. Molly's words felt as if they had come from his own heart. Ted could never have expressed it like that. So he said finally, his voice full of feeling, "Today I ran down the beach. I ran and ran. I felt like I had to escape from something. Then I saw a gull and I wanted to fly off and follow it. That's what you mean, Molly, isn't it?" She had described it so perfectly. That was what his life had felt like lately. Like it had been lived inside a cage — a beautiful, very precious cage. No matter how much he loved Chris, being with her felt that way. Now standing in the damp sand, on the dark beach, beside a girl he barely knew, Ted felt a funny, knotty pressure behind his eyes. Then he realized he was just about to cry.

The sun was dipping low, the beach was almost dark now. The reflection of neon lights from the boardwalk sparkled on the water.

"So, Mr. Jock, how fast do you run?" Molly suddenly said. Beneath the boardwalk it was too dark for Ted to see her face.

"Why?" Ted met the challenge in her voice.

Molly didn't answer. She emptied her fist of stones and tore off toward the beachfront. Ted followed in hot pursuit. She was fast and strong, but Kennedy's star quarterback had very long legs. In spite of her head start they reached the water at the same time.

"I won, I won!" they both screamed at the same time.

"I'll show you who won!" Ted cried breathlessly, and began splashing water in Molly's face. She squealed and darted out of range. Ted pursued her along the water line. Finally he tackled her from behind.

The next thing he knew, he was sprawled on his side in the foam, right at Molly's feet. She had her hand around his wrist. She was looking down at him, grinning triumphantly. "Like I said, I won!" she taunted as she pulled Ted to his feet.

He rubbed the side of his leg. His skin stung where he had hit the sand, otherwise he wasn't hurt. "How — how did you do that?" he sputtered, trying to catch his breath. She had really knocked the wind out of him. He slicked back his hair and anchored his toes in the sand. For a second Molly was all blurry in front of his eyes.

"Akido, body building — all that 'jock' stuff!" she said archly.

"All that what?" Ted roared and lunged toward Molly. Before she could duck, he had grabbed her again and pinned her down to the sand. They were still at the water's edge, just below the tideline. The waves washed over them. Molly forced her head up out of the water. Her lips were only inches from Ted's. "Can your Akido get you out of this predicament?" he taunted, aware her heart was racing just like his.

"You bet it can!" Molly said fiercely.

Ted prepared to block her next move. As soon as he relaxed his grip on her arms, Molly squirmed free. She reached toward Ted and firmly wrapped her arms around his neck. "Akido can get me out of anything — if I want it to." He lowered his face towards hers.

Her lips were incredibly soft and sweet like cotton candy. It was a light, gentle kiss. But it wasn't a shy kiss. Kissing her felt so natural, lying there in the waves, beneath the stars, the distant sounds of the boardwalk drifting over them. Molly broke off to catch her breath. Ted pushed her hair off her forehead, brushing the water from her face. She held his face between her hands and gazed into his eyes. For a dizzying moment Ted felt his spirits soar high above the water into the swirling stars. He pulled Molly toward him and held her tight, hugging her with a kind of crazy desperation that frightened him. His lips found hers again, and they kissed for a long time, while the water washed over them.

Ted had never felt like this kissing anyone before, not even Chris. The thought of Chris set off a warning bell in his head, and he came crashing down to earth. He couldn't do this to Chris. Lying on the beach kissing Molly was so unfair to Chris. His shoulders tightened slightly. Molly pulled back from him and searched his face.

"Is something wrong?" Molly's voice trembled

103

slightly and she struggled to catch her breath.

Ted looked into her eyes. He hesitated only a second. When he spoke, his words came straight from his heart. "Wrong? Oh, Molly, nothing's wrong, nothing at all. This is the first thing in my whole life that's ever felt so right." He jumped to his feet and scooped her up into his arms, then ran with her along the beach, kicking up the waves. She screamed with laughter and buried her face against his wet chest. And Ted couldn't tell as he kissed her then if he was laughing or crying.

Chapter
8

Ted drove around Chris's block three times trying to work up the nerve to knock on her door. Finally he gave up. He raked his fingers through his tangled hair and sand sprinkled down on his neck and shoulders. Creating a commotion at the Austins' wasn't the way to begin a serious conversation with Chris. And he couldn't just ring the doorbell, walk in, and tell her. That would be too cold, too abrupt — like a lie. There had been too much between them for him to simply blurt it all out like that. He had to be alone with her someplace, some quiet, private, dark place where he wouldn't see the look in her eyes when he told her. Yes, that was it. It had to be a place where he could hold her and explain the feeling in his heart.

He remembered the phone booth outside the 7-Eleven that was halfway between his house and Chris's. It was an old-fashioned closed-in booth that only truckers used late at night when they pulled off the interstate. No one would hear him there. He'd call her, now before it was too late, and tell her he needed to talk. Maybe she'd come out and meet him. *Tonight*. That would be best. No, tomorrow night, after the game, would be better. He wouldn't feel as tense and on edge as he did now if he waited until after the game.

The game. Ted's car swerved within the lane for a second. Then he regained control. He had forgotten all about tomorrow's game. His thoughts drifted to his parting scene with Molly, just a few hours ago. She had asked him if he could drive her home. It took him a minute to remember his MG was back in Rose Hill and he had come to Ocean City on the bus with the team. They had run together toward the parking lot and found the bus idling at the far end near the locker rooms. Ted had shouted over his shoulder as he ran ahead to catch the bus. "Tomorrow. I'll be here tomorrow. I have to see you again. There's so much I have to tell you."

It was crazy leaving her this way. He felt like he'd known her forever in spite of the short time they'd spent together, but he hadn't had the chance to tell her anything yet, even about Chris. Then the bus had started up and Ted broke into a final desperate sprint across the concrete. The driver had spotted him and stopped the bus. Ted hopped in. Molly was waving to him, mouthing something he didn't catch before the door closed.

He stumbled to an empty seat at the back and looked through the window, watching her grow smaller and smaller beneath the starlit sky, until the road curved around and he lost sight of her.

Now, back at Rose Hill, Ted realized he couldn't meet Molly tomorrow. He couldn't skip the game on such short notice. And he couldn't even call her to explain. Molly hadn't even had time to give him her phone number and he didn't know the name of the aunt she was staying with. He had no way to get in touch with her. "You're so dumb, Mason. Sometimes you're such a loser." Ted moaned and rested his head against the steering wheel of his car.

When the phone rang, Chris was sitting on Brenda's bed painting her stepsister's nails silvery white. They had been talking about the weekend, and Greg.

Chris couldn't seem to stop talking about Greg. Everything about him was so interesting — so different, yet so familiar. Chris didn't tell Brenda that part: how talking to Greg felt so right, as if she had known him her whole life.

"He wants to go into business — but not like his dad. He actually plans on opening something like a mining colony on the moon, or growing vegetables in a space station to feed starving people on earth. Can you believe it?" Chris said with an excited little toss of her head.

Brenda laughed. "I can believe a lot of things. But don't tell Sasha. I'm afraid our environmentalist friend would start an after-school group to look into growing vegetables organically on a space station."

At the mention of school, Chris's face tensed up. "Brenda, tell me the truth. Do you think everyone will think it's strange that Greg and I are friends?"

Brenda looked up but Chris didn't meet her eyes. She kept her attention focused on Brenda's hand. Brenda let out a thoughtful sigh and asked, "Why do you ask that, Chris?"

"He's just a kid, a sophomore. I don't even think he's sixteen yet. But I guess it doesn't matter between friends," Chris said casually, "sophomores and seniors hanging out together. It doesn't look *too* weird, does it? I mean, he doesn't even drive yet!"

"Look weird?" Brenda scoffed. "Nothing about Greg looks weird, Chris. Besides, I think all that age stuff is nonsense, even if it weren't just between friends." Brenda avoided Chris's eyes as she said that.

Chris smiled and took Brenda's other hand. "Do you think Ted will like him?" Her tone was smooth and even.

"Ted? Oh, you mean when they meet — this weekend." Brenda gave her sister an uneasy glance. "Yes, I think so. Greg is very likable. Brad's been impressed with him all year. That's how I met him. Brad kept talking about this crazy, enthusiastic freshman, so I finally went to a student council meeting to see the guy. Greg immediately got on his soapbox to push for his

108

crew team project. He's a guy who really goes after what he wants," Brenda said quietly. "I admire that. Especially since he wants to put that business savvy of his to work helping people. He talked to me after the meeting about Garfield House and had some great suggestions for fundraising projects. We're going to try a few out next fall."

Just then the phone rang. Both girls jumped for it. Chris reached it first.

"Ted, it's you!" she exclaimed. "Wait until you hear my news. So much has happened."

Ted was silent on the other end.

"Oh, I'm sorry." Chris slapped her hand to her head and giggled apologetically. "I didn't even ask you about the game. How'd it go? Did you win?"

"The Ramblers won," Ted said simply. "Listen, Chris," he added after a pause. "You and I have got to have a talk soon. How about tonight? Can you get out a bit, go for a drive in the park?"

"Ted Mason, are you nuts?" Chris scolded. "It's past eleven. Dad's not going to let me out at this hour, tomorrow being a work day and all." Chris lowered her voice and said softly, "Can't our little drive wait until Friday because — " a teasing note entered her voice " — because Friday we have somewhere really special to go."

"We do?" Ted sounded confused. "I'm sorry, I don't remember. I'm sort of tired now. I wanted to talk to you sooner than that. How about tomorrow?"

"Tomorrow's Congressman Barnes's dinner party. I promised to help out at his house. No, it'll have to be Friday. And don't be so silly. How could you possibly remember our plans — I just made them. You aren't going to believe this." Chris pushed her hair off her face and flopped down cross-legged on the floor. "I met a friend at work — Greg Montgomery. He goes to Kennedy, but you probably don't know him — he's just a kid, a sophomore." Chris grinned and toyed with the fringe on Brenda's rag rug. "His folks have a big place down on the Eastern Shore and he invited us out there this weekend. A whole weekend sailing on the Chesapeake Bay — they've got a yacht and all sorts of other boats. You'll really love it, Ted. Brenda and Brad are going and Dad said it was okay." Chris paused to catch her breath. "I didn't get a chance to ask you first, but I figured — "

Ted broke in. "No, Chris. Not this weekend. I can't do it. We've got a game up near Maryville on Saturday, a doubleheader."

"Oh, Ted!" was all Chris could manage at first. "Can't you cancel — just this once?" she pleaded.

"I don't believe you, Chris." Ted suddenly sounded edgy and annoyed. "You're the one who insisted it was important to attend all the games this summer — oh, never mind. That's not the point now. The point is I can't go . . . and I need to talk to you somewhere alone. Soon. It's important."

Chris frowned. She waved at Brenda and covered the mouthpiece of the phone with her hand. "I think Ted's having trouble with the team again!" She raised her eyebrows, then took her hand off the phone.

"We can't talk about it now?" she said, trying to focus her attention on whatever Ted's problem was this time. It was hard. She really wanted to talk about sailing, about the weekend and the beach.

"No. No, I can't." The tone of Ted's voice scared Chris. Something bad must have happened. Coach Beely must have given him one of his famous man-to-man post-game chats. Maybe he kicked Ted off the team. Ted wouldn't want to talk on the phone about that. Chris heaved a deep sigh. At any rate, sailing with Greg was out.

"Okay, Ted. I understand. We'll see each other Friday," Chris said, trying not to sound disappointed. "I'd better call Greg now before it gets too late. I had told him yes earlier tonight — but now. . . ." Chris forced herself to brighten up. "Why am I being such a baby?" she sniffed. "We can go another time. He said they always have lots of room for guests."

Ted didn't say anything for a minute. "Listen, Chris, this is silly. Just because I can't go doesn't mean you can't. Why don't you go anyway, without me? Brenda, Brad, and you. I know you'd have a great time and it's supposed to be really hot again," Ted encouraged.

"Go without you?" Chris gasped. "I — I don't know." She looked quickly over at Brenda. Brenda had her eyes trained on a magazine. She didn't seem to be listening to the conversation.

"Go, Chris. You'll have a good time. Just — let's make a date for Monday night. Okay? I'll talk to you then."

Chris giggled self-consciously. "You know, Mason. Sometimes I think it was unfair of you to get brains and brawn! You're a genius. Okay, I'll go then . . . but I'll miss you. I love you, Ted!"

"Uh, me, too," Ted murmured after a long pause. Then he hung up.

Ted closed his eyes and rested his forehead against the phone. "Hey, man, don't hog that phone, will you?" Ted turned around. A small line had formed outside the booth. "Sorry," Ted muttered. Jamming his hands into his pockets, he headed back to his car.

Was he crazy? Chris sounded so elated to hear his voice. The way Chris had said "I love you, Ted" had cut right through him. Ted's resolution wavered. He rubbed his hand across his forehead and kicked a can down the cement walk. Suddenly a year's worth of loving Chris flashed through his mind. He thought of never holding her again, never kissing her. They had shared so much together, so many good times. He had been so in love with her. He still loved her. He just knew they weren't right for each other anymore. Nothing in this crazy world made sense. How could something that had once seemed so right seem so wrong now? His stomach knotted up, and his head started pounding. He bit his lips, hard. They tasted salty, salty like the spray from the waves on his face as he raced his shadow down the sunny beach. And sweet like Molly's kisses.

Ted squared his back, slipped the key into the ignition, and took a deep breath. He knew what he had to do. Monday night he'd tell Chris. He'd see her after she got back from her sailing weekend, and he'd tell her right then it was over. How he would tell her was beyond him. He'd never find the right words. But even with the wrong words, he had to explain. It was over. It had been over for months now. But neither of them had looked to see that the distances between them were growing. Ted Mason and Chris Austin were a twosome whose time had run out . . . months ago. Ted finally realized it had been over even before he met Molly. And it would still be over if he never found Molly again.

Chapter
9

"Phoebe Hall, now look what you've done!" Phoebe's kid brother, Shawn, whined as the bus pulled away from the curb. "We've missed our stop!"

Phoebe looked up from her book. "Oh, Shawn," she groaned, "why didn't you tell me sooner?" She yanked the stop signal but it was too late. Phoebe looked out the window and watched Michael's house go by. She'd be late for her singing lesson — again. Four blocks later she pocketed her book, grabbed Shawn's knapsack, and ushered him off the bus.

"You should have drived," Shawn pouted, kicking a stone angrily before him as Phoebe hurried down the street.

"Driven!" Phoebe corrected automatically. Shawn was miffed at her and she didn't blame him. He hated the long, slow bus ride across town, and so did she. It wasn't her fault her mother's station wagon was in the shop for repair, though. But she knew it was the detour to Sasha's parents' bookshop, and the forty minutes she'd spent picking out a book on dreams that had really made them late. At least the book was proving helpful, and now she felt better. It took most of the bus trip to find what she needed to know. Her dreams about Griffin had probably not been a premonition. It had been something more complicated than that. Phoebe didn't quite follow the author's reasoning, but he said right there, in black and white, that when you fell in love you often dreamed of the person you really truly loved for the first time in your life.

Somehow that made her feel better about her decision. Dreaming of Griffin didn't mean she was destined to see him again, even if he was back in town. She would call Woody after her lesson with Miss Spinelli and tell him she didn't want to talk to Griffin. She didn't even want to hear his name.

"Shawn, you're here! You're here!" Paul Rifkin cried, running to the front yard. He was brandishing the garden hose and was dressed in his bathing suit and Mr. Spock ears. Phoebe squealed and darted out of range of the water. Shawn threw his knapsack on the grass and gleefully chased after his friend. Phoebe shook her head and grinned. Michael's mother had the job of watching both boys tonight. Phoebe hadn't been in the mood to drag Shawn to her singing lesson, but Paul's suggestion of a sleepover turned out to be a good one. Phoebe was glad to have Shawn out of her hair, and out of the house. Ever since the ten-year-old's day camp had closed, Shawn had been driving her crazy.

She retrieved his knapsack from the wet grass and started up the broad stairs leading to the porch. A voice floated out the open window of the music room. Phoebe caught her breath. It was a familiar voice, a man's voice, singing "Lullabye of Broadway." "I'm going crazy," she murmured, putting one hand on the porch railing to steady herself. The past twenty-four hours she had thought about Griffin so much she actually imagined she was hearing his voice.

She swallowed hard, took a deep breath, and listened. This time she heard nothing, not even the sound of conversation coming from the house. In the backyard the boys were screaming at each other. Phoebe shook her head to clear it and pressed the doorbell. "How crazy." She smiled to herself. "Just plain crazy."

The big white door opened, and Miss Spinelli greeted Phoebe with a kiss. "You're here. I was beginning to wonder if you were coming."

Phoebe hugged her teacher and looked over her shoulder into the room. She found herself staring straight into Griffin Neill's eyes. He was standing right there, in the front hallway of Michael's house.

"What are you doing here?" she gasped.

Griffin cleared his throat. "Auditioning. Everyone at Maryville told me I should study with Miss Spinelli." He sounded so casual. His eyes held Phoebe's a long, searching moment.

She felt like she couldn't breathe. She averted her glance, then squeezed her eyes shut. This couldn't be happening. It was all some crazy dream. In her dream book she'd read about waking dreams. They were strong, like this, a kind of vivid memory that came up during the day when you thought about something — or someone — too much.

"Phoebe — "

Miss Spinelli was saying something. Phoebe opened her eyes and found Griffin still standing there.

"Why don't you go into the music room and start warming up?" Miss Spinelli said. "You're running late today and I need to talk to Griffin for a few minutes." She ushered Phoebe past Griffin.

His shirt brushed her arm as she passed. "Sorry," she mumbled, without returning his smile.

Fifteen minutes later Phoebe pleaded a sore throat. Miss Spinelli treated her with some hot tea and sent her home. She felt crummy about her lie. But there was no way she could sing right now. She could hardly breathe just thinking about Griffin finding her, knowing he was somewhere nearby. It was crazy running into him here. Griffin had timed his audition perfectly, too perfectly. Woody must have told him about her singing lessons. Yes, that was it. He had planned their meeting, Phoebe was suddenly sure of it.

117

She left the house and walked across the front lawn, eyes focused straight ahead. The boys were still horsing around in the backyard. She could hear them shouting and splashing in the round plastic pool. She didn't turn and yell good-bye, just headed for the corner and the Plexiglas shelter of the bus stop.

The honking horn startled her. She looked to her left and noticed a beat-up old truck parked on the corner. It must have been red once. Now it was mainly rust-colored and patched with tin. Griffin rolled down the passenger-side window.

"Need a lift?" he said. He slid across the front seat and opened the door. When Phoebe didn't move, he climbed out and started toward her. Her mouth went dry and her heart started pounding. She had forgotten how gracefully he moved, how comfortable he seemed with his body.

Shawn's high childish voice rang out across the yard. "I've got flippers *and* goggles, Paul, in my knapsack. PHEEEEEBEEEE!" he cried.

"What!" Phoebe said, too sharply, suddenly afraid Shawn would see Griffin.

"You going home now?" Shawn poked his head around the corner of the house. He waved good-bye to Phoebe. He didn't notice Griffin.

"Yes, sweetie," Phoebe answered, more like herself. "Be good, okay? And I'll see you at home tomorrow."

Shawn didn't hear. He was playing with Paul again and didn't even glance at Phoebe. Phoebe looked into Griffin's eyes.

"Okay. Give me a lift then." Her voice was tight and cold. "Let's get out of here." She scrambled into the front seat and slammed the door. Griffin walked around to the other side and climbed in. Phoebe huddled close to the door, as far away from Griffin's side as she could get.

She stared stonily out the window as Griffin made a U-turn and headed across town.

"Do you want to stop and get something to eat?" Griffin finally broke the silence.

"No!" Phoebe practically shouted. They were stopped at a light near the mall where Michael worked.

"Okay, okay, I just asked," Griffin said testily, glancing at Phoebe. She was sitting very straight now, staring out the window, not looking at anything in particular. Griffin made a left turn, then a right, and headed toward the east side of town.

Suddenly Phoebe faced him. Her voice shook as she said, "Why were you at my lesson? How did you know when I would be there? What else did Woody tell you?" Her eyes were flashing, her cheeks flushed.

"Woody?" Griffin looked over at Phoebe. "He told you about me, then? When I talked to him this morning he said he hadn't yet." He sounded puzzled, a little hurt.

Phoebe gave Griffin a long, suspicious look. He didn't look like he was lying. A small vein throbbed in his temple. He was scared and nervous and had a hungry look about his face, as if things hadn't been going too well for him. But she knew he'd had a job all summer and Woody had said he'd be working all next year at Maryville.

Griffin turned to look at her again. Phoebe quickly looked down and studied her hands. "Woody told me you were still studying singing. I remembered your lessons were on Thursday afternoons. That's why I auditioned today. I can't even afford lessons now, I just came to see you," Griffin confessed. "I needed to see you, Phoebe."

Phoebe was afraid to respond. She had rehearsed her speech to Woody all last night. "Tell Griffin I don't want to see him and I don't want to hear from him. Tell him there's someone else." But sitting next to Griffin now the little speech didn't quite work out, not when she knew in her heart she had needed to see him, too. Last spring when she hurt so much she had really believed she might die from a broken heart. But she didn't die, she just got angry. All summer long her anger had been there inside her chest, cold and hard. She had even hated Griffin for a while and she wanted him to know that. Part of her wanted to hurt him back and part of her wanted to know what it felt like being near him again. In the past, whenever she'd been within a mile of him her soul had soared. She had felt like singing and dancing and hugging the whole world. She had felt alive in a way she had never felt before, so alive that sometimes it hurt inside. Had loving Michael changed all that?

Thinking of Michael suddenly brought Phoebe

back to earth. She must have been crazy, jumping into Griffin's truck like this. Suddenly it seemed very urgent to get far away from him. She glanced out the windshield, looking for a bus stop.

"Hey," she yelled. "Where are you taking me? This isn't the way to my house." Griffin had just made a left at the stop sign beside the old factory. A second later he pulled into the weedy lot of the abandoned Rose Hill railroad station, the place he had brought her the first night they kissed. Griffin stopped the car. He didn't get out and he didn't look at her.

Phoebe was furious. "Griffin Neill, take me home right now. You have no right, no right at all to bring me here." Her voice was shaking, tears started building behind her eyes. She forced them back. "I don't know what kind of game you're playing, Griffin, but I'm not interested. I just want to go home. If you won't take me, at least show me where the bus stops."

"Game?" Griffin repeated incredulously. He turned around in his seat. His face was livid. "Phoebe, this is no game. I bought you here because I thought — I thought it might still matter to you what we felt for each other."

"What *we* felt for each other?" Phoebe gasped. "Last I remember you didn't feel very much for me at all, Griffin! As for what I felt about you, that's over," she declared adamantly. "It was over last spring, when you and that — that Sara Carter — " Phoebe couldn't even finish. She yanked open the truck door and jumped out.

The air was hot and sticky but she felt cold and frightened. She kicked her way through the weeds, conscious of Griffin following behind her.

He vaulted up onto the dilapidated concrete platform and held down a hand. Phoebe ignored it and stayed below, leaning back against the mossy cement wall and staring straight ahead.

Griffin squatted down on his heels. Grass sprouted through the concerte at his feet. He yanked up a handful and tore it as he spoke. "Phoebe, I know, oh, I know how I hurt you. I never wanted to. What happened between me and Sara was some crazy infatuation. I should have realized that then, but I didn't. Right from the first time I kissed her it was still you I was kissing, no matter how hard I tried to forget you." Griffin's voice broke. "Phoebe, it didn't work. No matter what went on with Sara, I was always thinking of you."

Phoebe remained very still. The damp cement was rough and cold against her bare back but she was afraid to move, afraid to breathe. More than anything she was afraid to speak. Ever since Woody had told her Griffin was back, she had tried to imagine seeing him again. The details were always fuzzy but she had fantasized this moment. In her fantasy she would tell him how much he had hurt her, and then she would hurt him back. But none of it seemed to matter anymore. She had fallen in love again and everything with Griffin was over. She didn't even want to be his friend.

But she didn't know he still loved her. She

had never expected that. She had never expected him to be kissing Sara, thinking of her. And she knew he wasn't lying, because she knew exactly what he was thinking about. It was just like what had happened to her with Michael last spring, and just the other night in her dream.

When she finally spoke her voice didn't seem to be her own. "Griffin, I can't see you again. Please take me home." She sounded so calm, so in control of herself. Chris should see me now, she thought.

"How can you say that, Phoebe?" Griffin jumped up and began pacing back and forth on the platform above her. "Just like that — " he snapped his fingers " — you say 'I can't see you again. Take me home.'" His imitation of Phoebe's voice, her very intonation, was so perfect it was cruel.

She cringed slightly and hugged her arms to her chest. She took a deep breath.

Griffin waited a minute. When Phoebe didn't respond, he leapt down beside her. "Don't you understand?" He grabbed her by the shoulders. "I love you, Phoebe. I don't think I can live without you."

Phoebe looked up into his eyes. They were dark with pain and they cut through her. "Please, Griffin, I can't talk about it. I just want to go home." She deliberately took his hands off her shoulders and took a few steps toward the truck.

"I don't believe you," Griffin said angrily. "I look into your eyes and I think you're lying."

"Lying?" Phoebe repeated incredulously. She

spun around and faced him. He was only inches away from her. She took a few steps back to widen the space between them. She didn't want him to touch her again.

"Lying about your feelings. I can see, I can *feel*, here," Griffin tapped his heart, "that you love me, that you're hurt but you still love me. Phoebe, I *know* what you're feeling."

"What I'm feeling!" Phoebe retorted angrily. "You don't know the first thing about my feelings. And the love you see in my eyes, maybe it's not for you, Griffin." Phoebe bit her lip. She hadn't meant to tell him that way. He still loved her and she no longer felt like she had to hurt him back. But she was so confused. She didn't know what she felt for him. And she knew that she did love Michael. And he was something separate from Griffin. She didn't want Michael entering Griffin's world. Michael was *now*, Griffin was *then*.

Griffin eyed Phoebe steadily. "Are you trying to tell me there's someone else?"

Phoebe took a deep breath and said quietly, "Yes, there's someone else. There has been for a while. Woody didn't know or he would have told you." She didn't meet Griffin's eyes as she started toward the truck.

Suddenly Griffin's hand was back on her shoulder. He wheeled her around to face him. He put his hand under her chin and tilted her face up toward his. He made her meet his eyes. Phoebe looked into them. The effect was magnetic, the way it had always been. "Tell me that again. Look me straight in the eye and tell me there's another guy and you love him." Griffin's face was pale, but his jaw was set as he added, "And I'll go away, Phoebe."

Phoebe didn't even blink as she said, "I love someone else, Griffin." Looking directly at him like that, Phoebe had to tell the truth.

He took his hands from her shoulders and reached in his pocket for the keys. He walked ahead of Phoebe to his wreck of a truck, his proud shoulders stooping slightly. His whole body looked wounded.

Suddenly Phoebe couldn't stand it. She rushed up behind him and grabbed his hand. "Oh, Griffin, I'm so sorry." The words tumbled out before she knew it. "I'm so sorry it has to be this way," she stammered, still holding his hand. She hadn't meant to hurt him like this.

Slowly Griffin turned to face her. His eyes were watery and one tear had started its way down his cheek. Phoebe reached up to wipe it away. Griffin took her hand and gently kissed it, his eyes never leaving hers. He pressed her fingers against his damp cheek. His skin was so soft, so smooth. Phoebe couldn't resist when he drew her closer. His hand was warm against her waist where her halter didn't quite meet the top of her shorts.

As if they had a will of their own, Phoebe's arms tightened around Griffin's shoulders. He caressed her face, her hair, the damp skin on the back of her neck, his eyes drinking in every bit of her. Phoebe felt hypnotized watching him look at her like that. Then he bent to kiss her, just like in her dream. And just like in her dream, before his lips sealed hers, a voice cried out from deep inside her, "Oh, Griffin, Griffin."

Chapter
10

Clutching the receiver of her new phone, Phoebe closed her eyes and leaned against the bedroom door. Her hands were shaking so much she had already dialed the wrong number twice.

"Congressman's Barnes's office. May I help you?" Chris sounded calm and efficient. Phoebe opened her eyes, sank down to the floor, and hugged her knees to her chest. Good old steady Chris. Just hearing her voice made Phoebe feel better.

"Chris. It's me, Phoebe." Phoebe rubbed her arm across her face. She had finally stopped crying, but her eyes still burned, and her head hurt, and the air conditioning was making her shiver.

"Hi, Pheeb. What's up?" Chris asked brightly.

Phoebe swallowed hard. "Chris, something happened. I have to talk to you. I really do."

"Oh, Phoebe, I can't talk now. You know that. I'm at work," Chris reminded her.

"Oh, Chris. It's important!" Phoebe started pleading, then stopped. She had just pictured Chris, sitting in front of a big desk in a very official office, looking every inch the rising young politician, listening to her best friend's latest sob story. The picture didn't quite fit. Neither would Chris's reaction to the news about Griffin. Phoebe suddenly realized that. Her first impulse had been to run home to phone Chris, hoping to hear her say, "It's okay. A few stolen kisses, that's all. It's no big deal." But she knew Chris would never tell her that. Chris would never lie to make Phoebe feel better about Michael, about facing Michael tonight. Phoebe stifled a sob.

"Pheeb!" Chris's voice sounded worried. "Hey, are you still there? Are you okay? You don't sound so hot. I mean, if it's serious — "

Phoebe willed her voice to remain steady. "No, it's not that serious." She forced a laugh. "You know me. I get dramatic. It was just something dumb, something about Michael," she added, not really lying.

"Hey, tonight's Springsteen, isn't it?" Chris said. "You lucky dog."

"Uh, yes. It's tonight. In fact, I'd better go. It's getting late." Phoebe checked the old brass alarm clock on the table near her bed. It really was late. In less than an hour, Michael would be there. "And Chris," Phoebe added hastily, "have a good time this weekend."

Phoebe hung up the phone and put it back on

her night table. It was a Garfield phone and somehow all wrong for the conversation she had just had. The silly cartoon figure of the fat orange cat usually made her laugh, no matter how awful she was feeling. Shawn had picked it out himself when her father had wanted to surprise her with a phone for her birthday. But today she looked at it and was frightened. Any minute now, or tonight, or tomorrow, it would ring, and Griffin would be on the other end. He had said he would call.

After the miserable scene at the old railroad station, they had driven to Phoebe's neighborhood in silence. They had been sitting in the truck a few blocks from Phoebe's house because she wouldn't let him drive her all the way home. She didn't want anyone to see them together. Griffin was leaning against his door, facing her. Phoebe sat on the other side of the lumpy front seat, her knees drawn up to her chest.

"I've got a place now, Phoebe. I'm living with roommates in an apartment over a barn up in Maryville," Griffin had said.

His black T-shirt had a sparkling picture of the swirling Milky Way, with an arrow saying: I LIVE HERE. For the first time that afternoon, Phoebe had smiled. Maryville didn't look much like a star-studded galaxy.

Griffin misunderstood her smile.. "So you'll come then and see me there? Soon?" He sounded so eager.

Phoebe had stared at Griffin, unable to believe he was asking her to see him again. Hadn't it

129

been hard enough just this once?

"Griffin, I can't," she had answered with a shake of her head. "Let's not see each other again. I didn't mean for that to happen back at the station. Really I didn't. I was telling the truth about the other guy. It's a new thing." Her voice was very firm and strong. "But I love him."

Griffin had leaned his cheek against the steering wheel and eyed Phoebe intensely. His voice was calm but insistent. "Phoebe, I hear what you're saying. But what I feel — what we *both* felt back there at the station — oh, how can I believe you love another guy?" Then he had reached across the seat and pushed the damp curls off her face. Her hair was a mess, her braid had come all undone. His touch had been tender and Phoebe shivered when he took his hand away.

"But I do," Phoebe had insisted, feeling tears well up behind her eyes. How could she make him understand when she didn't understand herself? Kissing Griffin should seem wrong, as if she had betrayed Michael, but it had seemed right. It was a bittersweet, tender moment between them. Phoebe never wanted to forget it. And she didn't want to feel it was a bad thing. The hard bits of anger in her heart had melted away with Griffin's kiss. Kissing Griffin didn't mean she didn't love Michael. It felt like she loved them both. That thought made Phoebe's heart stop. She didn't see how it was possible to love two people so very much.

Phoebe had opened the door then, and jumped

out of the truck. "Good-bye, Griffin," was all she had said.

"I'll call you soon, Phoebe. I love you," he had called after her.

Phoebe hadn't answered. Instead she put her hands over her ears and ran as fast as she could down the block toward her house. She had raced right inside, past her father's study, without even saying hello. She had slammed the door to her room, and leaned against it with all her might, wanting to shut the whole world out. But she couldn't shut out her feelings, and she began to cry. She cried softly so her father wouldn't hear, but she could hear plainly a small voice in her heart crying out, "Michael, Michael, what have I just done?"

Janie Barstow had never been to a baseball game before, and standing at the edge of the Annapolis ballpark, she wasn't sure she was going to like it. The sun was too bright, and she felt self-conscious in her shorts walking in front of a bench full of jocks. She wasn't even sure they were Ted's teammates. She tugged her sun hat over her eyes and put her hand on Henry's arm.

"Uh, how do we know which one is Ted?" She eyed some guys in green uniforms warming up. They were all tan, all blond, and uniformly brawny.

"He's on the other team, Janie," Henry replied patiently. "The team wearing red and white shirts that say Ramblers. Ted's number thirty-three. They're taking batting practice now. Come on, let's try to catch him before the game starts."

Ted went down swinging. He tossed his bat into the dirt and started over to the bench. He'd already been dropped from the starting lineup. After his poor showing at the plate just now, Ted might as well hit the showers. Beely would never put him in to pinch hit. Maybe he'd even ask Ted to quit. Ted actually savored that idea for a minute, especially today. He could walk off the Annapolis playing field, right to his car, and head for Ocean City. It would be a three-hour drive to the beach, but maybe Molly would still be there waiting for him. He had promised her he would turn up.

"Ted?"

Ted spun around, half expecting to see Molly. "Janie. Henry. What are you two doing here?" Seeing two old friends from Rose Hill brought a smile to his face.

"You won't believe this," Henry laughed. "I had some appointments in the local boutiques. We decided to drop by and see the game. Janie's never been to one."

Janie wrinkled her nose in embarrassment. "You don't have to announce that fact to the whole world." She glanced uneasily at the players milling around the field. "Besides, that's not the *only* reason we're here." Janie tapped a Polaroid camera dangling from her shoulder. "Henry's got this great idea for a new line of designs. Clothes for women based on professional sports uniforms."

"Sounds like Phoebe would love it," Ted laughed.

Henry nodded. "Actually, she was my original inspiration. I love the way she puts kooky boys' clothes together and manages to look so feminine. Then I was watching the Orioles last weekend and decided to come up with some designs inspired by baseball uniforms. Today I figured I could get some live action pictures during a real game."

"And," Janie said shyly, "maybe you wouldn't mind if I snapped a few of you now, before the game starts."

"Snap away!" Ted said a bit sarcastically. "In fact you can take my picture all afternoon if you want. I'm benched today."

Henry frowned. "Trouble with the coach again?"

Ted shrugged. "No. Trouble with my game, as usual, but thanks for asking." Ted always forgot Henry's father was a football coach, and although Henry didn't like playing sports, he knew a lot about them.

Ted walked Janie and Henry over to the grandstand, then settled himself down on the Ramblers' bench. The game went by in a haze. In the back of his mind he knew his team was losing and part of him cared. But most of him wanted to be far from Annapolis, back in Molly's arms on the beach.

"Mason, you're up next." Coach Beely's voice broke into his reverie.

Ted responded automatically to the coach's order. He got up, selected a couple of bats, and walked into the on-deck circle. After a couple of practice swings he realized he had no idea what the score was, or even what inning it was. He glanced at the scoreboard. Top of the ninth, two outs, two men on base. The Ramblers were down two to one. He quickly checked the bench. Beely had gone through all his other pinch hitters. "Fats" and Lofredo were on base. A single might tie the game. A fly ball or grounder would lose it.

With a small, despairing shake of his head, Ted stepped into the batter's box. A weak cheer rose up from the seats behind first base. Ted turned around and squinted into the grandstand. Janie and Henry were flashing him a victory sign. Then another cheer rose up, a louder one, from down the third-base line. Ted craned his neck. A group of guys he'd never seen before were chanting his name: "MASON, MASON, MASON." In the middle of the group, standing on one of the seats waving a Ramblers banner, was a small figure in a blue-and-white-striped shirt. It was Molly Ramirez.

Ted grinned and closed his eyes. Molly had found her way to the game and here she was, cheering for him, even though she had said she hated all that rah-rah stuff. It seemed like some kind of miracle. Ted said a quick prayer and settled into his stance. He willed his hands steady, took a few deep relaxing breaths, and focused his attention on the pitcher. Ted never even saw the ball. He heard the sharp thump of it hitting the catcher's mitt. "STRIIIIKE ONE!" the umpire cried.

Ted stepped out of the box and rubbed some rosin on his hands. His heart was pounding, his hands sweaty. Relax, he told himself. Loosen up. Behind him Molly's spirited voice still led the cheers. "GO MASON. GO MASON. GO MASON."

This time, as the ball left the pitcher's hand, Ted knew it finally had his name on it, carved in big, bright neon lights. It seemed to roll toward him slowly and steadily. He felt like he was moving in slow motion. He brought the bat around and it connected and Ted felt an enormous power surge through him. He didn't need to hear Molly's screams to know he had done it. The ball sailed far out of the ballpark. Ted watched it, until it was lost in the sun, until he was absolutely sure he had won the game for the Ramblers.

On the way to home plate, he was careful to touch all the bases. As soon as he made it all the way around, Fats and Wally and Tommy Lofredo grabbed him and hoisted him up on their shoulders. Ted couldn't remember ever feeling happier in his whole life. The entire team had cleared the bench and was running toward him, cheering and slapping him on the back. "Good work, Ted," Coach Beeley said to him. Then the umpire said something to Beeley and everyone had to settle down and play out the inning. The home team crowd was filing out before the last out. Everyone knew the game was really over. But Ted sat there, shoulder-to-shoulder with the guys, joking, making small talk, waiting for the Ramblers to take the field. He stood patiently in right field through Wally's nine strike-out pitches, waiting for the game to end, waiting to see Molly again.

"Ted! Ted!" Everyone seemed to be calling his name. He fought his way through the crowd toward Molly. She was jumping up and down, and he could make out the top of her curly dark head among all the others.

"Surprise!" she shouted as he pulled her into his arms and spun her around and around. They were standing on the pitcher's mound. Wally and Coach Beely were both talking to Ted at once. But Ted only had eyes for Molly. He was so happy to see her. "I forgot, yesterday, to tell you about the game. I'm sorry." He was holding her tight, wondering how she had found him. What in the world was she doing here?

"Sorry?" Molly guffawed, and wriggled free of Ted's arms. "You're nuts, Ted Mason. I told you I would be here last night when you were running for the bus. Don't you remember? I said, 'I'll see you at the game.' " She was laughing at him, and Ted loved it. He tousled her hair and bent down to kiss her on the lips. He didn't care that the whole team was watching.

"These are the guys on *my* team." Molly gestured to the boys Ted had spotted in the stands. She quickly introduced him to her friends.

"Gosh," Ted joked, shoving back his baseball cap and scratching his head, "I hope you left some lifeguards on the beach!"

Molly giggled. "Oh, enough to keep the girls in Ocean City happy!"

"But we've got to get back now. There's a beach party tonight and some of us are 'on duty,' " a big blond guy explained. He turned to Molly. "Coming with us?"

Molly looked at Ted. Her hand tentatively touched his arm. Ted pretended to glower at the lifeguards and answered for her. "Are you kidding? Molly and I have a date tonight!"

Ted headed for the showers, whistling the Kennedy Fight Song. Funny how a home run and the right girl rooting for you could make a guy feel alive again. As Ted approached the dugout, he noticed Henry and Janie standing side by side on the first base line. Ted started toward them with a smile, then stopped. They were looking at him awfully strangely.

Henry poked out his hand a little stiffly. "Uh, good game, Ted. That was some home run."

Janie didn't say anything. She avoided Ted's eyes.

Ted's throat tightened. They had seen him kiss Molly. He started shaking his head, thinking he may as well explain that it was over with Chris. But Janic had already mumbled good-bye, and was dragging Henry by the hand toward his car.

Chapter
11

When Michael's van pulled into the driveway, Phoebe was at her bedroom window putting on her earrings. Monica, Peter, and Jeremy were already in the backseat, but Phoebe didn't notice them. She grabbed her bag off the bed, and dashed down the hall out the back door. She landed right in Michael's arms.

"Oh, Michael!" she cried, standing on her tiptoes to kiss him on the lips. She closed her eyes, and was relieved to find it was still Michael, only Michael, she was kissing. Suddenly she knew that she was home safe. She hugged him so tightly she thought her arms would break. When she pressed her face against his chest, his blue print shirt smelled new and was pleasantly rough against her cheek.

Michael gently broke away. His face opened into a big, beautiful smile as he said, "Hey, what's this?" He gave a quick sideward glance across the yard. Phoebe had forgotten her parents were sitting right there at the old green lawn table, having drinks with some friends. But at the moment she didn't care who saw her kiss Michael. He looked down at her, his finger tracing a pattern in her palm, and her smile widened to match his.

Phoebe met his eyes, then abruptly dropped his hand. Michael was smiling but his eyes looked puzzled, as if he were trying to figure something out. She backed away a step or two. Her fingers strayed to her face. She suddenly felt like the word KISS was written all over her. Griffin's kiss. She was sure Michael could tell she had been with another guy. She blushed and stuffed her fists into the pockets of her blue striped baseball knickers, as she walked quickly, head down, toward the car. Her heart was pounding and there was a funny ringing in her ears. She felt as if the ground was slipping out from under her.

Then Michael's hand was under her arm. His grip was firm, reassuring. "Hey. You okay?" He sounded worried. Phoebe hesitated an instant, then pulled her arm away. She was afraid to touch him.

"I'm fine. I just tripped," she said sharply. She opened the door, climbed in the front seat, and mumbled hello to the other kids. The whole way to the concert she sat staring out the window, carefully avoiding everyone's eyes.

Ever since Phoebe could remember, her mother had sworn Phoebe was the poorest liar she'd ever seen. "It's your eyes that give you away, Phoebe," she had said one time. "They're like your Grandma Kelleher's. That kind of green that changes color when you fib." Her mother had been trying not to laugh then. When you're six you tell such silly lies. It was a snowy day and Phoebe had come home from school crying, her bare hands hurt so much from the cold. She had lied through her tears about losing her mittens, the new furry ones she hated because someone had killed a bunny rabbit to make them. That afternoon, she and Sasha had buried them in the playground at school.

"BROOO-OOOCE — BROOO-OOOCE — BROOO-OOOCE!" Phoebe's head throbbed in time with the rhythmic chant resounding through the auditorium of the Capital Centre. She felt like she was the only person in there not yelling, jumping up and down, or having fun. Being in the eye of a storm must feel like this, Phoebe thought as she pressed her hands over her ears. The row of kids behind her was suddenly screeching. One of Springsteen's roadies had tossed something off the stage. A knot of girls tumbled into the crowded aisles to see what it was.

The cries of "BROOO-OOOCE" crescendoed to a fevered pitch.

"Why are they booing him?" Jeremy shouted across to Peter.

Peter kept clapping his hands, not missing a beat, and yelled back, "Stone, we're shouting 'Bruce, Bruce,' not 'BOO.'" He resumed his cry in unison with the thousands of Springsteen fans.

140

From the other end of their row, Jeremy enthusiastically joined in.

The rhythmic clapping broke into a round of hysterical screams and applause as a small, blue-jeaned figure bounded back and forth across the stage. "Hello D.C.!" Springsteen shouted. From her front row seat Phoebe could see the beads of sweat glistening above his headband. Up close like this he was even better-looking than his pictures. His plain white T-shirt reminded her of Griffin's. Phoebe glanced guiltily at Michael. He was sitting beside her, next to Jeremy, helping the photographer load a second camera. He wasn't looking at her or Springsteen.

With his back to the audience Springsteen stomped his foot and shouted to the musicians. "One-Two-Three-Four — "

Suddenly the familiar opening chords of "Born in the USA" rang out and the delirious audience sprang to its feet. Phoebe felt the wave of energy pulse down from the balconies, all the way to their row. Everyone was standing and stomping. The frenzied will of the crowd pushed Phoebe to her feet, and for a dizzying instant she was shoved forward toward the stage, right against the chest of a burly bouncer. Any other night she would have relished the fantasy of being shoved up on the stage and landing right in Springsteen's arms, but tonight, between the heat and crowd and the pounding in her head, she just wanted to scream and run out of the suffocating arena into the empty hills of the surrounding Maryland countryside. She wanted to throw herself on the cool ground beneath the open sky and be alone.

As the musicians hammered the driving rhythm of the chorus, several thousand voices took up the chant. Springsteen danced and clapped and waved the mike toward the audience. Monica grabbed Phoebe's left hand, Michael her right. Both of them were dancing and singing, shouting the words. Phoebe moved along with them, but she couldn't sing a note. She was struggling not to cry. It was the first time all night Michael had touched her hand.

Greg stuffed his tie into his pocket and held open the door of the sub shop for Chris. A blast of cold salami-scented air hit her in the face.

"Oh, how wonderful!" Greg sniffed and staggered dramatically against the door. "I'm starved, absolutely ravenous."

Chris looked at him in mock dismay. "After packing away all those hors d'oeuvres at Congressman Barnes's house?" Her eyes twinkled mischievously. "Back in the kitchen, Mrs. Barnes was distinctly overheard saying something about Mr. Montgomery needing to go on a diet!"

"Doesn't she realize I'm still a growing boy?"

Greg emphasized the word "boy" slightly and flashed Chris a winning smile.

She looked away in confusion. Ever since Greg had mentioned he was a sophomore, he seemed to be teasing Chris. She wasn't sure exactly what the joke was. At first, learning Greg was two years behind her in school had bothered her.

She'd never felt right about hanging out with kids younger than herself. In fact, she couldn't remember ever having a younger friend, girl or guy. But she felt so safe and comfortable around him, she was trying not to let his age get to her.

"Chris, Greg, over here!" Brenda was waving from the crowd's favorite corner booth. Chris settled herself in the seat across from Brenda, just as Brad walked up carrying a couple of subs and Cokes. He eyed Greg's rumpled linen suit.

"Hey, Montgomery, what's with the fancy duds? I thought this was a sailing weekend, not a meeting with the chairman of the board!"

"Fancy duds?" Greg scoffed. "These are our work uniforms!" He motioned toward Chris. "And the term is 'on board' not 'of-the-board', and I'm not chairman, but captain. From here on you'll all address me saying 'Aye, aye, sir!' "

Brenda arched her eyebrows and drawled in a low, sugary voice, "Aye, aye, sir! Or is it 'Captain'?" She gave an exaggerated flutter of her thick dark lashes. "I need to know, *sir*, because I'd like to ask the captain to stop pining over my sub — "

Chris felt a momentary pang of jealousy as she watched her stepsister flirt with Greg. But her jealousy gave way to a giggle, then was followed by a twinge of guilt. Brenda was only pretend-flirting. Besides, why should she care?"

Greg sprang up and saluted Brenda. "*She* definitely gets the job of first mate."

"And me?" Chris asked quickly.

Greg wriggled his eyebrows in a comic imitation of a silent movie villain and leaned seductively over her shoulder. "You, my dear, are my galley slave."

"What?" Chris gasped, suddenly blushing. She wasn't sure what a galley slave did, but somehow it sounded embarrassing.

"Well, I guess that makes me the fearless pirate who rescues all the damsels in distress!" Brad joked. Greg headed for the counter to place his order.

"By the way, the galley slave gets everything her heart desires — Coke, Super Salami Sinker Sub, Bombs Away Deluxe," Greg read from the menu on the wall.

"Diet Coke!" Chris mumbled, frowning. She pulled her wallet out of her bag. "Hey, here's the money," she called after Greg. He didn't seem to hear her, so she stuffed the money back in her wallet, her frown deepening.

"It won't kill you to be treated just this once," Brenda laughed.

"It's the principle that counts. Besides — "

"He's only fifteen!" Brad teased. "But with an eighteen-foot sailboat, and a place on the Eastern Shore, a Diet Coke won't make him or break him."

"It's still the principle of the thing. Just because he's a guy doesn't mean he has to pay for me. I mean, Woody never does." Chris caught Brenda's eye across the table and quickly looked away. Brenda had been giving her funny looks all week, every time she mentioned Greg, and Chris was getting tired of it. She'd have to speak to her later when they were alone. Her stepsister had a crazy habit of making mountains out of molehills. She'd been listening to too many kids with problems down at the halfway house.

"What about Ted?" Brad mumbled, between bites of his sandwich.

"Ted and I split everything, too." Chris said. "You know that. Hey, speaking of Ted, here come Janie and Henry. Weren't they going to Annapolis this afternoon? I wonder if they saw the game."

Chris waved. "Hi, guys!" She smiled as they approached. "Pull up a chair. Did you get to the Ramblers game today? Who won?"

Janie looked so woeful, Chris feared the worst. Had Ted blown his team's lead again?

"Uh, the Ramblers won," Henry said in a strangely clipped voice. "It was Ted's homer that won the game. Pretty exciting actually." Henry ruffled his hand through his lank blond hair and looked nervously around the shop "Where is everyone?" he said, not quite meeting Chris's eye.

"Springsteen!" Brad and Brenda chimed in unison.

Henry just nodded. Janie smiled weakly. "Peter must be on cloud nine!"

"In orbit, is more like it!" Chris laughed.

"Orbit? Who's in orbit — who took off without me?" Greg set a Bombs Away Deluxe in front of Chris, and a Super Salami Sinker at his own place. "I don't want my galley slave to starve!" he murmured into her ear, loud enough for the whole table to hear.

Chris groaned and Brenda introduced Greg to Janie and Henry.

"You're the guys with the clothing business, aren't you?" Greg said in an admiring voice.

Henry nodded, and looked from Greg to Chris and back at Greg again.

Janie tugged at his sleeve. "Henry, remember, we have to bring those subs home for the twins." She turned to Chris, still not meeting her eyes. "We promised to bring my sisters some sandwiches. Nice meeting you, Greg," she squeaked, and pulled Henry to the counter.

"What was that all about?" Brad murmured.

Chris giggled into her Diet Coke. "I think Ms. Barstow and Mr. Braverman were busy in the bleachers today and didn't quite have their eye on the game. Did you see how embarrassed they were when I asked about Ted?"

Brad chuckled and Brenda looked over at Greg and Chris. They were huddled closely in the booth, trading bites of their sandwiches and giggling. Chris looked especially pretty tonight in her softly gathered blue shirtwaist dress and her mother's pearls. Her cheeks were very pink and her eyes were sparkling in a way Brenda hadn't seen in a long, long time.

"Do we have to go in?" Phoebe said breathlessly as she toyed with the edge of Michael's collar.

146

They were standing in the doorway of a card store near the sub shop. Michael was nuzzling her ear. With each little kiss, Phoebe shivered. She was afraid if she moved, the spell would be broken. From the time Michael had taken her hand back at the concert, he hadn't stopped touching her. He had held her hand on the way out of the Capital Centre, and all during the long walk through the parking lot. Even on the Beltway when they were stuck in post-concert traffic, and the heat was suffocating, Michael's hand stayed on her shoulder, gently smoothing her skin. Phoebe couldn't understand what had happened between the time they left her house and the middle of the concert. Back home, she was certain he had looked at her as if she had betrayed him. Now she had never felt so much love pouring out of any human being.

"They're waiting for us," Michael said, his voice husky and low. Phoebe could tell that the last place he wanted to be was in the crowded sandwich joint rehashing the concert.

"Peter's good at taking care of himself," Phoebe assured him between kisses. She ran her fingers up the nape of Michael's neck and through his hair. It was thick and wild and curly. Not silky like Griffin's. The next kiss died on Phoebe's lips.

Michael broke away and laughed softly. "Phoebe Hall, what's getting into you?" He tilted her face toward the light. "Pheeb? What's the matter?"

"Nothing," she whispered, staring at her feet.

"I just was feeling guilty — " The word spilled out of her mouth before she could stop it.

Michael slapped his hand on the wall and laughed. "Like you said, Peter can take care of himself. But let's go in for a while. I could use a Coke before we head home. Anyway, I don't want you feeling guilty. It's not as much fun!" He gave Phoebe's hair a loving tug and ushered her into the sub shop.

Peter was perched on the edge of the counter, holding court. Peter had his sunglasses shoved up on his head, one arm slung over Monica's shoulder. He had taken a break from his play-by-play description of the concert to read a flier posted in the sub shop. "Brad, how could you not have seen this? It's been posted for weeks." Peter reached up to the bulletin board behind their usual table. "Can you read, or what? Listen." Peter used his best DJ voice. " 'Variety Records is proud to sponsor the first annual Potomac Raft Race. All high school students are welcome to compete. Proceeds from the race go to help a good cause — Garfield house, the halfway house for kids in Georgetown. So build those rafts — and be there!' " he finished with a flourish. "So, how about it, guys? The race is next Saturday. Let's meet at my house the day after tomorrow. We can put together a terrific raft. We'll make a party out of it."

"Sounds like something out of *Huckleberry Hound*!" Woody quipped. He was sitting on the edge of a table next to Kim.

"*Huckleberry Finn*," Jeremy corrected, not quite getting the joke.

"Darn, I can't be there!" Greg groaned. "None of us can!" He motioned to Chris and Brad and Brenda.

"That's okay, sailor," Peter said good-naturedly. "We'll need you next week. You're the one person here who really *does* know something about sailing."

"Well, I don't, and I don't intend to learn." Woody shook his head vehemently. "Like I told Greg the other day, I'm only good at floating dinghies in my bathtub. But I'll be part of your cheering squad."

Everyone booed Woody. "What a cop-out!" Chris laughed. Just then she spotted Phoebe and Michael. They were standing at the door. Phoebe looked strangely pale, Michael rumpled, but beaming like the sun. Chris remembered Phoebe's call that afternoon. Something really was wrong.

Phoebe slipped quietly into the corner of a booth and tried not to meet Woody's eye. She had caught his glance as she walked in the door, when Michael's hand was on her shoulder. She had forced herself to smile and wave at the crowd. Everyone was busy talking with Peter about the raft race and the concert, and Phoebe was grateful for that. She didn't have to say much or be social, and sitting apart with Michael seemed the naural thing to do. Since they were so new together, no one would blame them for sitting alone.

She felt Woody's eyes on her, and her cheeks started burning. Woody must have known she had seen Griffin. Maybe Griffin had dropped in at the Arena Stage after he left.

"Earth to Phoebe!" Michael said softly, setting a Coke in front of her.

Phoebe managed a weak smile. Michael slid into the seat next to her. He was looking at her as if he suspected something. Phoebe averted her glance and began rummaging in her bag for her sweater. "The air conditioning," she muttered, "it always gets to me." She shivered.

"Well, if it's getting warm you need — " Michael's arm stole around her, his hand lingering over the damp skin at the back of her neck. As Michael held her close, Phoebe suddenly couldn't tell if her heart was pounding because it was Michael's touch she was feeling, or Griffin's she was remembering.

Chapter
12

The boardwalk was crowded for a Thursday night. Molly and Ted sat on a bench near the entrance to Cheap Thrills, the new amusement park at the bottom of Ocean City. The silhouette of a gigantic Ferris wheel filled the sky and strains of honky-tonk music drifted down from the fairway.

Molly sat on Ted's lap, popping French fries into his mouth. Ted was almost totally happy right then. He couldn't remember when he'd ever felt so comfortable. Molly felt so good, so natural in his arms. The blue stripes on her shirt matched her eyes perfectly. Ted chuckled inwardly. She didn't look at all like an Akido black-belt champion, certainly not with his baseball cap perched saucily on one side of her head. The flashing neon lights made crazy patterns on her bare legs.

"Has anyone ever told you you've got great legs?" Ted smiled, brushing a bit of French fry off her knee.

"Wouldn't you like to know," Molly teased.

"I asked, didn't I?"

"Let's see now." Molly began ticking names off on her fingers. "Jim Lowe, Andy Saperstein, Marty Tonelli, Johnny Martin — I'm not sure he counts, really. That was back in the eighth grade — "

Ted grabbed her hand and folded her fingers down. "Stop, stop. I can't stand it. I'm the jealous type. Tell me you're putting me on, *please*."

Molly shook her head. "Nope. It's all true. I've dated lots of guys. I like getting to know lots of different people. I've never gone with just one guy — " She cut herself off.

"Before!" Ted finished her sentence for her, and brushed his lips gently against hers. They were salty from the fries.

Molly leaned back slightly and studied his face. "Before," she repeated quietly. "It's just too bad — " She broke off and pressed her cheek against his. She looked out over the ocean then back at him. Her fingers were playing with his hair. For the first time that night she wasn't smiling. Now her eyes were misty.

Ted cleared his throat. "Well, I have, Molly. In fact, I am, officially still — "

Molly's arm tightened around his neck. "Going with someone?"

Ted wished he could see her face better, but the boardwalk was shadowy and the lights were flickering behind them. "I wanted to tell you last night but there just wasn't time."

Molly slipped off his lap, staying close to Ted on the bench. She turned her face toward his and smiled the most beautiful smile he'd ever seen. "Listen, I'm the jealous type, too, but you live here. Of course a football hero has to have a steady girl. Tell me, is she a cheerleader?" she joked.

Ted flinched slightly. "Hey, that's not fair."

Molly looked down. "No, no it wasn't. I meant the other part, though. I have no right to think you'd have no other girl. I've dated guys here all summer long. We did just meet. Sometimes it's like that — falling in love happens so fast."

"But you don't understand." Ted was having trouble speaking. He just wanted to bury his face in Molly's hair, to tell her he loved her. "It's over between me and Chris." Saying her name out loud made breaking up feel more real. Ted felt he had taken a step through a one-way door. There was no going back now. "It isn't working anymore. I wanted to tell her last night As soon as I got back I phoned her. But it's not the kind of thing — " Ted floundered.

" — you say on the phone," Molly finished for him. She took a deep breath and pressed his hand between hers. "Ted, don't do it."

"Do what?" Ted asked.

"Break up with her because of me. That's crazy. I — I understand about there being someone else. I can live with it — I can keep seeing you and live with it. I don't know about you.

Maybe you shouldn't see me again, if it bothers you, seeing me and Chris. But it would be wrong to leave someone because of me. I'll only be here for another ten days."

Ted's back stiffened. "Ten days?" He grabbed her by the shoulders and cried out, "That's impossible," even as the truth slowly dawned on him. The world seemed to crumble at his feet. "You're going home."

Molly touched his cheek. It was a gentle, hesitant touch. Ted took her hand away and cradled it between his as he stared across the sand at the silvery surf beating at the dark shore. Distant screams from the roller coaster punctuated the silence between them.

"But we have over a week," Molly said solemnly. She kneeled on the bench and forced Ted to meet her eyes. "And I don't care who I have to share you with," she declared. "I'm not going to let jealousy or anything else spoil whatever time we have together."

Ted swallowed hard. There was this crazy lump in his throat. "But you'll be back, Molly, I mean, your aunt lives here, doesn't she? And I — I can go to California." He tried to laugh. "That's why there are planes and all. It's not exactly the Stone Age. You're only a few hours away. I'll save my money. I graduate in June."

"Ted, stop it." Molly jumped up and leaned back against the railing, glaring at Ted. Even in the dim light he could see the fire in her eyes. "I'm going home. I live there. You live here.

Nothing can change that. Just like nothing can change how we feel about each other right now."

"But that's why we have to see each other again," Ted insisted, pacing back and forth in front of her. "I mean, I could go to college there — I'm applying to Cal Tech — there's a good chance for a football scholarship there. Or you could come here, Georgetown, American U. Gosh, there are so many places. Oh, Molly, it doesn't matter as long as we're together."

"It matters." The sharp tone of Molly's voice startled Ted. "I'm sixteen. I can't leave home now. And I can't plan where I'll spend my life. Neither can you. I don't even know if I'll go to college." She reached out a hand toward Ted. "But that's beside the point. This is something special, Ted, and I just think we should make the most of it while we're *here*, together."

"But something like this can last forever," Ted said quietly. He heard Molly catch her breath.

"Yes," she said quietly. "I'm sure it does, sometimes." She pulled Ted down on the bench beside her. "If it works that way. But this is the end of summer. We live three thousand miles apart. All we have is now. Let's not waste more of our time together, sitting here getting all heavy, huh?" Molly's voice was very gentle.

Ted's hand shook as he touched her face, then ran his fingers across her lips, her cheeks, her eyes. He barely knew her. He'd barely have the time to know her. She was right. They had to make the most of their short time together. He

155

traced the outline of her nose. "You know, you must have at least a hundred freckles," he said in a deadpan voice.

"You creep! No one teases me about freckles and lives!" Molly roared and grabbed his wrist. But this time Ted was too fast. He slipped out of her grasp and darted down the boardwalk, weaving through the crowd with Molly hot on his heels.

They collapsed laughing against the gaudy neon sign at the entrance to the amusement park. ADMISSION: $4.00, a smaller cardboard sign said.

"Wanna go in?" they both asked at once.

Ted pushed his hat down over her nose. "Guess the vote's unanimous. Ferris wheel?"

"What a wimp!" She groaned in disgust, but pulled Ted's arm around her shoulder and held his hand tightly. "Roller coaster!"

The first car of Dead Man's Dive was halfway up the first hill. Ted sat with his arms wrapped around Molly. "Strange," she whispered, hugging him tight. "We're absolutely parallel to the stars."

Ted took a deep breath. "I know. I was thinking of that. Einstein might have made something of it, but all I can think about is what it'll be like to come down."

"You can't worry about coming down, Ted. It takes away from the fun of it." Molly laughed, but her eyes were serious.

Ted nodded slowly. "I won't worry, Molly. This is one ride I'm going to enjoy as long as it lasts." They were almost at the top now. Molly tightened her grip around his neck and nuzzled

156

his ear. Ted said what he had to say very fast. It was easier like that.

"But about Chris — it was over before I met you. It was Chris I was running from yesterday, on the beach."

Molly lifted her face toward Ted's. She looked puzzled.

"No. Molly, not *Chris* — but what she makes me feel, who I am when I'm with her, and who she can't help being. That's what I was running from. Lately, loving her's been like a cage for me — and it's not right anymore." Ted had been afraid to say that out loud, even to himself. Hearing the words, he was more sure than ever they were true.

As they approached the crest of the first hill, he added softly, "I couldn't help it if I ran right into you."

And then Molly screamed. The car plunged down the steep incline. She clung to Ted for dear life and shrieked until his lips found hers, and he kissed her for the whole dizzying ride.

Chapter 13

Beneath Phoebe's bedroom window, the summer roses were in full bloom. Their heady scent drifted up, enveloping her like a shawl. She sat on the windowsill, hugging her knees to her chest, watching the moon slip behind the thick-leaved branches of the old oak. It was hard to believe that pathetic scrap of light was last week's fat full moon. Phoebe thought back to the night of her party, the night when Michael had kissed her beneath the full moon and she had thought her heartaches had vanished forever. A tear spilled out of her eye, coursed down her face, and splashed onto the rosebushes below. Her shoulders started shaking and then she was sobbing, her head buried in her arms. Slowly the sobs died down, and she sat up very straight and wiped her face with the hem of her thin cotton nightgown. She wondered if she'd ever be empty of tears and able to sleep again.

A solitary car turned down Elm Street and pulled into a driveway a couple of doors away. It was the Halls' neighbor, Mrs. Emswiller, coming home from the night shift at Rose Hill Hospital. Charlie Brown, her beagle, began barking from his doghouse. The Subaru's headlights went out and as the white-uniformed figure climbed out of the car and hastened to silence the dog, Phoebe realized it must be past four A.M. She'd been sitting here for three hours now, ever since Michael had driven off with Peter and Monica and Jeremy, Springsteen's gravely voice on the tapedeck trailing a love song behind them. Phoebe had burst into tears then, and run into her room. She didn't know if the song sounded so sad because the words reminded her of losing Michael or leaving Griffin.

She had already decided she would never see Griffin again, and she planned to tell him that when he called, even though not seeing Griffin wouldn't change a thing about Michael. It was already too late. She was sure he suspected something, just as she was sure she had already lost him.

"I love you," he had said. The van was idling at the curb. Monica and Peter were talking quietly inside. Jeremy was asleep in the backseat. Phoebe's body was pressed close to Michael's. They were standing where no one could see them from the house, leaning against the corrugated tool shed. He had put his hand on her cheek and been surprised to find tears there. "Phoebe?" he sounded confused at first and then scared.

159

"Pheeb? I think — I think we really have to talk."

Monica's laughter rippled across the lawn toward them. "But not now, not here," Michael had added quickly. "Tomorrow, when I come over." He kissed her cheek and started toward the car. She stood staring at the ground, unable to move, unable to stop crying. She felt him stop. She knew he was standing there, waiting for her to say something, but she couldn't say a word just then. She couldn't tell him why she was crying and she couldn't say, "I love you" back. She hadn't stopped crying since then.

A blast of music shattered the silence of the deserted street, making Phoebe jump. She heard a car shift noisily into high gear, then saw a convertible, top down and full of kids, squeal around the corner. Someone threw a can into the street. Charlie Brown's startled howl started every dog barking up and down the block. Phoebe ducked back into her room, scared the kids had spotted her, sitting in the open window dressed only in her nightgown. She threw herself face down on her bed and buried her face in her ragged old teddy bear. She was still crying when the last dog's bark died off and when she finally fell asleep, dreaming of Michael's face. But the voice saying "I love you" in her dream was Griffin's.

It was Michael's voice that woke her.

"You're very beautiful when you're sleeping," he said.

Phoebe opened her eyes. The sun was pouring

in the window and across the bed. For a second she thought she was dreaming, the scent of roses was so strong. Her hand strayed to her pillow and touched a flower. She couldn't remember why it was there or when she had fallen asleep. She did remember crying her eyes out. Yesterday, last night, Griffin and Michael — and the ache in her heart — all seemed like parts of the same bad dream.

She turned her head toward the window.

"Michael!" she gasped. He was standing outside her window, leaning on the sill, picking the thorns off the stem of a rose in full bloom. "What are you doing here?" She sat up and yanked her nightgown over her knees. There was a faint smell of coffee in the air, but the house was very quiet. Her parents had left for work already.

"Watching you sleep." He tossed the rose over toward her. It landed near the one on her pillow and matched the brilliant orange bedspread perfectly. Phoebe had a feeling he'd been watching her a long time.

"How long have you been here?"

"Awhile."

She grabbed her pillow and threw it at him. "You creep!"

Michael ducked, but the smile was even wider on his face as he yelped, "Hey, is this the thanks I get for protecting you?"

"Protecting me?" Phoebe was laughing now. "From what?"

Then she heard Shawn's voice in the yard,

yelling something about the hose. Paul screamed something back. Phoebe had forgotten. Michael was supposed to be here this morning to bring Shawn home and help her baby-sit. They were going to go over some music for his mother's winter concert. And then she remembered he was also here to talk to her, like he had promised last night. Her heart stopped a second and her throat went dry. The smile died on her lips.

"Actually, a girl like you needs a lot of protection," Michael was saying. He peered meaningfully around the yard. "*They* wanted to wake you up by turning that hose on your window."

"What!" Phoebe jumped off her bed and backed into the corner between her desk and the closet.

"And then I can't believe you haven't heard it's not such a safe thing to sleep with your window wide open on the ground floor. Someone may get in," Michael said in a spooky voice.

Phoebe gulped. She hadn't thought of that. "In fact, I see my rival did!" Michael gestured dramatically toward Phoebe's pillow.

Phoebe stared at him, horrified. What was he talking about? What rival — a blush started up her neck. Then she noticed he was pointing at the teddy bear.

She sank against the closet door and started giggling in relief. "Michael Rifkin, get away from my window, *now*," she ordered. "Right this minute. I have to get dressed." She marched across the room and pulled the curtains shut.

Michael yelled from the other side, "Put on your bathing suit. These water demons out here are very serious about getting everything and everyone in sight very, very wet!"

Phoebe grabbed her clothes and headed for the shower. Halfway out the door she stopped. She looked back toward her bed. The rose was still lying there. She walked back into the room, a wide, goofy smile on her face. She picked up the flower very carefully and opened the fabric-covered journal she kept on the table by her bed. She lay the rose inside and closed the cover gently. She would keep that rose forever. No matter what Michael wanted to say to her later, she could tell from the look on his face she hadn't lost him yet. And she didn't intend to.

Two hours later they were down in the basement. Michael was at the piano coaching her through a tricky part of an aria she was supposed to sing at Miss Spinelli's winter concert. Phoebe loved the familiar Puccini melody but today she couldn't keep her mind on the music. Michael had told her to picture herself waltzing through a snowy square in Paris to get the feeling of what she was supposed to be singing. But she couldn't. She could only picture what Michael's face would look like when she told him about Griffin. Deciding to talk to Michael had been easy; finding the words to tell him seemed impossible.

"Phoebe, what's with you today?" he said, annoyed.

Phoebe gulped. "I'm not paying attention, I

guess." She was leaning against the old upright, rubbing the top of one bare foot with the other.

"Phoebe, you've got a wonderful voice and you could become a really good singer, but you have to work at it." Michael was using the reasonable, stern tone of voice he used when he lectured his kid brother.

Phoebe raised her eyebrows to the ceiling. "Michael, you know I'm serious about my music, you know I want to work on it, but. . . ." Phoebe's voice trailed off. Her fingers traced the shape of a faded decal peeling off the side of the piano.

"But?" Michael's tone softened. Phoebe looked so sad and lost and scared.

"But — we have to talk," she said, her voice steady and very, very soft.

Michael reached for her hand and smiled. "I know — "

His hand was warm and dry and very reassuring. Phoebe looked into his eyes. They were so kind, so trusting. Her courage seemed to fail her.

He pulled her down beside him on the bench, and put his hands back on the piano. Before she could say another word, he began talking. "Last night I felt such mixed vibes from you, Phoebe."

"Mixed vibes?" Phoebe pulled away to look at his face. His eyes were fixed on the piano keys. His hands strayed over them, as if feeling out a tune he didn't quite know yet.

"And there was so much I wanted to tell you — about us, about not being afraid, about all sorts of things." He turned to Phoebe with an embarrassed grin. "But words — words aren't really my thing. Not when I'm feeling so much.

"After I dropped off Peter, I drove around for a long time thinking about us. When I got home, everything I wanted to tell you was suddenly real clear. I wrote it down. There are just three words though — " Michael pulled a sheet of music out of his pocket. He smoothed it out and propped it up on the piano. He looked at it a second before he began playing.

It was a tune Phoebe had never heard before. It was a sad tune, a happy tune, a song that made her heart feel very big and full — as if she were in love with the whole world. Michael had the hint of a smile on his face as he played it. When the last note died down, Phoebe could still hear it playing in her heart.

"Michael!" She clapped her hands together. "That's the most beautiful song I've ever heard."

Michael faced her on the piano bench and just grinned. "Good. I'm glad you like it, Phoebe Hall, because it's yours."

"Mine?" Phoebe's eyes widened in wonder. "You wrote that for me?" she reverently touched the neatly penned music sheet. On the top of the page were just three words: "Love Takes Time."

Phoebe's eyes misted over. No one had ever written her a song before.

"There should be more words," Michael said. "I thought — since you're more of a writer — maybe we could think them up together." His voice was very soft, very gentle. Phoebe lifted her eyes toward Michael. She had never seen him look so vulnerable before. She threw her arms around him and buried her face in his neck.

"Oh, Michael, I'm not very good with words at all," she said.

Phoebe had no idea how long they stayed like that, just holding each other on the piano bench, rocking back and forth, not saying anything, not even kissing.

"Phoebe, the phone. Shawn's yelling that you have a phone call." Michael broke the silence.

"The phone?" Phoebe pulled away from Michael and the world seemed out of focus. "The PHONE!" she repeated, leaping to her feet just as Shawn yelled down again.

She bolted up the stairs and into her room. She picked up the receiver and yelled into the kitchen, "Paul, hang up. NOW!"

Before she even heard his voice, she knew it was Griffin.

"Pheeb?"

"Yes," Phoebe whispered. She sat down on the edge of her bed and closed her eyes.

"Who was that who picked up? Sounded like one of Shawn's friends. They must have some battle going on in there — or is that *Tom and Jerry* on TV?" Griffin joked.

"Uh — I don't know, really," Phoebe managed to get out. She was trying to take ten deep breaths. She opened her eyes, and spotted a petal from Michael's rose at her feet on the rag rug. She picked it up and closed her fingers over it.

"Well, since Shawn's busy — I thought I could come over. I'm at the phone booth at the mall."

"No!" Phoebe shrieked. Then with a worried look at her open bedroom door, she lowered her voice. "No, Griffin, you can't come over now." She reached over and closed the door.

"You — you aren't alone." The lilt went out of Griffin's voice.

"No, that guy I told you about, he's here with me."

There was a terrible silence at the other end of the phone. Phoebe fingered the fragile petal in her hands. At least now Griffin would believe there was another guy.

"Have you told him yet?"

"Told him what?"

"About us, about me coming back. About what we feel for each other." Griffin's voice was tight and strained.

"No, Griffin," Phoebe declared. "No, and I won't. Because there is nothing to tell him about us."

"Yesterday was nothing?"

Phoebe cringed. "I didn't say that, Griffin. You're being unfair. I told you yesterday and I'll tell you again. I can't see you anymore. It's over, what there was between us."

Griffin laughed bitterly. "You've got a funny way of showing something's over, Phoebe."

"I'll always love you." Phoebe hadn't meant to say that aloud. The words slipped out in a low whisper, loud enough for Griffin to hear. When

167

she realized, she held her breath.

Neither of them said anything for a minute. Finally Griffin spoke. "Please, Phoebe, see me just one more time. I think we can make it work again."

Phoebe was shaking her head, no, no. Seeing Griffin was no good. She knew that.

Griffin continued, a sense of urgency in his voice. "I'll be waiting for you tomorrow, out at Maryville. If we can't work things out then, I promise I'll never call again."

No, she wanted to say, but *yes* came out and she hung up quickly before Griffin had a chance to say good-bye — or "I love you" again.

Shawn burst into her room. "Paul and Michael are going now," he announced, then turned and flew back down the hall.

Then Michael was standing in the door, his music in one hand, Paul's bag of Transformers dangling from the other. "Sorry, Pheeb, leaving like this. But I didn't know it was so late. I promised Mom I'd have him home."

Phoebe managed a thin smile. "It's okay, Michael, I'll see you tomorrow, at Peter's. Remember, at the raft-building party."

"Who could forget?"

Michael bent down and kissed Phoebe quickly. "These kids," he murmured. Phoebe looked over her shoulder. Paul and Shawn were ogling them from over by the front door.

Phoebe didn't reply. She didn't trust her voice. She suddenly felt all weak inside. She should have told Griffin no. Now she'd have to tell him tomorrow when she saw him.

"By the way," Michael said, heading out the door, "who called just now?"

"Woody!" Phoebe squeaked, then said it again to be sure Michael had heard. "About the raft-building tomorrow." She pasted a smile on her face for Michael, surprised at how easy it was to lie.

Chapter
14

The next day, by the time Phoebe pulled into the Regional Theatre parking lot, her lie to Michael had begun to make sense. When she had walked out of her room yesterday afternoon she couldn't have said to Michael, That was Griffin Neill on the phone. He's back in town and I'm seeing him tomorrow to tell him I won't see him again. How could she have told Michael that, with Shawn standing a few feet away untangling a yo-yo and Paul munching a donut by the door? The way the kids stared at them made her feel like she and Michael were specimens from a teen romance comic book. Today, when she got back from Maryville, she could tell him the truth. The whole story — how much she loved him, what she'd been going through, how part of her would always belong to Griffin. She hated lying, and she was bad at it, but sometimes a person had no

170

choice. She resolved to straighten things out as soon as she got back to Rose Hill.

The whole way to Maryville Phoebe had planned her conversation with Griffin. She knew exactly how she would begin — by explaining what she meant yesterday on the phone when she said she would always love him. Phoebe had taken back roads and driven very slowly. She planned on being late. In just two hours she'd have to be back at Rose Hill. Michael was picking her up to go to Peter's. As she drove, she hummed the tune to the song Michael had written for her.

She spotted Griffin leaning against the white wood fence on the far side of the lot. She purposely parked her car near the entrance and started to walk very slowly toward him. Her heart was pounding, and she was beginning to feel out of control. She needed time to calm down, to go over her farewell speech one more time. She was having trouble breathing; the afternoon air was sticky and close, and it was very, very hot.

But halfway across the tarmac her footsteps quickened. And Phoebe's whole body seemed to develop a will of its own. She forced herself not to break into a run, not to throw herself into his arms. She hadn't felt like this on Thursday, even though she hadn't seen him for months then. Until they had kissed she had been so certain she never wanted to see him again.

Phoebe forced her hands into the pockets of her suspendered pants, and walked right up to

171

Griffin, stopping two feet away from him. She hoped he wouldn't kiss her hello.

"Hi," he said, without approaching to kiss her. He looked directly at her. Today his eyes matched the hazy overcast sky.

Phoebe swallowed hard. Her little speech had gone right out of her head. "Hi," she muttered, noticing he looked different today. His gray "I Love New York" T-shirt was clinging to his back with sweat. He looked rumpled and thinner than he used to and he needed a shave. But the color was back in his cheeks. He looked alive again, and all at once Phoebe knew he looked alive only because she was standing there with him. That scared her — and gave her a funny sense of power, something she'd never felt before.

"Let's go where we can talk." Griffin straightened up and hooked his fingers in his belt loops. He started walking toward the gate that led to the theater.

"Not there!" Phoebe said quickly, pointing at the huge red barn that was a playhouse now. Last time she had been here it was spring. Griffin had been rehearsing *West Side Story*. She had sat in the third row center and watched in horror as Griffin kissed his leading lady, Sara Carter, and watched him fall hopelessly in love. Phoebe had never wanted to come back there. Remembering that broke the spell of being with Griffin this time. Phoebe remembered exactly what she wanted to tell him. It was over. She could never bear being hurt like that again and even if there were no Michael, she never wanted to see him again.

Griffin led the way behind the theater into a meadow she'd never noticed before. On the way they passed some stagehands hammering together a plywood staircase. An ornately decorated pillar was propped against a tree. A woman was painting it to look like gray stones. It reminded Phoebe of the set from a horror film. She must have looked curious because suddenly Griffin spoke. "The balcony," he explained tersely. "Next fall, we're doing *Romeo and Juliet.*" He sounded like he was about to say more, but he abruptly fell silent. Phoebe nodded and pretended not to notice the crew's curious glances as she made her way past them. Some smiled at Griffin, but he didn't introduce her. Phoebe wondered if the last time Griffin had walked this way he had been with Sara.

Phoebe kept a good two feet away from Griffin as they walked across the field. Even when he held up the barbed wire fence at the edge of the pasture, and she crept under, she was careful not to touch him.

They filed along a narrow cow path winding up to the top of the hill. The meadow was empty except for a dead-looking tree on the hilltop and some cows clustered at the far end beneath a shady clump of oaks. Griffin suddenly stopped and pointed down below. "That's where I live." He was pointing to an old white barn that belonged to the next farm. Phoebe could see it had been renovated. There were curtains in the windows of the part that should have been a hayloft, and a TV antenna sprouted from the barn roof. Several cars were parked in the driveway — one was the Regional Theatre courtesy van, another was Griffin's truck. Phoebe remembered Griffin had mentioned roommates. He started down toward the barn, but Phoebe shook her head. "No, this way. I like the view up here," she said. She didn't want to go where Griffin lived.

At the top of the hill Phoebe stopped. She looked out over the valley. In the distance the Potomac was a winding sliver of light, and behind the mountains thunderheads were building. Phoebe recognized the familiar hump of Stormking Mountain. On the far side of Stormking was Fillmore Nature Preserve and Lost Lake, the lake where Michael had first held her in his arms. Phoebe imagined herself flying right off the edge of the hill, far away from Griffin. She'd glide across the valley, and land somewhere near her garden. In a few more hours it would be dark and the crickets in the backyard of her parents' cottage would be singing Michael's song.

Griffin started speaking. He was leaning against the leafless elm, picking dry bits of bark off its trunk. He didn't look at Phoebe, he stared into the distance. The vein in his temple was throbbing visibly.

What he said surprised her. He didn't start talking about their relationship — not right away. "I could have stayed in Minneapolis," he said. "I didn't get the lead in *West Side Story* there — the management wanted a big name, a

174

big draw. But I could have had other work at the Guthrie — there were other places, too, I could have gone. I didn't leave because of me and Sara. We're still friends," he concluded a bit defensively, shooting Phoebe a quick look.

Phoebe looked pointedly at the distant cows swatting each other with their tails and placidly chewing their cud.

Griffin took a deep breath, and kicked at the dirt. "I came back here because of you."

Phoebe frowned. "You've done that before," she said curtly.

Griffin bit his lip. "Okay. I deserved that. I came before because of you, and it didn't work then. But this is different."

"This is now," Phoebe said sharply. Everything's changed now, Griffin, she wanted to say, but the words just wouldn't come out.

"Last year was a crazy year, Phoebe. You must realize that. Meeting you and falling in love so fast, and leaving for New York. It was all so crazy — so wrong." Griffin was asking her to understand.

She did owe him at least that. "I know," Phoebe said, trying not to sound angry, but standing next to Griffin was making her angry again. "It *was* wrong," she added in a tight voice. "It was all wrong."

Griffin caught his breath. "You don't mean that."

Phoebe closed her eyes. All she had to do was say, Yes, yes, I mean that, and it would be over. She'd never see him again. Instead she said, "No,

175

I didn't really mean that." She rubbed a hand across her forehead. She was sweating and the air was heavy and sticky and seemed to be pressing in on her. Even in this wide open space she was having trouble breathing. Thunder rumbled in the distance.

"I thought a lot about us, and about what happened with me and Sara. It won't happen again," he said. "Not ever." He turned toward her as he said that. His eyes were clear and intense and Phoebe felt as if she were looking right into his soul.

Griffin's glance held hers. Phoebe couldn't look away and her angry protest died on her lips. Griffin wasn't lying when he said that. He was too honest.

"That's the truth, Phoebe," he stated.

Phoebe felt the tears well up behind her eyes. She tried to will them back. "I know. I can see you mean it," she stammered. Her next words tumbled out. "It's *your* truth — for today."

"My truth?" Griffin frowned. A pained, angry look crossed his face. He took a step toward Phoebe. "I've never lied to you, Phoebe. Never — except that time in New York about getting that part — but never with something that counted, you know that. I didn't lie to you about Sara." He was standing very close to her now, both his fists clenched at his side. Phoebe caught her breath. Griffin was trying as hard not to touch her as she was not to touch him, as if he knew touching her would somehow demolish all her arguments about not seeing him again. And

176

Griffin didn't want to win her back that way. Phoebe suddenly loved him for that.

She took a few steps back, putting the tree between them. She said in a very soft voice, "You don't know what I mean, do you?"

Griffin didn't answer.

"You fall in love all the time, Griffin — with everything you do. That's part of why I love you."

Griffin looked up quickly, and started toward her. Something in Phoebe's face stopped him. She continued speaking, the words coming out in spurts, though she had thought about them for a long, long time. "And when you are in love with your next role, your next break, your next golden opportunity, there's no room left for me, for anybody not part of your world — at that moment, in that place." Phoebe could hardly get the words out. "There are girls who will love you in spite of all that, but not me, Griffin. I can't — I can't let myself love someone with a life like that."

"Let yourself?" Griffin repeated incredulously. He raked his fingers through his hair. His voice shook with emotion as he said, "You can't turn love on and off like that. You, of all people, Phoebe Hall, should know that. You can't 'let' yourself love me, but I can't stop myself from loving you, either." Suddenly his hands were on her shoulders. He forced her around to face him. "Can't you feel it, Phoebe? You can't tell me you don't feel it, what's between us. It's — I don't know." He dropped his hands to his side, and stared up at the lowering sky. He spread his arms wide, and cried, "It's bigger than us, it's like we're meant to be together. It's as if something brought me back here — keeps bringing me back here — to you. I can't fight it. And you can't tell me you don't feel it, too." Tears were forming in his eyes now and Phoebe couldn't bear to watch him. She didn't dare try to respond. Her heart was saying, "Yes, I know, I feel it, too," but her mind was flashing danger signals at her. And somewhere inside her head, like background music, Michael's song was playing over and over. Phoebe pressed her hands over her ears, and started walking very quickly up the hill. She had no idea where she was going. She walked faster and faster, finally breaking into an awkward run, her flipflops slapping at the uneven ground, just as the first big drops of rain splashed on the meadow.

"Phoebe, Phoebe!" Griffin was shouting. She could hear him running behind her, following her. And then there was a bright flash of light, followed instantly by a crack of thunder. Phoebe suddenly grew afraid, remembering something scary about lightning in open spaces. She headed toward the trees hedging the far side of the pasture.

"Phoebe, stop!" This time Griffin sounded scared. Phoebe didn't turn around. She had reached the barbed wire fence. Just beyond was the forest. She scrambled through the fence and heard the sound of something ripping as the hem of her pants caught on the wire. Phoebe pitched forward onto the wet leaves of the forest floor.

Griffin's hand was instantly on her arm, pulling her up to her feet. He was gasping for breath. "We can't stay here. It's too dangerous." It was pouring now, and the sky flashed lightning, followed instantly by cracks of thunder.

Griffin grabbed her hand and pulled her after him deeper into the woods. Phoebe could hardly catch her breath. "I can't run this fast, Griffin."

"It's not far now," he cried, and helped her up a slippery outcropping of rock.

A second later Phoebe found herself inside a shallow cave. The rain still whipped in and she cowered toward the back wall. Her foot touched something and she jumped. She looked down and found it was a beer can. There were lots of them, along with charred wood from old fires. The ancient stone walls were carved with names: TOMMY AND LISA, MEGAN LOVES BRUCE, T.M. AND C.A. FOREVER, SIGMA RHO GIRLS WANT TO HAVE FUN!

Phoebe carefully read all the inscriptions, wondering if T.M. was Ted Mason, and trying to avoid looking at Griffin. He was still holding her hand, and Phoebe was shivering.

"You're cold," Griffin stated. He hesitated only a moment, then his arm was around her, his hand chafing her shoulders.

Phoebe pretended not to notice. She rubbed the rain off her face and squeezed the water out of her braid. "My pants — I tore them," she said in a sad voice, amazed that at such a moment something so silly could seem so important.

"You sound so sad, Phoebe," Griffin whispered softly. "Have I made you this sad? I didn't mean to do that."

Phoebe's heart was in her throat. She slowly looked up at him, her eyes filled with tears. "Griffin, you told me a long time ago I had to be brave, I had to do what I felt in my heart, love who I really loved. That was a gift you gave me, telling me that."

Griffin's hand tightened on her shoulder. He bent over her, and touched his lips lightly to her forehead. Phoebe kept talking in a small frightened voice, her hands dangling limp now, by her sides.

"It was easy then. I didn't love Brad anymore. I loved you. Now — " Phoebe could hardly get the words out. "I love you — but I love Michael, too. I really do." She was sobbing, and Griffin pulled her close against him, stroking her head as she whispered, "I don't know. I can't tell what's the right thing to do this time."

Griffin didn't answer. He lifted her face toward his. He held her head between his hands and kissed her gently on each cheek, wiping away the tears with his lips. With his fingers he smoothed her forehead, her lips, her temples. His eyes were so full of love, Phoebe felt her knees buckle. "No, Griffin, stop." She shook her head, but her body seemed to be speaking in a different language. Her eyes, her face, her arms were saying "Yes." She didn't resist when he lowered his face toward hers.

Chapter
15

Phoebe pedaled her bicycle cautiously down the wet pavement, steadying the two half gallons of ice cream in the rickety basket. Peter Lacey's house was only a half mile more away and before she got there she needed to get her story straight in her head. She knew something was wrong with the story she had told Michael on the phone. She knew because Michael had fallen strangely silent when she told him she had gotten back late to Rose Hill because of Ted and the Ramblers ball game up in Maryville.

When Michael had phoned from the party, she was still in the shower. She had just begun shampooing her hair for the third time. She had come back from Maryville wet and shaken and desperately afraid her mother would see her looking so distraught as she ran by the study. She had torn into the bathroom, locked the door, and jumped into the shower. Only then did Phoebe let herself break down. She slumped against the tiled wall, letting the warm water wash over her and drown out her sobs. She was utterly and totally confused.

Loving Griffin this time around wasn't making her happy at all, and yet each time she saw him she couldn't bring herself to tell him she never wanted to see him again. Her determination just dissolved the minute she was face-to-face with him.

Her mother had knocked three times on the bathroom door before Phoebe heard. "Michael's on the phone."

"Just a minute," Phoebe had yelled, as she frantically rinsed the shampoo out of her hair.

"Hey, Pheeb, where've you been? I have to leave soon for that gig at Wolftrap. The raft's almost built — and everyone wants their ice cream." Michael's voice sounded light enough. He hadn't suspected anything.

Phoebe clutched the towel around her and thought quickly. "Oh, I forgot to tell you. Chris called last night, before she left for the shore. She needed to give something to Ted and she didn't have time before she left, so I said I would do it. So I went to the game in Maryville. I thought I'd be back sooner. It was a good game, and I got kind of involved. I came home and jumped in the shower. I'll be there soon. I promise. I'm riding my bike over, 'cause Mom needs the car."

She surprised herself at how good she sounded:

182

out of breath, as if she were excited by the game, not like she had been crying. The excuse didn't even sound too improbable.

"The Ramblers game in Maryville?" Michael repeated, as if not quite hearing right.

"Yup," Phoebe said. She had one leg in her old pink overalls, one leg out. She stood like that a second, holding her breath. In the silence that followed she knew Michael hadn't believed a word she said. And by the time she wheeled into Peter's driveway she still hadn't figured out why.

"Pheeberooni!"

Woody was the first to spot her. He was waving from the side yard. The whole crowd was gathered around a heap of rotten-looking wood. For a minute Phoebe thought they were about to start a bonfire. Then she realized the pile of boards must be the raft.

Woody jogged over toward her and grabbed the ice cream. "This better be good," he said. "We waited long enough. What'd you do, go clear to the North Pole to find a cow cold enough to — " Then he looked into her eyes. He stepped backward. "Something happened? It's Griffin, isn't it?" he whispered, placing his arm lightly on Phoebe's arm.

Phoebe didn't know how to answer. For a second she wanted to pour out her soul to Woody, tell him everything. But she knew this wasn't the place to talk, and Woody might not be the right person to talk to. He was, after all, Griffin's good friend.

Michael walked up then. Woody gave Phoebe

183

a panic-stricken look and made a beeline for the kitchen, clutching the ice cream to his chest and shouting hysterically across the yard, "I scream, you scream, we all scream for — "

"Ice cream!" the other kids finished Woody's chant with a whoop.

Phoebe stayed in the driveway fiddling with the streamers dangling from the handlebars of her bike. She didn't meet Michael's eyes as she said, "Hi, Michael."

He just stood there, not saying anything right away. Finally he cleared his throat and said simply, "Better late than never. I'm glad you finally came." Phoebe awkwardly turned her face as he bent to kiss her so he wouldn't kiss her on the lips. She'd have to wait for him to drive her home to tell him. Phoebe decided then and there, even if she stayed at Peter's just ten minutes, she'd leave with Michael. She'd make him put her bike in the van, and she'd tell him what was happening with Griffin, just like she promised Griffin she would. After the rain had stopped, they had walked down the hill toward his truck. Griffin had said, "Tell Michael soon about us. I'll wait until then to see you again. But I want to be open about this. I don't want to hide from people. I can't hide what I feel about you." The intensity of his voice when he said that still reverberated through Phoebe like a bell. But she didn't have to make it worse by pretending nothing had changed between her and Michael.

"So, PheebeJeebe, where ya been?" Peter greeted her with a bowl of the Chocolate Chocolate Chip ice cream she had brought. Phoebe knew she couldn't eat it but she took it anyway and mushed it around with her spoon. Michael must not have told them what she had said about the game. Phoebe wondered why. For a frantic minute she searched the crowd: Rob and Sasha, Janie and Henry, Kim, Woody, Monica, and Jeremy lying on his stomach in front of the raft, mysteriously absorbed in snapping close-ups of the rotten wood. No, Ted wasn't there. He couldn't be. There really was a Ramblers game today. Phoebe had seen the sign posted at the gas station in Maryville.

She pasted a smile on her face and lied again. "At the ball game up in Maryville. I went to see Ted." Out of the corner of her eye she saw Janie whisper something to Henry. Woody flashed her a frantic look. Phoebe nervously began embroidering her story. "In fact, he was quite the hero. There were four outs and — I think it was the bottom of the third inning — and Ted came to bat, and — "

"Four outs?" Jeremy looked up from his camera. "Peter just finished explaining baseball to me and he said there were — "

"Phoebe is crummy at sports," Michael suddenly butted in. "I guess she got kind of mixed up — after all, the storm there was pretty wild. That tornado touching down near the stadium would have gotten me pretty confused, too."

"But I thought the game was called in the first inning," Monica said innocently.

Phoebe's heart sank and she blushed scarlet.

185

What tornado? The storm had been violent, sure, but she hadn't seen any tornado. Of course, she hadn't exactly been looking. Phoebe suddenly felt queasy. Michael had tried to help her — even though he knew — and now *everyone* knew she was lying. But at least no one knew why.

"Here's Ted — let's get it straight from the horse's mouth." Kim laughed genially, giving Phoebe a worried look.

Phoebe watched as Ted climbed out of his MG and waved at the crowd. When he walked up, Sasha handed him some ice cream. Ted looked at it and grinned. Phoebe frowned as Ted put the bowl aside on the grass and walked over toward the raft.

Ted was Kennedy High's Ice-Cream-Eating Champion. Nothing killed the legendary Mason appetite. His hands were balled in a fist but he smiled his normal smile at his friends and said, "You've got to make this stuff float?" He shoved his baseball cap back on his head. Sand trickled down his neck, out of his hair.

"Hey, watch it, mister!" Peter whacked Ted on the shoulder. "You've got some nerve showing up here at the eleventh hour and criticizing our masterpiece. Where have you been, anyway?"

Phoebe wanted to run. She didn't want to hear what Ted was going to say. She was so embarrassed at being caught in a lie she wanted to die.

"Maryville — the Ramblers game. It was a good one. We won," Ted said easily.

Peter gaped at Ted, then looked quickly at Phoebe. Everyone except Phoebe and Jeremy exchanged startled glances. Janie's hand flew to her mouth and she ran into the house with Henry following.

Phoebe was still staring at Ted, as Jeremy said, "Well, mate, while you've been playing baseball, we've been working. Come on, you're a big chap. Lend me a hand here, we need to lash these ropes around this end." Ted bent to the task, as Jeremy kept babbling. "By the way folks, what's a tornado?"

"A windstorm," Ted answered. "Like a funnel. They have them in the Midwest a lot and on the plains. Now and then we get them around here."

"Pretty violent, I guess. Didn't hurt anyone, did it, today, up in Maryville?" Jeremy asked innocently.

Ted's back stiffened. Keeping his head down, his eyes fixed on the knot he was tying, he mumbled, "Don't think so."

Phoebe could hear the fear in his voice. What was Ted hiding?

"Phoebe, I've got to go now." Michael was still standing next to her. She didn't dare meet his eyes. She took the empty ice cream bowl from his hands.

"I'll take this to the kitchen," she murmured, "then, can you give me a ride home? I don't feel very well."

She started toward the house, not looking at Michael. She knew he would drive her home. They would finally be alone and she could tell him the truth.

"Okay. I'll put your bike in the back," he said.

Phoebe hurried into the brightly decorated kitchen. She put the dishes into the sink and leaned back against the counter to catch her breath. Her eyes were focused on one of Mrs. Lacey's bright abstract paintings, but Phoebe wasn't looking at the painting. She was desperately trying to figure out how to tell Michael about Griffin, where to begin, how to make it all not hurt so much.

"Pheeberooni!" Woody had crept into the kitchen, a woebegone look on his usually merry face. "Oh, Pheeb, what's happening? What have I done?"

"You?" Phoebe gave him a short little laugh. "You haven't done a thing." The words came out all tight and funny. She sounded like she was angry at Woody.

"I shouldn't have told you about Griffin. I should have gone to him myself and told him about Michael. You've seen him, haven't you?" Woody concluded flatly.

Phoebe just nodded. Woody looped his thumbs in his suspenders and let out a loud sigh.

She glanced at Woody and her face softened. "Woody, it's not your fault. Even if Griffin hadn't told you, hadn't asked you to speak to me, he would have found me sooner or later. He would have picked up the phone and called. I'm glad you told me first. It helped — knowing what to expect." Phoebe's voice shook slightly.

Woody started putting his arm around her. "No, no, don't do that." Phoebe cowered away. She didn't want anyone touching her today. She suddenly felt so fragile, as if the next time someone touched her she might break.

Woody drew back. He looked hurt. Phoebe's next words startled him. "We know why I lied, but what about Ted?" she wondered aloud.

Woody shook his head from side to side. "Beats me, but something's wrong — really wrong. And I wonder if it has to do with Chris and that new guy. Ted's the jealous type."

"Michael's leaving. Phoebe, where are you?" Sasha called from the yard.

Phoebe flashed Woody a pleading look. "Wish me luck!" she stammered, and walked slowly out of the room.

"Good luck, Phoebe," Woody said softly. Then he kicked himself in the shin and slammed his hand against the counter, once, twice, three times, until his palm stung. He grumbled loudly, not caring who might hear him, "When I get hold of Griffin Neill, I'll — " Woody couldn't imagine exactly what he would do to Griffin, but dunking him in a vat of hot oil seemed too kind a punishment. Hurting Phoebe, as far as Woody was concerned, was a capital crime. And no matter what she had said, he felt like an unwilling accomplice.

The van was idling in a little cul-de-sac behind the monuments in Rose Hill Park. To the west, where the storm had been, the clouds were gold, and Phoebe thought she saw the faint remains of a rainbow. She shifted uncomfortably in her seat. Out of the corner of her eye Michael's cello in the backseat looked like another person. She loved his cello but silly as it seemed, whenever Michael brought it somewhere, Phoebe felt like it was somehow alive, capable of eavesdropping. She gnawed the inside of her lip until it hurt. Then she started on her nails.

Michael was listening to the radio, making sure the concert at Wolftrap that night hadn't been canceled because of the weather. He found out it was still scheduled to go on. Phoebe sighed with relief. She wanted to talk to Michael now, get this whole horrible scene over with, and try to begin her life again. A life with Michael in it, Griffin outside of it.

"Ted and Chris — " Michael started. Phoebe straightened up in her seat.

"Ted and Chris?" she repeated.

"Let me finish." Michael stared straight ahead out the windshield. He was grasping the steering wheel so tightly his knuckles were white. "I think it's obvious they've been on the rocks for some time now."

"No, it's not obvious to me," Phoebe said quickly. She wasn't in the habit of talking about Chris's problems with anyone.

"Stop it, Phoebe." Michael turned toward her, his usually kind face was taut and livid. "Stop pretending. I didn't know. I was too dumb to put one and one together until this afternoon." He shook his head in disgust. "Next time the two of you should get your lies straight."

"Lies straight? The two of us?" Phoebe gasped in horror. Somehow, some way, he had seen Griffin. He had met Griffin and found out — but how? where? — not this afternoon?

"Ted telling such a baldfaced lie — and you — " Michael stared at her. The hurt in his eyes went so deep, but what did any of this have to do with Ted? Phoebe couldn't understand.

"What's Ted's lie about the game have to do with me?" she asked.

Michael practically snarled at her. "Well then, who were you with all day — Santa Claus?"

Phoebe's mouth fell open. "*Me and Ted!* You think I spent the day with Ted? Michael, I'd never do that. I'd never betray my best friend. Chris is my best friend — " Phoebe's voice broke off. Had she really just said that — about not betraying her best friend?

An expression of doubt flickered across Michael's face. He studied Phoebe intently. "Then — "

"I wasn't with Ted Mason," Phoebe declared flatly. Her heart seemed to be stuck in her throat, but she closed her eyes and forced out the words. "I was — "

"Oh, Phoebe!" Michael cried, and buried his face in her hair "I'm sorry. I'm so, so sorry. I shouldn't have thought that — not for a minute. I'm so dumb!" He pounded the steering wheel. The horn honked. They both jumped. Phoebe startled herself by laughing. And then they were both laughing, and Phoebe couldn't stop. She doubled over until her sides ached, until her laughter turned to tears.

Michael pulled her toward him. "I didn't mean to hurt you, Phoebe. I love you so much I get jealous, I guess." He was stroking her hair. "Don't cry, Phoebe, please. I promised I'd never make you cry like this."

"Michael, stop. Stop saying that. Right now." Phoebe pulled away brusquely. She rubbed her arm across her nose. She had to tell him. She had to tell him *now*. But sitting next to him it was impossible. When he held her like this it was that wonderful feeling again — as if she were suddenly, completely safe. Phoebe felt back on course, as if she weren't skidding off the edge of a precipice. No, now wasn't the time to try to talk. Phoebe suddenly wasn't so sure of what she had to say, anyway. "Your concert," she smiled through her tears. "I don't want you to miss it."

"Being with you now, I almost wouldn't care," Michael said, but he released the brake and drove Phoebe home.

She had one foot in the driveway when she turned to him. "But Michael, we do have to talk. I have to explain — about today — something happened." Her voice grew very small.

Michael reached over and put a finger to her lips. The deep, soft look in his eyes took her breath away. "I don't need an explanation." He turned on the ignition and drove away.

Phoebe watched his van round the corner and head toward the Beltway. She stood there a long time. The look in Michael's eyes said he loved her a lot, that maybe even what happened with Griffin really didn't matter, not if she had the strength not to let it.

Chapter
16

"Brenda! What are you doing?" Chris groaned, as her stepsister motioned from the far side of the dock.

"Stand closer together! I can't fit you all in the picture!" Brenda yelled, looking through the viewfinder of Brad's Polaroid. "I want to get the lighthouse in, too. Move over, Greg, closer to Chris."

Chris gritted her teeth. She was sandwiched between Brad and Greg, trying to keep her balance on the rocking boat. Brad's arm was lightly around her waist; Greg's around her shoulders. His hand tightened slightly as they all moved closer together, sending a shower of electric sparks down Chris's arm and spine.

"Smile!" Brenda snapped, and the camera spit out a square black-backed picture. "That's it!" She smiled as Brad started toward her.

Greg's hand lingered a minute on Chris's arm. Chris quickly moved away. "I love seeing these develop right in front of your eyes. It's like magic," she said a little too brightly as she craned her neck over Brad's shoulder to see. Her arm was still tingling where Greg had touched her.

"There we are!" Greg exclaimed as the shadowy picture grew more and more distinct: Brad, wearing the jaunty sailor's cap Brenda had bought him that morning at the marina; Chris, looking a little stiff, her sunglasses perched on top of her head, her hair blowing across her mouth, half-obscuring a surprised smile; Greg, looking down at Chris, his face not turned toward the camera.

"An important historical document — for the Montgomery/Austin/Davidson archives," Greg said excitedly. "Hey, Brad, can you get copies of these?"

"Copies?" Chris gulped. No one should see this picture. It gave totally the wrong impression, as if there really were something between her and Greg, and that was absolutely ridiculous. *Ridiculous*. Ted would die if he saw this.

"I don't think you can get copies of these," Brad was saying, "Let's just take another one."

Chris thought quickly. "But I want a picture with Brenda in it, and then one of me and Brenda and Brad — " Chris pretended to pout.

"And *me* and Brenda and you," Greg said, handing Brad the camera.

"Me first!" Chris tried to sound playful, not

nervous or overeager. "Here, give me the picture, you three get over there. Brad, the camera please." Chris lay the picture on the blue railing. Her hands were trembling as she focused the camera on the threesome, posing by the helm. Brenda was now wearing Brad's new cap. Chris took a small step back, then another.

"Chris, watch out!" Brenda screamed. Chris's elbow struck the rail and the photo fluttered into the waves below. just like she planned.

"What happened?" she gasped innocently, spinning around. "The picture — " she cried in dismay. "How dumb can I be?" She looked up contritely. Brad and Greg were looking down at the water. Brenda was glowering at her. "Sorry, Bren. I didn't mean it. Here, we can take another," Chris mumbled, shoving the camera in her stepsister's hands. "It was an accident," she said defensively.

"Chris Austin, sometimes you're too much!" Brenda muttered. She pulled her bluejean jacket tightly across her shoulders and started to make her wobbly way across the deck, arms folded across her chest.

"Bren?" Brad looked up.

Chris nodded in Brenda's direction and said curtly, "Over there." Chris yanked down her sunglasses and glared out over the waters of Chesapeake Bay. Brenda should learn to mind her own business, especially regarding Chris and Ted and this nonsensical idea she had about Greg, Chris thought. Her stomach knotted up. Seasick, I'm getting seasick. The perfect touch

196

to the perfect weekend, she thought sarcastically. Her next thought was more of a lament. If only Ted were here.

"Be careful!" Greg cried out in warning. A sudden swell heaved under the eighteen-footer, sending Brenda flying into the rail. Brad's cap flew off her head into the water. The next wave pitched the prow downward, and hurled Chris into Greg's arms. In the background Brad was yelling, "Cap overboard! Cap overboard!" Brenda's throaty laugh floated across the deck. Chris was still clinging to Greg; the fall had knocked the wind out of her and she was unable to disentangle herself from his arms. His hands were strong as he helped her to her feet, never taking his sparkling blue-green eyes off her face. For a second his lips were very close to hers, and she had the panicky feeling he was going to kiss her any minute.

Instead he cleared his throat and said, "The captain of the *Love Boat* is needed at the helm!"

"Sorry I fell like that!" she mumbled as he steadied her over at the rail.

"I'm not," she thought she heard him whisper, But she wasn't sure. She glanced up. Brenda was staring from across the deck, a knowing little smile playing along her mouth. Chris's face tightened and she gave her stepsister an icy stare. Brenda looked a little green around the edges, and for a second Chris was happy as a clam that Brenda had gotten seasick the minute they left dry land.

Chris turned away from her sister and stared

straight ahead. Brad was fussing with the sails, Greg was at the helm. They had changed the boat's course and were heading for a point across the mouth of the bay. Chris leaned out over the water. The spray stung her skin and her hair whipped angrily across her face. But the fresh breeze cleared her head, and the water was less choppy now. She leaned back against the rail, closed her eyes, and inhaled the clean sea air. What a confusing weekend this had been so far.

That morning, when they had set out from the sprawling Montgomery beach house, Chris had spotted the boat from the dinghy. "The *Sally Ride*! Oh, Brenda, look! Someone's named their boat the *Sally Ride*!" she had exclaimed delightedly.

"I'm glad you approve — because that's the boat we're taking out today." Greg grinned.

Chris couldn't believe her ears. "You mean that's your boat?"

Greg nodded vigorously.

Brenda giggled. "You see, Chris has this love/hate thing for Sally Ride. She hates her because she beat Ms. Austin to the honor of becoming America's first woman astronaut, and she loves her because — "

" — she is America's first woman astronaut!" Brad finished enthusiastically.

Chris was trailing her hand in the water as the dinghy slowly motored through the low wake area. "And she's brave, and a symbol of a woman getting to do what she sets out to do. Being a woman didn't stop her. That's why I admire her."

198

A fierce determination colored Chris's voice, but she didn't look up from the water. Greg naming his boat after her own heroine was a crazy coincidence, one more thing they seemed to have in common. She had been having a wonderful time here with Greg. Being with him felt so perfect and she felt so guilty having such a good time without Ted.

"You look so dreamy." Greg had walked up. Chris looked up at him, startled. Her grip tightened on the rail as Greg propped himself back on his elbows and stood next to her. Chris squinted toward the horizon. They had already circled the lighthouse and were heading back west. The sun hung low on the horizon. "Thinking of Ted?" he asked.

"Ted?" Chris echoed his question. She looked away guiltily. She had barely thought of Ted all day, just when Brenda took that dumb picture, and once last night. She had been riding in the cramped backseat of Brad's Honda with Greg. Brenda's arm was around Brad's neck as he drove, her delicate fingers toying with his straight dark hair. The car was little, and Greg so tall his leg had pressed against hers the whole way to the shore. She kept thinking, Ted, Ted, why aren't you here?

"No," Chris answered finally. "I wasn't thinking of Ted at all."

"I didn't think so!" Greg said.

Chris swallowed hard and casually put a few feet between them. She pretended to look at the water. Behind her sunglasses her eyes were closed tight. She felt like she was losing her balance — losing control.

Greg turned to face the rail. The soft golden hairs on his arm brushed her hand. "After all, Ted's not here," Greg announced.

"He can't help that!" Chris said a bit shrilly. "I feel bad he's not. He would love this." She gestured broadly around the bay. It was a perfect day. White sails dotted the blue waters. The sky was a darker blue now than before and the light was getting low. Soon it would be sunset. Yes, she really did wish Ted had been able to see all this.

"In fact, I've been wondering when I get to meet him," Greg said, the mockery back in his voice.

"Why, next week of course," Chris said. "Yes, first thing next week. Why don't you come along to the movies, or meet us at the sub shop? The rest of the crowd will be there and — "

"When did you last see him?" Greg said. He was toying with the logo on his polo shirt, looking straight ahead.

"Saturday," Chris answered promptly. "At Phoebe's party. I told you about Phoebe's party." A week ago. Chris hadn't seen Ted in a week. She hadn't realized that until now. She got a tight, funny feeling in her chest. She hadn't felt like this since Sunday night when she'd gone to bed all lonely and scared. She hadn't been scared since Monday, and she had hardly thought about Ted at all since then. Monday was the day she first met Greg. She hadn't felt nervous or scared or lonely or afraid of losing Ted — not since

Monday. Something definitely didn't make sense.

"Hmm. Saturday. That's a week ago." Greg sounded like a doctor considering a diagnosis.

Chris could feel his eyes on her. She forced herself to take a deep breath. "Greg," she started, "I think something's going on here."

"Ah, you finally noticed," he said with a funny, tight laugh. "I was beginning to wonder —" He moved a step closer.

"No, Greg." Chris put up her hand to ward him off. "You don't understand. I mean I like you, but. . . ." Her eyes strayed toward the back of the boat. Brad was standing with his arms around Brenda's waist. She was leaning against him. They were looking back toward the mouth of the bay. They reminded Chris of her and Ted — the way she felt sometimes in his arms, at this time of day, when they were off somewhere alone. Watching Brad and Brenda she decided she had to tell Greg how much she loved Ted.

That would stop him. He had everything all mixed up. She was too old for him. She was dating another guy. He had to get that straight in his head.

She turned to face him. Suddenly he had one hand on each side of her, grasping the rail.

"Greg!" she cried, pushing her hands against his chest. She wanted to push him away, but somehow his lips found hers. It was a light, gentle kiss that thrilled Chris in a way no kiss had thrilled her for a long time. They stood like that for a long moment; the only sounds were the keening gulls and the furled sails snapping in the breeze. Her hands were still pressed against Greg's soft knit shirt. He smelled so clean, so fresh, like the whole outdoors. No, kissing Ted hadn't felt like this in a long, long time.

"Greg," she gasped, backing away, her pink cheeks suddenly crimson, her heart racing. She glanced quickly toward the back of the boat. Brad was facing away, but Brenda had her head cradled on his shoulder, and she was looking right at Chris. Chris couldn't see her expression from here, but she knew for sure that Brenda had seen them.

Chris scrambled away from Greg's side. "That was wrong, Greg. That was really wrong." Her voice was suddenly cold and tight.

"Wrong?" Greg pulled off his sunglasses and looked Chris right in the eye. "It didn't feel wrong to me," he said intently. "I don't think it felt too wrong to you, either."

"You don't know what I feel! I love another guy, Greg — Besides, besides — " Chris fumbled for the right words. Suddenly nothing felt clear or precise anymore so she blurted out, "You're too young for me, Greg. You're just a kid, even if there weren't Ted. I mean, you don't even *drive* yet." Instantly she regretted saying something so dumb.

He didn't take his eyes off her face. "What's driving got to do with kissing?" he said slowly.

Chris wrapped her arms across her chest and stormed up to the bow. She glared into the distance. The bright sun hurt her eyes, even through her sunglasses, but she didn't care. Greg had no right to take advantage of the situation just because Ted wasn't around.

She sensed him close behind her again. Her whole body went rigid. She kept her back turned as she said, "I want to go back, Greg. I'm feeling a little seasick." Chris's voice was tight and strained. The muscles in her neck had gone hard. Her fists were clenched inside her jacket pocket.

"Funny thing about that, how suddenly seasickness comes on. Come to think of it, you must be contagious, Chris. I'm feeling a bit sick myself right now!" Greg snapped in annoyance. He turned and was back at the helm in a couple of long strides.

Greg's kiss had turned Chris's weekend into a disaster. Finding Laurie Bennington on the Montgomery dock when Greg anchored the little dinghy threatened to make it an absolute catastrophe.

"Surprise," Laurie cooed. "Bet you didn't expect to find me here." She smiled. Her smile was sincere enough, and Chris had to admit, a few weeks away from Rose Hill at her dad's spiffy new condo here on the Eastern Shore had done Laurie a world of good. She looked more relaxed, less made-up, and very happy.

Laurie looped her thumbs in the pockets of her red cropped pants and tossed her dark hair off her face. Her greeting was friendly enough but her searching hawk eyes looked from Greg to Chris to Brad and Brenda, and then behind them.

"Where's Ted?" she asked.

Chris gulped. "Baseball. He had to be at a Ramblers doubleheader up at Maryville."

"Too bad," Laurie said smoothly, but she kept watching Chris's face. Chris shriveled slightly under her probing glance. Laurie continued breezily, "Word was out down at the marina that Greg had company from Kennedy High. I decided to check it out. Dick and I thought you'd like a little surprise."

"Westergard's here?" Brad looked around eagerly.

Laurie nodded. "For the weekend. He's off jogging now. Thought we'd come back though, after dinner."

Chris's heart sank. Well, at least Kennedy High's walking grapevine didn't have telescopic eyes. She couldn't have seen what happened on the boat, but Chris had a feeling Laurie didn't have to. Greg's usual smile had darkened to a scowl. Brenda was irritable. At least Brad looked as if nothing worse than losing a cap had happened. Chris didn't even want to know how she looked. It was bad enough knowing how she felt.

Two hours later Chris was still trying to make sense of her feelings. The sun had set, the fog had rolled in, and she sat alone on the veranda steps, looking down at the beach where Brad and Dick had built a small fire. Laurie and Brenda were talking as they toasted marshmallows, and now and then scraps of conversation or a burst of laughter rippled back to Chris. If Ted were

204

here, Chris thought wistfully, I'd be down there, too.

The lighthouse beacon scanned the distance, marking a soft, eerie path through the fog, and the buoys sounded a mournful tune. Chris couldn't remember when she'd ever heard anything so sad. Tears started down her face, but she didn't bother to wipe them away. No one could see her here in the dark, not even Laurie, who'd been watching Chris out of the corner of her eye all night.

The only thing Chris felt made sense right now was wanting to go home. She couldn't wait to be back in her own room where she could pick up the blue princess phone and call Ted. She needed to hear Ted's strong and cheerful voice. Easygoing, wonderful, fun-loving Ted. Suddenly Chris's heart ached with love for him. And she felt so guilty, not just about kissing Greg — that had been an accident. But when she got home tomorrow she would tell Ted she was sorry, she would try again not to be so serious, so uptight, so righteous about everything. Sitting there just then, the scent of bayberry drifting in from the dunes, Chris would have given anything in the world to roll time back one week, and to say, "Yes, Ted, let's go on that moonlight swim."

Chris would talk to him tomorrow. Then these other feelings would go away.

Suddenly she was aware of Greg's tall, strong presence behind her. Chris could feel him standing very close and her throat went dry. She didn't move. She kept her chin pillowed on her knee, trying to ignore him, but her heart began to pound. Greg's presence somehow scared her and she tried to swallow back her tears.

Neither of them spoke for a long time. "That's a nice sound," Greg finally broke the silence. "The wind in the grass."

Chris didn't want to listen to Greg's nice sound, but she couldn't help but hear it — the sharp, high dune grasses rubbing in the wind.

"Yes. The sound's nice," she said. She suddenly felt silly. Greg was just a kid. He might look eighteen but he was just a kid. Some of her friends in school had younger brothers Greg's age. She didn't feel afraid of them. She would tease them, make fun of them. Some of them even had crushes on her. That was it. Greg had a crush on her. Looking at it that way gave Chris courage. It's up to me, she thought. I'm older. I know better. I'm in control of the situation. She repeated that to herself several times, then cleared her throat.

Then Greg spoke first. "Sorry about my over-reacting on the boat today."

Chris frowned in the dark. He was apologizing, not for the kiss, but for being angry afterward.

"Ted is my boyfriend and whether he's here or not I don't kiss other guys — and I love him," Chris declared flatly.

"I know," Greg mocked. "And when you grow up, you're going to marry him."

"It's possible. Yes, in fact we have talked about it!" Chris retorted. Then she swallowed hard. Marry Ted? It was true. Ted had said something once earlier in the summer, how they might some day get married. That crazy day with Wesley and Sasha at the Naval Academy. They were standing outside the beautiful old chapel. That whole day seemed very far away right now.

Chris rubbed her hand across her forehead. She was suddenly getting a terrible headache. It was all that sun and wind today.

Greg dropped down beside her on the steps. Chris pressed herself closer to the banister. There was enough space between them as he leaned back on his elbows, his legs stretched down to the narrow boardwalk leading down to the sand. "Well, I don't believe it. I don't believe you'll marry Ted. I'm not sure I believe you're in love with him."

Chris narrowed her eyes at Greg. "You have some nerve, Greg Montgomery. You don't know the first thing about me and Ted. You have no right to act as if you know what I'm feeling, especially about Ted," she said in a cold, angry voice.

She couldn't see Greg clearly on the dimly lit porch, but for the first time since she met him, he didn't sound so sure of himself. "You're right. I'm sorry. I guess I just wanted that to be true. I wanted you not to love Ted," he said with a tight little laugh. "I'm used to getting what I want, Chris." The self-assurance momentarily fled his voice. "I can't help it, Chris. I really like you. I thought — I hoped — you liked me, too."

Chris breathed in sharply, then sagged slightly against the steps and looked down at her hands, neatly folded in her lap. Greg didn't have a crush on her. She knew that from his voice, just as she had known it from his kiss that afternoon. And thinking of all that had happened in the past week — and the past few months — Chris knew in an instant she'd never marry Ted. She didn't love him anymore. Chris clasped her hands together very tightly. She didn't want to burst into tears in front of Greg. She also didn't want to reach out and touch him. If she did, she knew she'd fall apart.

"Marrying Ted's not the point," Chris said gently, as though she were talking to a child. "That's between me and him. The point is, I like you a whole lot, Greg, as a friend, a good friend, but not as more than that."

Greg whipped around. "That's how you kiss your good friends?"

Chris inhaled sharply. "That's unfair, Greg," she managed, though her voice came out shaky. Chris felt like she was losing control again. She would never tell him exactly how his kiss had made her feel. When she was fifteen, no sophomore guys she had dated kissed quite like that. "You startled me — "

"Did I?" Something in his voice started Chris's stomach churning. He wasn't mocking now. There was a sad sort of tender feeling in his voice. Chris was glad she couldn't see his face. He sounded like he really believed she had been waiting for him to kiss her. She stood up and started up the steps. Sitting too close to Greg, she'd begun to feel cornered, trapped.

Greg got up, too. He followed her to the door. She could see his face now beneath the porch light, his jaw strong and determined. Suddenly Chris remembered Brenda saying he always went after what he wanted. Then Laurie's laugh rang out across the beach and Chris became self-conscious.

"People will see us!" She hissed and ducked further into the porch shadows.

"Ah, well, I know a quiet little place — " Greg's voice was following her in the dark.

"Greg, stop it. Listen to me." Chris's voice trembled. She clenched her hands and struggled to regain her self-control. "You're too young for me. Guys fifteen and girls seventeen don't date. They don't hang out together — not like that."

"Is that because guys fifteen don't drive, or is it a rule and regulation in the Kennedy High Student Handbook?" He paused, then quipped, "I've always liked breaking rules." To prove his point, he pulled her toward him.

"Greg, NO!" Chris's voice rang out loud and clear, and she pulled free from his grasp. She ran into the house and up the back stairs. She slammed the door to the room she was staying in, and leaned against it, trying to catch her breath. She rubbed her arm where Greg had grabbed her. It didn't hurt; it felt wonderful, and the tears were already starting down her face when she heard Laurie calling from outside.

"Oh, Greg, there you are. We're leaving now. Where's Chris? I wanted to say good-bye."

Chapter
17

Chris padded down the long hallway toward Brenda's room. She paused outside the door, nervously folding and unfolding the collar of her pink cotton robe. The theme from *Masterpiece Theatre* filtered upstairs from the living room, and then her stepmother's voice, followed by her father's. Chris took a deep breath, pursed her lips, and knocked on Brenda's door.

"Brenda," she said curtly, "it's me. Can I come in?"

Brenda didn't answer. Chris walked in anyway. Brenda was in the middle of the room, unpacking her knapsack. She looked up at Chris with a sullen expression on her face.

"What do you want?" she snapped. It was the first time she'd said anything to Chris in twenty-four hours.

Chris stood straight as an arrow and tossed

her hair off her shoulders. "I just wanted to be sure you won't tell Ted about Greg and what happened on the boat." Her face was stony, but her eyes pleading.

"I won't tell Ted." Brenda sounded somewhat offended. "I don't tell your business to anybody." As an afterthought she added, "Neither will Brad."

"Brad?" Chris repeated. She tightened her grip on her robe. Chris had forgotten about Brad.

"He's not blind — neither is Woody, or Phoebe, or Janie — or the rest of the crowd for that matter," Brenda suddenly sputtered.

"They didn't see what happened on the boat," Chris said, a note of fear creeping into her voice.

"They didn't have to!" Brenda declared, with an exasperated toss of her head. "Chris, every time you've been with Greg — at Sticky Fingers, at the sub shop, around town — everyone's noticed. Everyone's wondering what's going on. I mean, it's been pretty obvious." Brenda sat back on her heels and regarded her stepsister. "Oh, Chris," her voice softened. "I know this complicates things between you and Ted — but Greg and you, you seem so right together. You're both so darn stubborn and determined to have things your own way!"

Chris's jaw clenched. "Brenda! I didn't come in here to hear your opinion about Greg and me — or Greg and Ted — or whatever point you're trying to make."

Brenda's shoulders tensed. "Well, maybe you didn't — but you're going to have to listen,"

Brenda declared hotly, throwing some T-shirts on the floor. "You managed to ruin everyone's weekend —"

"Me!" Chris retorted "*I* ruined everyone's weekend? Montgomery's the one — it's him. The whole drive home he pouted like the baby he is!"

"And you? Exactly what did you do? Pout! At this point I think you two 'babies' deserve each other." Brenda put her hands on her hips and glared at her stepsister. "I don't think I have any more to say about this. I'm tired. I want to go to bed now."

Chris bit her lip and headed for the door, but she didn't open it. "Brenda, listen, I'm sorry. I didn't mean to yell at you. I'm upset. I don't know how to handle Greg, and I'm scared some crazy story will get back to Ted."

Brenda was at Chris's side in an instant. She hesitated a second, then awkwardly patted Chris's shoulder. Chris didn't pull away, and her body slowly relaxed. "Nothing's going to get back to Ted, not for a while yet. Laurie won't be back until next weekend. You have time, Chris. Chris," Brenda was pleading now. "Talk to Ted — I think you've got something to work out with him. I think you like Greg, Chris, I really do."

Chris's shoulders stiffened again. "Yes, I do have something to work out. How to convince Greg I don't like him that way. Can't you see, Brenda, he's really just a friend." Saying the words somehow reminded Chris of Phoebe — of talking to Phoebe about Michael. But Michael wasn't too young and Griffin was already out of the picture when Michael came along, almost.

"Lying never helps," Brenda said. Her voice was quiet, the kind of voice she probably used when she tried to help kids in her rap group at Garfield House. Chris gritted her teeth.

"Brenda, I'm not one of your runaways down at the halfway house. And I'm not lying!" she sputtered. "I'm not. And maybe you should just mind your own business for a change. Anyway," Chris added defiantly, "even if half of what you said is true, why should it matter so much to you?"

Brenda considered Chris's words. She propped one hip on the corner of the desk. "It matters — because I've always envied you that — telling the truth easily, not running away, facing things." Her words came out in spurts, jagged. Talking about envying Chris never came easily to Brenda.

"I'm not running away." Chris dismissed Brenda with an annoyed wave of her hand.

"Yes, you are. You're running away from the truth, away from what's really happening with Ted and you, away from your feelings about Greg. You might as well be telling an out-and-out lie — to yourself and to both of them. It's just unfair. And it's not like you to be unfair."

"Well, I'm sorry I've let you down," Chris said tightly, "but it's just none of your business, Brenda."

"Whatever's going on with you and Greg is affecting me, too — and Brad. I mean *we* have to pretend with Ted that nothing's different."

"You've seen Ted?" Chris asked, a little too quickly.

Brenda closed her eyes and shook her head. "No, I haven't, but he lives here in Rose Hill. I will see him and so will you." She walked over to her bed and began twirling the fringe on her spread.

"There's nothing to pretend about, anyway," Chris said stonily, from over by the door.

"Chris, I don't get it. I know — you know, that I know — things haven't been too hot with Ted. A week ago, you were really a mess. And he hasn't called or dropped by since then."

"He called the other night. You were here. You heard the whole thing," Chris reminded her.

Brenda grew thoughtful. "Yes, I was here. I heard." She rocked back and forth on the edge of her bed. Something was wrong. Brenda sensed it. Something was wrong with Chris, but something was wrong with Ted, too. She had heard something tonight. After they'd dropped off Chris and driven Greg home, Brad and Brenda had gone off to the sub shop. Henry and Peter were talking in the back booth. Brenda had heard them saying something about the game being canceled in Maryville Saturday and Ted lying about it. Then Henry had spotted her, and changed the subject. A few minutes later he walked out looking vaguely embarrassed.

Brenda looked over at Chris. She was digging at the shag rug with her toe, her beautiful face all tight and hard, her lips trembling. Chris didn't suspect anything was wrong with Ted. Brenda sure wasn't going to be the first to mention it — not until she knew for certain.

Chris inhaled sharply and opened the door. "Good-night, Chris," Brenda said gently.

Chris didn't say good-night. She didn't trust herself to say anything. She walked very carefully to her room. She took off her robe and draped it neatly on the back of her chair, then sat down stiffly on the foot of her bed and began brushing her long blond hair. She brushed and brushed with hard, vigorous strokes, until her scalp tingled. She looked straight ahead. Ted's latest football trophy stood on the dresser. His picture was beside it, tacked to the wall between the red and gold Kennedy High pennant and Chris's framed National Honor Society award.

She looked past all that right into the mirror, right at the reflection of Chris Austin, sitting very straight, very still, very tall, the big blue hairbrush poised midair in her hand. She stared at herself sandwiched between the pictures of Sally Ride and Geraldine Ferraro. "I don't love you, Greg Montgomery. I love Ted. I do, I'm *sure* I do," she whispered and slumped down, crying, into her pillow.

Phoebe sat cross-legged in the middle of her bedroom floor, solemnly mending the hem on her suspender pants. The air conditioning was on already, the window closed, so she didn't hear the soft, persistent rap on the glass at first.

When she did, she paled slightly, and whispered, "Griffin?" He had promised not to visit her yet. She jumped up and opened the curtain.

"Chris?" she gasped and threw open the window. "What are you doing here?" She looked at the clock. It was ten A.M. "Why aren't you at work? Why didn't you come in the front door?" In the next instant she took in Chris's old jogging shorts, the slightly torn alligator T-shirt, and her red-rimmed eyes. "Chris, what's wrong?" Her voice dropped to a whisper.

Chris sniffed and swallowed hard before speaking. "I need to talk, Phoebe. I need to talk to someone. I called in sick today because I — I — just couldn't face it. I can't face it alone anymore." Phoebe stared in disbelief at the tears streaming down Chris's face. Something very terrible must have happened. Chris almost never cried in front of people, certainly not in the middle of the day, in the middle of the street.

"Let's go down to the river," Phoebe said, ducking back in her room for her sandals. A minute later she came around the back of the house, carrying a box of tissues. She had tucked a couple of sodas and some candy in her pack. Phoebe had her doubts she could be of much help to anyone now, but Chris was obviously in trouble. At least she could be there to listen.

"Did you walk over?" Phoebe asked.

Chris nodded. "Yes, I mean, no. I ran."

"Take my bike. I'll borrow Shawn's."

Along the riverbank in Rose Hill Park, the giant rhododendrons still dripped from the weekend rains. Phoebe sat very still though the ground was uncomfortably damp against her bare legs and she was very frightened. She had never seen Chris cry like this, not over Brenda, not over any of her terrible fights with Ted, not since Chris's mother died and Phoebe and Chris had first found this place to have their heart-to-hearts. She still had no idea why Chris was crying now. The whole way there they hadn't talked. Phoebe was almost afraid to touch her but she had never seen anyone look so terribly unhappy. So finally she murmured, "Poor, poor Chris," and threw her arms around her and held her as she sobbed.

Chris's tears slowly subsided. "Phoebe, I don't know what to do. I couldn't face going to work today. I had to lie. It's just like Brenda said, I'm becoming a terrible person." Chris choked up again.

"You're not a terrible person. You couldn't be, Chris Austin," Phoebe declared, yanking out some tissues and stuffing them in Chris's hand.

"Brenda was right, she was right last night, but I couldn't tell her. I was too proud then. I'm too scared now." Chris scrambled to her feet and walked toward the river, ducking beneath the old willow. For a crazy minute, Phoebe was scared she might jump in. Of course the river wasn't deep here, and Chris could swim, but Phoebe hurried to her side, anyway.

"Something happened with Brenda?" Phoebe asked, puzzled. The two stepsisters had been getting along so well for months now.

"No. Well, we had a fight last night." Chris swallowed hard. "But it's not about Brenda, it's Ted."

"Ted." Phoebe said. She stuffed her hands in the pockets of her shorts and asked very carefully, "What happened with Ted?" She held her breath, not sure she wanted to hear. Ted had been lying to Chris. Everyone knew that after Saturday. Someone must have told Brenda about the ball game, and last night Brenda. . . .

"I still love Ted." Chris sniffed and reached for another tissue to blow her nose. "I really do. But — "

"What has he done?" Phoebe fought to keep her voice even. She was suddenly very afraid to hear. She remembered the sand falling down his neck, out of his hair. She suddenly could see the whole scene Saturday afternoon, every awful detail. He had been down at the beach, lying in the sand, and there was only one reason to lie about it.

"Ted? Oh, nothing. *He* hasn't done a thing." All the pink went out of Chris's cheeks. "It's me," she confessed in a horrified whisper. "Greg — he kissed me. I kissed him back. And Phoebe, it's so awful. I haven't felt that way kissing anyone. I think I'm in love with him," she wailed, burying her head in her arms, and sobbing into the mossy trunk of the tree.

Phoebe drew in her breath sharply. She closed her eyes. This couldn't really be happening. Chris wasn't telling her this. She must be dreaming. She stood there still as a stone, afraid to open her eyes, afraid to breathe.

"Phoebe," Chris's anguished voice was pleading. "Please don't think it's so awful. I mean, I haven't told Ted yet. I didn't know until last night how I felt. I thought it was impossible to feel this way. I thought I loved Ted too much. And Greg — he's so young."

Phoebe opened her eyes. "Oh, Chris," she cried, wrapping her arms around her friend. "I wish I could help you, tell you what to do." She was crying now, too. "I understand how you feel, really I do. But something so similar is happening to me. I'm the last person to tell you what to do." She felt so awful. "Griffin is back, Chris."

Chris's mouth fell open, her eyes widened. "Here? In Rose Hill?" She gave a furtive look around the park.

"No. Maryville." Phoebe's voice sounded hollow and flat. She stared down at her feet and watched the progress of an earthworm across the grass. She didn't look up at Chris as she said, "So you see, I don't know how to help you. I don't know what to do myself. And with me and Michael — we're just at the beginning — it's not like you and Ted."

Chris caught her breath. "That's not fair, Phoebe. You sound just like Brenda, as if it's a foregone conclusion Ted and I are washed up. I'm not convinced about that. I'm not sure I want to leave Ted." Chris's voice grew angrier with every word.

219

Phoebe looked Chris squarely in the eye. "But what about Ted? What does he feel? Maybe he's tired of fighting with you all the time. Ted hates fights. You know that. You found Greg. Maybe Ted — " Phoebe abruptly cut herself off. She had no proof Ted had another girl friend somewhere.

Chris sank down on a bench. "I know. Maybe Ted's figured out about Greg — everyone else has. But he hasn't seen us together. He hasn't even met Greg yet. Ted gets so jealous. I think that's why he hasn't called since last week when I couldn't meet him late one night. Maybe I've lost him, Pheeb," Chris said desolately. "Maybe it's better that way. I'm getting pretty tired of fighting, too," she admitted, wiping her eyes.

Phoebe sat down next to Chris and handed her the box of tissues. "And what about Greg?" Phoebe asked gently, her heart aching for Chris.

"Greg? What about him? It's impossible. No matter how he makes me feel, how much I love him, it's wrong." She stood up and stomped back over toward the riverbank. She folded her arms across her chest and hugged herself tightly. She turned around toward Phoebe, a familiar, set expression on her face. "I can't see him again. That's that. And I guess I have to tell him soon. I have to face him. I just can't believe I'd fall in love — and — " Her voice faltered.

"And break all the rules?" Phoebe said quietly from the bench. The bench was high and her feet didn't quite touch the ground. She suddenly felt small and vulnerable like a little girl, except when she was a little girl the rules were so much clearer — rules to the games you played, what your parents said you could or couldn't do. Phoebe said it aloud. "I don't think there really are rules about who you love, Chris — there are no rules about how old the person you love should be, and no rules to keep you from loving someone, even if loving him is hurting someone else you love so terribly it makes you feel like dying inside."

Chris regarded Phoebe for a second. "Pheeb, you said Griffin's back. Have you seen him?"

Phoebe closed her eyes and nodded. "A couple of times. I tried to tell him to go away." Phoebe opened her eyes and looked directly at Chris. "But I couldn't. Because I don't want him to go away. Not really."

"And you still love Michael, too," Chris stated quietly, looking down at Phoebe on the bench. Phoebe glanced up and met her eyes. The ghost of a smile crossed Phoebe's face. "Chris, you aren't lecturing me. You aren't telling me how awful I'm being — like that time when I broke up with Brad."

"No. I wouldn't do that now." Chris bit her lip and returned Phoebe's dim smile. "I couldn't — in all honesty — could I?" The girls smiled shyly at each other. Chris finally said, "I just wish you had told me sooner. It must have been awful for you." Chris didn't sound accusing, just a little hurt.

"Me, too!" Phoebe took a deep breath. Nothing was over, nothing was solved, but she didn't feel so alone anymore, so afraid. "But Chris." She took Chris's hand and pulled her down by her side. "Listen to me. I know I've told you — *everyone* tells you — not to give so much advice, and now I'm going to sound just like you. I can't say what to do about Ted. But about Greg — you're dead wrong. He's not too young. If it feels right to you and you love him, there's nothing wrong with it."

Chris shook her head in despair. "But how will it look, Phoebe? I've got a lot of responsibility at school this fall. I'm student body president, all that stuff. I can't run around with underclassmen — "

For the first time in a week, Phoebe really giggled. " 'What will the neighbors think?' " She imitated Chris's refined voice perfectly. Chris blushed and lowered her gaze to the ground. Phoebe tugged her hand. "Chris, people *will* talk — let them. What difference does it make? Besides, I think Kennedy's grapevine could use something new and exciting to talk about. You might single-handedly liberate a few people. After all, you've always wanted to do something very brave. Letting yourself love Greg — even though he is younger — is pretty brave."

Chris studied Phoebe's face for a long time. She nodded slowly. "Phoebe, I don't know how I'll face the kids with Greg, but I think, maybe, I do love him. Besides," she said more brightly, "I won't have to face them alone, will I?"

Phoebe smiled. Chris almost looked and sounded like her old self.

222

Chris shook her head. Her lips trembled as she said, "And Ted. Well, I guess that's going to be tough, but no tougher than kissing Greg behind Ted's back. Ted and I were supposed to go out tonight, but I haven't spoken to him yet."

A shadow flitted across Phoebe's face. Chris squeezed her hand. "And you? What are you going to do? What's been happening, Phoebe?"

Phoebe sagged back against the bench and shook her head slowly from side to side. She twirled one thick red curl around her finger as she spoke. "I don't know. I know I love Michael — I love him in such a wonderful way — but it's not like loving Griffin. Nothing's like loving Griffin. Oh, Chris," she cried, her huge eyes filling with tears. "Whenever I see Griffin, or hear his voice, I can't resist him. It's like a magnet. No, it's more than that."

Phoebe drew her knees up to her chest and buried her face in her arms. Her voice was all muffled as she spoke. "He said I was his other half. And that's just what it feels like. I can't picture my life without Griffin — I never could. I just thought he'd always be far enough away that it wouldn't matter."

Chris's touch was gentle on her arm. "Phoebe, then why do you sound so unhappy?"

She glanced up white-faced at Chris. "Because as intense as being with Griffin feels, it feels awful, too. He said it was like Romeo and Juliet with us — and Chris," Phoebe broke down, "they had such an awful ending."

Chris stroked Phoebe's head, and let her cry a

bit. "But you and Griffin don't have to. Anyway, *Romeo and Juliet* is just a story. But what about Michael? How do you feel with him?"

Phoebe looked up with a lovely smile. "Happy, as if my whole world's gotten very wide and very big and very full of wonderful experiences and wonderful people." She spread her arms out and looked up at the sky. "Do you know, Chris — do you realize how many more people I've met around town, at school, just because of Michael?"

Chris nodded vigorously. "I like that about him, too. He's really made a difference in our crowd."

Phoebe looked at Chris and smiled a sad smile. "I know. I can tell from the way you're smiling now that it's clear as day. Michael's who I should be with. I know that. But then there's this other thing I feel that's bigger than me. I keep trying to tell Griffin to go away and I just seem unable to do it. I feel like such a weak person." Her voice got small.

"Nonsense, Phoebe Hall." Chris frowned. "You're a very strong, determined person. A very special person," she added softly, then bit her lip. "But I can't tell you what to do. I don't — I don't like Griffin as much as Michael."

Phoebe looked up surprised. "You never told me that," she accused.

"I have no right to. Besides, it's not who *I* like. And Griffin is a very special person, too — like you. And Michael — in another way — is, too. So it's hard. But Phoebe," Chris paused. "I think a person — every person — has a right to be really, really happy. Greg makes me that, right now — really happy."

Phoebe's tear-streaked face brightened into a smile. "Thanks, Chris. I know that," she said, remembering Saturday, and Michael. She still didn't know what he meant about not explaining things. . . . But if only she could be strong enough, she knew exactly what she had to do.

Chapter
18

If Phoebe could see me now! Chris groaned inwardly, and slouched down further in the driver's seat of her car. Chris had once said she'd never be caught dead at the gory horror flicks they showed at the Rose Hill Drive-In. Plenty of other kids had already seen her and a couple of nasty comments had filtered their way into the open window of her Chevette as she and Greg drove down to the front row. No girl drove a guy to the Drive-In. She must be making some kind of town history, she thought wryly. At least no one she knew had seen her. The only reason she was here was to be alone with Greg, away from the crowd.

He had his long legs drawn up to his chest, and his eyes were on the screen. They had the sound off but Greg had warned her he knew every line of *Attack of the Killer Tomatoes* by heart.

Chris smiled slightly as she watched him watch the movie. He had the same rapt expression on his face as Phoebe's kid brother Shawn did every time he saw *Star Wars*. For a second Chris's heart stopped. Maybe Greg really was too young.

He looked away from the screen just then. "Want some popcorn?" he said. He hadn't said very much since they'd arrived. Neither had she. At first she was uncomfortable, certain that everyone was watching her with this cute, but very young, guy. Then she rememberd Greg looked at least eighteen, and by now no one was even watching the movie.

"Popcorn?" Chris repeated, then shook her head. "I'm thirsty, though." She watched him awkwardly work his lanky frame out of the small car. He stood up and stretched to his full height. Looking at him like that, a crazy electric feeling ran from the tip of her toes to the top of her head, a wonderful sensation. Then her stomach turned to butterflies and she got the same excited, nervous feeling she had earlier that night, when she had opened the door to find Greg standing there, a bunch of wilted daisies in his hand, a concerned expression on his face, and so much love in his eyes. "You weren't at work today. They said you were really sick. I called you, but you weren't home."

She almost threw her arms around him and kissed him then, but she restrained herself. There were things that had to be talked about — and there was Ted, who hadn't yet returned her calls.

"I wasn't sick," she said. "I just needed some time to think." She didn't have to say more.

"Let's get out of here," Greg had said then, shoving the flowers in her hand. When she came back from the kitchen, he was standing on the porch, rocking back and forth on his heels and looking around the neatly manicured front yard of the stately brick home. He had never been to her house before. "I pictured you in a place like this. I like seeing how people live," he said.

It felt funny walking down the flagstone path to her car and going around to the driver's side and getting in. It was such a silly thing, but she had never driven a guy on a date before. And that's what this was, their first date, even though they did have to work out some things.

Right now she couldn't help thinking she wanted to skip over all that because she knew exactly how the night was going to end and she wanted to skip right to the ending.

They sat facing each other with one popcorn, one Coke between them. Chris had kicked her sandals off and had her feet on the seat. She dug her toes into the upholstery and said to Greg, "I called Ted today."

Greg paused for a second, then stuffed a fistful of popcorn in his mouth. "And?" he mumbled.

"He wasn't home. He wasn't at Ramblers practice, either. I called the stadium. They haven't seen him since last week. I — " Chris pursed her lips. "I think he suspects something — about us."

"About *us*, Chris?" Greg's voice was teasing.

Chris looked up straight into his laughing eyes.

228

His hand reached out gently and brushed her cheek. "Tell me about *us!*"

Chris drew back and pretended to pout. She folded her arms across her chest, and leaned back against the door. "Not much to tell, is there?" For a second she was scared to hear Greg's response.

"Not much for Ted to know, is there?" Greg imitated her voice and grinned. "Of course, we could change all that." He fed Chris a piece of popcorn. His finger grazed her lip. An incredible shot of warmth rushed through her. "We could give Laurie Bennington plenty to gossip about. We have a whole five days to work something out." Greg sandwiched Chris's bare foot between his feet. He had come to her house straight from work. His pants were rumpled and he was wearing soft cotton socks. Chris didn't pull her foot away.

Her heart was thumping like crazy but she was afraid. She said, "I don't want Laurie to gossip about us. I don't want people to talk. I'm afraid of that." She had never admitted that to anyone but Phoebe before.

"People talk," Greg said flatly. "They'll talk more about us — because Ted's a hero around town, and because I'm a mere sophomore, and because you're so many important things at school — including most beautiful girl on campus."

Chris blushed prettily, then gnawed her lip. "That's what Phoebe said, about giving people something to talk about."

"Phoebe knows about *us*?" Greg wriggled his eyebrows and lowered his voice. She had her hands primly clasped together on her knee. Greg placed a hand on top of hers.

Chris was finding it hard to talk. She was a little embarrassed. "Yeah. She's my best friend, I needed someone to talk to."

"I like her," Greg said. "She's a very sensitive person."

"You've hardly said five words to her," Chris said. "How do you know that? It's true, though, she is a wonderful person."

"I don't know how I know that, Chris." He combed back his hair with his fingers. "I'm pretty good at feeling people out when I first meet them. And I got a good feeling about Phoebe."

"And me?" Chris teased, squeezing his hand.

Greg didn't answer. His blue-green eyes searched hers for a long, long instant. Then he pulled her toward him across the seat and kissed her.

This time Chris didn't feel guilty or confused about his kiss, not one bit. She finally surfaced, and ran her finger across his smooth cheek. "But Greg, we should — at least till I talk to Ted — try to keep a low profile."

"This low enough?" He captured her by the wrists and pulled her toward him, this time touching each of her cheeks and her nose lightly with his lips before he kissed her. She pretended to struggle a few seconds, then relaxed into his arms. He nuzzled her ear and said softly, "As for keeping a low profile — I think the only person

230

who doesn't know about us is Ted."

"Greg!" Chris sat up suddenly. She straightened her shirt and scrambled back to the driver's seat. "What are you doing?"

He had reached over and turned up the sound. An awed, strained voice filled the car: "My God! It's worse than we thought. These are cherry tomatoes!"

Chris squinted in disbelief at the dumb scene on the screen. A man in a white lab coat and a group of other men — some with cameras, some with guns — were being pursued by a platoon of giant red balls hurtling across a field.

"This is the dumbest thing I've ever seen!" Chris cried. "What are they doing?" She pointed to the red things.

"Those are the cherry tomatoes. Wait until the big beefsteak ones start destroying Earth. Look, we're getting to the good part now." He sounded so happy, so buoyant.

Chris rested her head on the steering wheel and groaned. "I never, ever should have let myself fall in love with a younger guy. It was dumb, dumb, dumb." She peeked at Greg. His eyes were transfixed on the screen. "Just like Shawn," she groaned.

"Who's Shawn?" Greg's head snapped around.

"Oh, another younger man I see once in a while." Chris pretended to brush a crumb off her shirt before curling up in her seat and snuggling into the crook of Greg's arm. His body suddenly tensed. After a second she whispered, with a happy smile, "He's only ten."

Greg drew her back into his arms and looked down into her eyes. "Robbing the cradle, are you?" He laughed, and bent to kiss her.

"But what about the killer tomatoes — don't you want to see what happens to them?" Chris opened her big blue eyes very, very wide.

"I've seen this movie already," he murmured as he lowered his lips toward hers. "It's funny, but every time I see this movie the good guys always win."

Chapter 19

At Michael's house Phoebe was helping Miss Spinelli clear the table. It had been a lovely dinner, but Phoebe hadn't been able to eat a bite. Earlier that afternoon she hadn't been able to sing, either. Miss Spinelli hadn't yelled at her. All she had said was, "Everything beautiful is meant to be used, Phoebe, not just looked at, or talked about, or kept in a glass cabinet. Your voice is beautiful. Don't keep it in like that, all bottled up. It's as if you're afraid to let it free. Give it to people, share it. Singing's like being in love, Phoebe; it should make you — and the people around you — very, very happy."

Phoebe had been thinking of that as she cleared the table. She carried the stack of plates very carefully into the kitchen. They were beautiful plates, with an airy floral design that reminded her of something very old, very delicate,

233

very rare, like something you'd see in a museum. But she knew Miss Spinelli used them every day, even when company wasn't there, because Michael had told her once.

She put the plates down on the counter and pushed open the heavy swinging door. She had one foot in the dining room, one foot in the kitchen, when Michael's mother looked up from the sink and said, "Your friend, that nice looking actor, he won't be coming back for lessons. Too bad. He's not a great singer, but he has a pleasant voice."

For a minute, everything went out of focus and Phoebe couldn't catch her breath. She looked frantically up at Michael. He was standing near the table, holding Paul's Spock ears in his hand. He didn't look at Phoebe, but as he went past her into the kitchen she could sense the tension in his body. He must have heard. Now he knew for sure about Griffin. He'd probably known all along.

Phoebe smiled her way through dessert, afraid to look at Michael. She heard herself laughing at Paul when he read excerpts from his new story book, *Fat Men From Space*. She heard herself answer Miss Spinelli, "Yes, I'd love to do that new piece, 'Musetta's Waltz,' at the Christmas concert." But Phoebe had a feeling she might never come back to this house, not after tonight, not after Michael drove her home and confronted her with what he knew.

But Michael didn't confront her. He didn't say a word on the way home. He kept the country

234

music station on low, and hummed along with a few tunes. Phoebe sat scrunched up in the passenger seat, feeling very small and not very brave. Before she knew that Michael knew about Griffin, she had every intention of telling him, but now she felt embarrassed and ashamed.

He pulled up to the curb. Phoebe sat very still, staring at her hands. He didn't flick off the radio. Any minute now he would. Any minute now he would say, "I know, I know Griffin's back." Phoebe clasped her hands tightly in her lap and waited.

"It's getting late," he finally said. He had parked where there was no street lamp, and she couldn't see his face. His voice sounded okay, a little sad, maybe. Why didn't he ask her about Griffin? Was it possible that even though his mother had mentioned him, Michael didn't think Phoebe had seen him? But if that were the case, then why was he suddenly acting so cold? He hadn't touched her once the whole way home.

"Uh, yes, it is late," Phoebe answered at last. She felt like she was on her first date, waiting for something to happen, waiting for him to kiss her, or waiting for him to tell her, It's been nice, I'll call you sometime. This was crazy. There had been too much between them for Phoebe to pretend something bad wasn't happening. She burst out, "Michael — "

"I have a rehearsal tomorrow." His voice was even, strong, determined. "I can't hang out here tonight. I have to go home." He had never talked like that to her before, his voice all short and clipped with all the music missing from it. He hadn't even sounded like that Saturday, when he thought she had been hanging out with Ted. He gripped the steering wheel tightly, and in the dim light she could see his jaw was tense and set.

"Michael, I have to tell you something," she began. "It's important. Remember Saturday, I said I wanted to explain — "

Michael reached across the seat and flung open her door. " 'Night, Phoebe," he said, and pecked her lightly on the cheek. He might as well have slapped her. That's how she felt, rejected and abandoned. He had never not walked her to the door before.

Michael drove to the corner and turned out the headlights where he sat and watched Phoebe's house. The ground floor window in the back was hers. He watched as the light came on and then flicked off again. Only then did he turn on the ignition and head back up Elm. He wanted to be sure she was safely inside.

At the flashing light he made a left, toward the school. He had the chapel key in his pocket and a terrible need to be alone. The lot was empty except for a shadowy gray Saab parked over by the theater. "Darn!" Michael muttered. Charlie was there, too. Well, maybe later he'd go back to the chapel and they'd jam some and he would lose himself in the music, and forget about the mess with Phoebe.

He parked next to Charlie's car, then walked

across the faculty parking lot toward the baseball field. Michael climbed way up into the grandstand. He took a long, deep breath. It was late but still hot. Last time he'd climbed up here it had been spring, the night he had first kissed Phoebe. He hadn't meant to kiss her, but he couldn't help it. He had wanted her for so long, ever since the first time he'd heard her sing at the Christmas concert.

Michael leaned back and dug in his shirt pocket. He pulled out the harmonica Charlie had given him last week. He did a quick scale and rapped it twice against the back of the wooden seats. Then he put it to his lips and began playing a low, mournful tune. Michael's eyes were closed as he played, and he didn't notice Charlie climbing up the narrow bleachers to settle beside him. But then he heard a second harmonica harmonizing with his and he opened his eyes and kept playing. When the song ended, the two of them sat silently under the stars.

"Nice tune, Rifkin," Charlie finally said.

"Thanks. I wrote it for Phoebe."

"It needs words."

"We're working on it," Michael said, his voice shaking slightly. He tugged at his hair, and rested his forehead in his hands. "I'm not sure we'll finish it."

Charlie kicked absently at the concrete stairs. "That guy, he's back." It was more of a statement than a question.

Michael nodded. "I thought so. I figured it out before tonight. My mother just mentioned some-

237

thing about Phoebe's actor friend auditioning for a lesson."

"Wanda saw him last week at the Arena Stage. He was trying out for some part. She thought you knew."

"I haven't mentioned it to Phoebe," Michael said quietly. "I feel like I'm competing with a ghost." His voice tightened. "She almost told me tonight. I didn't want to hear it. If she said she'd been seeing him, I'd have to do something about it, like go punch him out, or break up with her. Something."

Michael didn't know what to make of the fact that Griffin was back in town. He knew he still loved Phoebe. Nothing had changed in that repect, but she had been acting strangely lately. Hot and cold. But so had he. He was trying so hard to be patient, hoping she'd come around when she got her feelings all straightened out. It was getting harder every day, but he loved her so much, he was willing to wait a while longer.

"You don't have to *do* anything. Let it be," Charlie broke into his thoughts. "You did the right thing, Michael. Sometimes words aren't the best way."

Michael put the harmonica to his lips and blew out. The notes escaped like a sigh.

Charlie slapped him on the back. "Give it time, Rifkin. Give it time."

Chapter
20

Ted bounded up the stairs to his room two at a time. He stopped only long enough to rip a note off his door. His kid sister had written in big block letters: CHRIS CALLED THREE TIMES!!! He shoved his cap back on his head and took a deep breath. Then he crumpled the note, pushed open the door, and tossed his gym bag in the middle of the cluttered floor. The room was hot and Ted was already sweating from the long drive home. He peeled off his T-shirt and dumped it on a chair already heaped with clothes. He rummaged in his bag and pulled out three smooth white stones and a handful of shells. Very carefully he laid them on top of his bookshelf between last year's Statewide Football Championship trophy and a picture of Chris. Then he flopped down on the edge of his bed. When he pulled off his sneakers, sand spilled out over everything.

He hesitated only a minute before reaching for the phone.

The instant it rang, Molly answered.

"Ted?" She didn't whisper. That meant her cousin was still downstairs watching *Top Ten Video,* Ted's shoulders relaxed. That meant tonight they could talk a long, long time.

Ted threw himself down on the floor, stuffing his gym bag beneath his head, and propping his feet up on the edge of his desk. "How'd I do?" he asked, laughing. He couldn't quite picture Molly in the room she shared with her cousin Kara. Still, he knew she had been waiting there by the phone ever since he pulled away from the curb and headed home — so she could pick up on the first ring and not wake the rest of her family.

"Two hours and twenty minutes. I'm impressed!" Molly answered. "And to think just a few days ago it took you three whole hours for the trip between your house and here."

Ted jumped to his feet and walked over to his window. The telephone cord toppled a pile of clean laundry stacked on the bed. He leaned out into the warm night air. His bedroom faced east, and until now that had always bothered him, because the sun streamed in at the crack of dawn. He had even brought a black window shade the day school closed last June so he could spend the summer sleeping in. But facing east right now didn't seem bad at all. He looked out over the quiet streets below, and imagined clear across the state to Ocean City. He tried to visualize Molly's aunt's house as he said, "Didn't get a ticket, either!" But he couldn't picture it at all. He had never even been there.

"Don't brag about breaking any speed records. My Uncle Pete's a state trooper!" Molly warned. After a pause she added, "I guess you didn't get to call her yet. It's so late again." He detected a hint of disappointment in her voice.

Ted's smile faded. "It's worse than that. There was a note on my door. Chris called three times tonight. I feel so awful about this — "

"Ted," Molly started: "Don't. I don't mean to push you. It really doesn't matter now, does it?" Her voice grew so soft, so wistful. Ted couldn't speak for a second.

"It's hard for me Molly," he whispered. "It's so hard — I can't believe there are so few days left."

"Don't, Ted," Molly begged. "Let's not talk about that. It's hard for me, too," she admitted quietly.

Neither of them said anything for a second.

"Molly, don't worry. I'm not going to let not telling Chris get in the way. It's just the raft race that's getting in the way. You would love it. It's not white water stuff like you're used to. Our raft looks like something that's already been torpedoed, but I really think it's going to be fun. I wish so much you could be there. I have to go no matter what. I'm one of the few guys who knows something about rafting and boats." Ted sounded

241

desolate now. "Saturday's our last day together. I can't believe I can't spend it with you."

Molly sighed. "It's better this way, Ted. It would be awkward with Chris and all. Really it would. I'll meet you later, after the race. Maybe you can tell her on Saturday, but if not, it just doesn't matter now." Molly paused, then began talking very quickly, as if a lot of words strung together could block out her feelings. Her voice was bright and cheerful. "Don't forget we've got a date to go to Cheap Thrills Saturday night. My aunt and uncle are going to some party and won't mind if I come home late."

"Good thing about that," Ted said huskily. He was glad Molly couldn't see him now, his eyes filling up with tears. He had promised her tonight that he would live just for the moment, for the next few days. It didn't even matter about Chris anymore. He had tried to reach her a couple of times, but she'd been out. He still wanted to talk to her, explain how he was feeling. He owed her that much. By now the whole crowd had probably figured out what was going on anyway. Between Janie and Henry seeing him with Molly, and that dumb lie about the Ramblers' game, it had to be pretty obvious.

Chris had probably heard already, too. That must have been why she called tonight. He would tell her first thing Sunday, after Molly was gone. Ted caught his breath. He couldn't quite picture a Sunday, or Monday, or the rest of his life without Molly.

"Ted?"

Ted lifted his head from his hand. He realized he had been quiet a long time. "I love you, Molly Ramirez," he said, closing his eyes. Tonight in her red blouse she had looked like a flower, a very joyful flower.

"I love you, Ted Mason," Molly whispered. "Good-night."

"Good-night."

Molly hung up the phone and flopped face-down on her bed. She picked up her sandal and flung it across the room. It hit hard on the opposite wall, barely missing Kara's framed photo of Judd Nelson. Molly instantly retrieved it, and contritely rubbed her sleeve against the black smudge on Kara's cheerful flowered wallpaper.

She stomped back to her bed, and sat down holding her sandal between her hands. Maybe it had been a mistake, loving Ted. From the minute she first looked into his kind blue eyes, she was lost. Falling in love like this must be what drowning felt like. In her advanced lifesaving course last year, someone had described it just like that: The undertow pulled at you, and you fought and fought the waves, until finally something in you gave in, and you almost gratefully went under.

Molly shivered. She should never even have let herself talk to Ted, to flirt with him. Every other guy had been so easy to have a good time with, to stay friends with, to say good-bye to when it was time, or when the sparks sort of fizzled out between them. But nothing would fizzle out with Ted. Molly knew that was true from the bottom of her heart.

That was why she had never told him exactly where she lived in the Bay area. She had never even let him drive her all the way home here to Ocean City. After Saturday night she didn't want to see him again. She didn't want to hear his voice on the phone. She didn't want him to write. One word from Ted after Sunday — after she got back to California — and she'd be lost. She'd somehow run away — run the whole way back to Maryland into his arms. And she couldn't do that. She had promised her mother, the night her father died, that she would never, ever run away like that again.

And Molly Ramirez prided herself on keeping promises.

Chapter
21

The sun was bright, the air clear, and Phoebe had never heard the birds sound so joyful before. She sat in her station wagon, gazing up at the eaves of the sundrenched barn and wishing it were a rainy day.

She closed her eyes, gripped the steering wheel tightly, and replayed last night's conversation with Chris one last time in her head. Chris had made her go through a role-playing exercise on the phone, something she'd learned from Brenda. Phoebe had to pretend Chris was Griffin. She had to picture him coming to the door, how she would feel when she saw him. She would tell Griffin to come outside, and then she would tell him she had decided to stay with Michael, that she loved Michael more, even though Phoebe wasn't exactly sure that was the truth. She wanted a different kind of life, she would explain, not the wild, crazy, impulsive life Griffin gave her, but something happier, something that Michael could give her. Phoebe knew it was going to be impossibly hard, but she had to do it because she knew it was the truth.

She climbed out of the car and very slowly walked across the deserted barnyard, past the Regional Theater van and Griffin's truck. She stood still a moment, one hand poised on the barn door, ready to knock.

She closed her eyes, said a quick prayer, and knocked softly. Once. Twice. The third time she forced herself to knock loud. The door opened. She looked up.

A guy wearing a Regional Theater Stage Crew shirt stood facing Phoebe. She felt a sudden sense of relief that it wasn't Griffin. For a panicky moment she hoped he wouldn't be home.

"Uh, is Griffin Neill here?" she stammered. Walking in from the bright light, everything looked dark to Phoebe. She blinked a few times to let her eyes adjust to being indoors.

"Sure, come on in." The guy yelled into the dark depths of the barn, "Hey, Romeo, Juliet's here." He winked at Phoebe, and lowered his voice. "Bob Jacobs just called. Griffin got the part — but act surprised, he'll want to tell you himself. You're Phoebe, aren't you?" He strolled across the sparsely furnished space, and filled his mug from the Mr. Coffee machine on the kitchen counter. He motioned Phoebe toward a lumpy couch in one corner of the room, then climbed the blond wood staircase, two steps at a time.

Phoebe hadn't moved since she came in. She stood right at the door, clutching her car keys in her hand. She recognized the sagging canvas couch from Griffin's apartment in New York. It looked even shabbier here with the bright sunlight pouring through the tall east windows of the barn. Her eyes had adjusted now. The whole house smelled of sawdust and new wood, and was airy and bright.

Griffin appeared from somewhere in the back. He had his old blue workshirt on, the same one he'd been wearing the first time Phoebe had ever seen him. It was unbuttoned, and a towel was draped around his neck. He was rubbing some shaving cream off his cheek.

He saw Phoebe and the sleepy, groggy look lifted from his face. His whole body seemed to wake up into a smile. He tossed the towel down on the floor behind him. Then he crossed the huge room and scooped Phoebe up in his arms.

"Oh, Phoebe! You're here! At last, you're here!" he cried, his voice deep with feeling. "This has been the longest week of my life."

He buried his face in her hair and cradled her in his arms. Phoebe held him tight, and pressed her face into the soft skin of his neck. He smelled woodsy and sweet. Tears coursed down her cheeks, onto his neck, down his bare chest. Griffin didn't seem to notice, or if he did, he didn't care. He spun her very slowly around and around the room, and carried her across to the couch. He set her down and gazed into her face and kissed her, not closing his eyes. Each kiss seemed to say, "I love you." Phoebe returned his kisses, savoring them. This moment would have to last her a long, long time. The rest of my life, she thought. She could barely see through her tears, but she needed to memorize Griffin and everything about him.

Suddenly he pulled back. "Phoebe, why are you crying?" he asked, still smiling. His touch was gentle as he smoothed her curls off her forehead. Phoebe couldn't answer and she couldn't turn away. "Phoebe?" he repeated. First a puzzled look, then a flicker of fear registered on his sensitive face.

"You did talk to Michael, didn't you?" Griffin sat up and seemed to hold his breath. Phoebe sat up, too. She swung her legs down over the edge of the sofa.

"Griffin, I didn't have to. My decision — it — it doesn't exactly have to do with Michael — it's between me and you," she stammered in a halting voice. She paused.

"Can we go outside?" she finally suggested, her voice barely audible. She glanced around the barn. Music drifted down from above and she heard someone moving in a room behind her. She stood up. Her knees were weak and her whole body was trembling.

Griffin sat a moment longer on the couch. He looked a bit dazed. He raked his fingers through his hair and stared blankly at Phoebe, then followed her out the door.

Phoebe went around to the far side of the silo,

the part that wasn't renovated yet. No one from the barn could see them here. Phoebe leaned back and pressed her hands against the gray weathered boards, watching a tabby fluff of a kitten explore a ladder lying nearby in the dirt. When Griffin walked up, the kitten mewed and bounded over to his feet. Griffin bent and gave it a cursory scratch behind the ear, then jammed his hands into his pockets. He took a deep breath, leaned his head back, and rested one foot against the silo wall.

"People look their whole lives to find what we have," Griffin said. "We're very, very lucky." His voice was quiet, full of awe.

Phoebe considered his words. They didn't change her feelings. They didn't change what she had to do. But they were true. "Yes, Griffin. I feel very lucky — having known you."

A shadow of a frown crossed his face. "I feel more than lucky — *knowing* you, Phoebe Hall." He corrected her tense. "In fact today — " he reached down for her hand. She let him take it, but it lay limply between both of his. "Today you really brought me my big break. I got the part. I'm going to play Romeo in the fall. Here!" He waved one hand toward the meadow rising behind them, the meadow where they had walked last week. On the other side lay the Regional Theater Barn. She let her hand drop from his.

"I heard. Your roommate just told me. I'm glad, Griffin, and I'm proud." Phoebe's voice trembled slightly. "I think it's the beginning of really wonderful things for you, Griffin." Phoebe swallowed hard and hid her hands behind her back.

Griffin squatted down on his heels and traced a pattern with his finger in the dirt. He looked up at Phoebe and considered her face, then closed his eyes for an instant. His voice was quiet but strained. "You didn't talk to Michael. I kept my part of the promise. I didn't see you all week, I didn't even call." Suddenly Phoebe realized he knew, he knew just what she was going to say.

"I — I had hoped you'd like it here. I've been thinking of beginnings, too — I thought you could come here and live with me, Phoebe. I mean, it's not too far from school for you and — " Griffin sprang to his feet. He stood in front of Phoebe. A light breeze blew across the barnyard pond and his shirt billowed slightly behind him. He was brushing the dust off his hands.

"No, Griffin. I can't. I can't do that," Phoebe murmured.

Griffin met Phoebe's eyes. "No, I guess you can't, not now. But in June, after you graduate — you'll be almost eighteen then, Pheeb, your parents can't stop us and — "

"It's not my parents stopping me." Phoebe's voice trembled. "I'm stopping me. I don't want to be with you anymore, Griffin." That wasn't how she had planned to say it. She hadn't visualized this scene at all. But maybe Chris was right — pretending what might have happened had made her strong, made her see the right thing to do. And now she had done it.

A terrible silence fell between them.

Then Griffin began talking very fast. He sounded almost desperate. "After June, I might have work in Hollywood. A big agent is coming out here in the fall looking for a new romantic male lead. He's heard about me, Phoebe. We can go there together. Nothing can keep us apart there." Phoebe was suddenly frightened. Griffin was pretending not to hear her, not to understand.

She grabbed Griffin's shoulders and made him look her in the eye. "Griffin, listen to me. It's over. I don't want to live with you. I don't want to go to Hollywood, or anywhere, with you. Don't you see, Griffin, it's *your* life we're talking about, what will happen to *you*, where *you* will be going. But it's not *my* life," Phoebe cried.

Griffin stepped back, as if Phoebe had struck him. He ran his fingers through his hair, then reached for her. Phoebe slipped out of his arms. Griffin took a deep breath and exclaimed, "I don't have to do those things. If you want something different, we'll stay here. You'll study singing. That's what you really want, isn't it? You should have that. We don't have to go to Hollywood. You mean so much more to me than all of that stuff."

"Stop it, Griffin. That's not true. You told me to always tell the truth," Phoebe declared angrily. "The truth is, you can't help being who you are, doing what you're meant to do. And you're meant for big things . . . very big things." She suddenly wanted Griffin to understand how much

251

she believed in him. "You're a very talented person, Griffin. I saw that the first time I saw you on the stage. You opened up just like a flower in front of an audience. You're doing what you're born for. You're lucky to have the chance. Some people never get to do what they want, but you'll get all the chances in the world, Griffin. You'll make it all happen in a very big way. You're going to have some kind of famous life, and I'm not meant for that. I'm not meant for your world, Griffin." Phoebe's voice faltered, but she kept her eyes on him.

"My world?" Griffin groaned, and slammed his hand against the silo wall. "You don't have to love my world, Phoebe, just me." Griffin rubbed his temples with his fingers. "If I could change who I am, I'd change, just to be with you. But I won't give you up, I *can't* give you up. It's not a choice between being with you or not, at least not for me. You really are my other half, Phoebe. We belong together, like Romeo and Juliet." The way he said that made Phoebe's heart stop. She turned quickly toward the silo and tried to catch her breath.

When she turned around her lip was trembling but she wasn't crying. She willed herself to stay dry-eyed. If she broke down now, Griffin would kiss her again, and then —

She fished in her pocket for her car keys and kept talking in a quick, urgent voice. She had to say everything now, fast, so he couldn't stop her. She wanted to finish what she had started, and leave. "Yes," she said, her words coming out in torrents now. "You and I are just like Romeo and Juliet. I feel it, too. It's such a sad, sad story, Griffin. I don't want to live such a sad story. Ever since I met you, life has been more intense than I ever knew it could be. It's also hurt more than I ever thought it could, and I can't stand a life like that. I want to have a happy ending, and I know I can't with you."

Phoebe started across the yard. She half walked, half ran, with Griffin following close behind her. His voice was pleading, and the pain in his voice stabbed her like a knife. She stopped for a second, and he caught up with her. His hand closed on her shoulder. Phoebe shut her eyes, and willed herself to walk away. He didn't try to stop her. She reached the car, opened the door, and climbed in. She didn't even look at Griffin. She acted as if he didn't exist anymore, although she was aware of his hand on the open window, and she could feel the familiar surge of warmth rush through her, as if he were touching her and not the car.

Phoebe started up the driveway, very slowly. Griffin walked beside the car. She speeded up a bit, bouncing in the ruts, and drove right past the neat white farmhouse and the garden. She glanced in the rearview mirror. Griffin was standing in the middle of the road, halfway down the long drive. His hands hung limply by his sides. He looked so desolate, so lonely. His whole posture expressed such sorrow. It was the saddest sight Phoebe had ever seen, until she caught sight of her own pale reflection.

She turned onto the blacktop and headed south. She drove until she couldn't see Griffin's barn from the road, or the hill with Griffin's elm or the forest behind with the cave and the beer bottles and the corny graffiti-ed hearts. Then she pulled over to the side of the road and turned the engine off.

She sat listening to the sounds of the afternoon: the distant whirr of a tractor, the hum of traffic on the interstate over the next hill, the caw of crows. She rested her head on the back of the seat and closed her eyes and sat there for a long time. She didn't cry. She felt as if her soul had been wrung out and she was dry as a desert inside.

Chapter
22

Phoebe didn't have a watch on but she knew she must be very late. She had gone to Griffin's early in the morning. Now, as she drove west toward the river, the sun through the windshield hurt her eyes. The lot at the entrance to Potomac Park was jammed. She parked at the end of a glistening line of cars along the shoulder of the road and hurried through the picnic grounds. A rock band was blaring down by the river. Then a voice — it sounded like Peter — came over the loudspeaker. Phoebe quickened her pace. The picnic tables were heaped with coolers and baskets but no one was around.

The race must have started already and Phoebe had promised she would be there. She had told Michael, when he volunteered to be on the crew, that she wouldn't miss it for the world. Phoebe stopped beneath a big banner flapping

in the breeze: FIRST ANNUAL VARIETY RECORDS/
GARFIELD HOUSE BENEFIT RAFT RACE. She
pushed up her sunglasses and rubbed her eyes
hard with her hand, then pressed her fingers
against her temple. She hadn't cried at all since
leaving Griffin, but her whole face seemed to
ache and her eyes burned. Inside she still felt
hollow.

She swallowed hard and forced herself to walk
more quickly up the little hill. It's over with
Griffin, she reminded herself. He was now past
tense in her life. Phoebe felt numb and terrible
inside, but she knew she had done the right thing.
It was the hardest thing she'd ever done in her
whole life, but now she had to do something even
harder. She had to meet Michael's eyes. She had
to be brave enough to look in them long enough
to see if she had any future in them. She pulled
down her glasses and the rim of her pink sun hat
and ran down the hill toward the milling crowd.

"Pheeberooni! Up here." Woody's voice was
calling from somewhere.

"Where are you?" Phoebe yelled back, standing on tiptoe. She was in the middle of the
crowd now, and she couldn't spot a single familiar face. Not that she could see many faces.
The world seemed to be a blur of bright shirts,
bare shoulders, and very pointy elbows. Phoebe
hated being short at times like this.

"Over there, Phoebe!"

Phoebe looked up and gasped. "Dick Westergard — I haven't seen you in ages — and

Laurie." At least eagle-eyed Laurie couldn't see her eyes behind these glasses.

"I just *love* that outfit, Phoebe Hall." Laurie pecked Phoebe on the cheek. Phoebe tried not to cringe. She liked Laurie better now, but she still didn't trust her, especially when she was upset. Laurie had the keenest nose for gossip at Kennedy High. Some sixth sense must have brought her to the raft race today, Phoebe thought to herself.

"Same old overalls," Phoebe stammered aloud, stuffing her hands in the pockets. "New shirt, I guess." She had brought the bright pink-and-white-striped oversized shirt with Chris. Chris had said something new would make her feel better.

"Woody's over there." Dick smiled, and motioned to his left. "Want anything from the concession?"

Phoebe shook her head and headed off toward Woody.

He was standing on a picnic table, a megaphone in his hand, some cheerleading pompoms lying in a colorful heap at his feet. "Hi. The view's better up here." He reached down and helped Phoebe up beside him.

He was grinning and looked straight ahead when he said, "You're pretty late. The race should have been over by now, but it hasn't even started yet."

Phoebe gave a little self-conscious laugh. "Sorry, Woody."

"You've been with Griffin just now, haven't you?" Woody said softly.

Behind her sunglasses Phoebe closed her eyes. She nodded slightly. She didn't trust her voice. But Woody deserved to know. He felt so responsible. "It's over, Woody," she managed to say, "and I'm so afraid!"

"Any room up there?" Laurie's voice was behind them.

Woody frowned, then answered cheerily, "Sure, Bennington, hop on board the cheerleaders' express. Hey, Westergard, how ya doin'?"

Phoebe let Woody do the talking. She scanned the crowd. Their table was close to the judges' stand. She spotted Peter Lacey and waved. He flashed her a victory sign, then went back to talking with some very good-looking guys in National Park Service T-shirts. One girl was with them and they were all wearing OFFICIAL JUDGE banners. She'd never seen a female Park Service lifeguard before. Looking at her, Phoebe decided she'd like her if she knew her. She was so lively and cute, as she talked to someone Phoebe couldn't see.

Phoebe forced herself to look toward the water. The crews were tugging their rafts back upstream to the starting place. It wasn't a long course, but the first third of the race wouldn't be visible from where Phoebe was. At first she didn't see Michael. She noticed Greg in a yellow life vest that looked too short. Everyone was wearing yellow vests. Brad's was too tight. Kim's was too long. Henry's was too loose. Monica's looked okay and kind of cute over her yellow and black bikini. Phoebe smiled. Sasha, allergic to the sun, was swathed from head to toe in some kind of white gauzy outfit topped by a big straw hat. She trudged beside the other kids, busily taking notes. The smile faded from Phoebe's face. Michael was standing right there, a few yards away from her, looking straight at her. He was at the back of the raft, half in the shallow water.

"Look, Phoebe, there's Michael." Laurie began waving. "He's looking this way. Look. Look." She grabbed Phoebe's arm and pointed it toward him.

Phoebe couldn't even fake a smile. Not when she saw the expression on Michael's face. How long had he waited for her by the parking lot? She'd left a message with his mother last night. He hadn't been home when she called from the mall. "Tell him I'll meet him there when the race starts, about noon. I've got to run an errand for my mom first," Phoebe had lied, and hung up quickly.

Laurie's hand was still on her arm. Phoebe glanced at Laurie's watch. Four P.M. She glanced back toward Michael again, but he had already turned away.

For the first third of the race Ted's mind was a blur. His body went through the motions — paddle in, paddle out — but his timing was off. He was slightly out of rhythm with the rest of the crew. He couldn't keep his mind on anything. He was too busy thinking about Molly. She had turned up at the race, as a judge, no less, and she had had no time to warn him.

He had spotted her right away on the viewing stand and had run right over to the platform where she jumped into his arms. He buried his face in her hair before he remembered where he was. Chris was probably somewhere in the crowd and Peter had been standing right there, his mouth hanging open.

"Uh, Ted, no fraternizing with the judges," Peter had joked. Ted had felt terrible. He wondered who else had seen.

"I couldn't call." Molly knelt down on the platform. She talked very quickly in a low whisper that Ted could hardly hear. "They assigned us this morning. Is she here?"

Ted nodded, and put his finger to his lips. Molly glanced back at Peter and took a deep breath. "Gosh, sorry about that. He's a friend?"

Ted nodded.

"I'll meet you later, in the lot," Molly said.

Ted unzipped the pocket of his trunks. "Here's the car keys. Wait for me. The car's parked down along the road. I just got here. I overslept. After the race I have to talk to Chris, Molly. She probably saw what just happened, or someone else did. I have to tell her before they do."

Then Ted had run the whole mile back along the riverbank, his open life vest flapping in the wind. He never did get to buckle it before the race started, and he never found out the name of the one crew member he didn't know.

"Paddle, paddle! All together, like one person," Greg yelled from the stern. "Hey, Mason, put your shoulder into it. We're supposed to be winning this race for Garfield House!"

Ted's attention snapped back to the present. Who was the guy on the back of the raft? How did he know Ted's name? Ted felt vaguely annoyed he'd been singled out, but his body responded to the command. They pulled around the bend of the river. The leaky raft looked terrible, but somehow it rode the water well.

Out of the corner of his eye, Ted saw two of the three other rafts fall behind. One was another crew from Kennedy, the other had a flag with the colors of Carlton High. Up ahead was the raft from Leesburg. It was a homemade raft all right, but the crew looked like they were the regular Leesburg varsity crew team.

For an instant Ted forgot about Molly and Chris and everything except how Kennedy's honor was at stake. He turned around and flashed the tall blond guy a victory sign, then dug his paddle into the swiftly moving water of the Potomac. This time he put his body into it, and his voice joined in with Greg's. "Come on guys, we can do it."

"Girls can, too!" Kim challenged, and flashed Ted an impish grin. Stroke for stroke they dug into the water, and began slowly gaining on the Leesburg raft.

"Leesburg?" Brad suddenly bellowed, and Ted felt the raft surge forward, right through the dayglo orange finishing line tape strung across the water. "We did it! We did it!" Henry leapt up screaming, and toppled the winning crew and their paddles into the cool waters of the Potomac.

They all surfaced sputtering and laughing, and pushed the raft before them as they kicked their way toward shore.

Ted's eyes were stinging from the water, and he couldn't make out the faces in the crowd pressing toward him. Then he felt a firm hand squeeze his shoulder.

"You're something else, Mason. That was great. You should go out for crew next year."

Ted was looking into the eyes of the guy who'd been manning the rudder. He'd never seen him before today. He looked very much the sailor except that his life vest was too short. Ted had lost his somewhere in the river. He rubbed the water off his face and grinned. "Thanks, man. I might take you up on that." He slicked back his wet hair and stuck out his hand.

Greg paused only an instant, then firmly shook Ted's hand. "Greg Montgomery."

Ted didn't react to Greg's name, though it was familiar. He just grinned and tipped his hand to his head, wondering where Chris was, wishing he could run up to Molly and hold her, the way Henry was holding Janie now.

Greg watched Ted smile and tip his hand, and act as if he'd never heard his name before. He knew Chris hadn't told him about them yet, but Chris said Ted suspected something. Greg had his doubts. Ted wasn't acting suspicious. Too bad this was Chris's old boyfriend. Mason seemed like a really nice guy, and Greg decided he liked him.

Well, maybe after this stuff with Chris is water under the bridge, we really can be friends, Greg thought. He searched the crowd for Chris's blonde head. She was wearing the S.S. *Sally Ride* sailor's hat he had had made up at the T-shirt store. He had to restrain himself to keep from folding her up in his arms. But in a few hours it would all be out in the open. Ted would know by then, and Greg could hug her in front of everyone.

Chapter 23

Chris hung back from the crowd rushing toward the river bank. Everyone was cheering and yelling, and Monica and Kim were being carried around by some guys. They were waving red and gold Kennedy pennants. Woody was dancing in front of the little parade, stabbing the air with his pompoms.

Chris couldn't walk up and join the fun, even though she should be leading the spirited Kennedy victory march. She didn't have the heart to force her way through the crush after what she'd just seen. Ted had innocently shaken hands with Greg, and now they stood there talking, looking for all the world like they were meant to be friends.

Ted had turned up so late, she had started to think he wasn't coming at all. She hated to admit that she almost wished he hadn't. After all, he must have heard that Greg was manning the rudder for the crowd's raft. But he did turn up and he looked a wreck. There were circles under his eyes like he hadn't slept all week. Chris's resolve to talk to him, to tell him it was over, almost broke down. If merely suspecting she was going out with another guy made him look like this, what would the truth do to him?

The crowd was heading her way. Chris slipped around the side and tried to catch her breath, then sank back against the viewing stand and brushed a tear from her cheek. She didn't want to hurt Ted. In a way she still loved him, but she knew she'd have to tell him now. She had no choice. It was like Phoebe said last night — you can't love two people so much at the same time.

Peter Lacey tried to quiet the boisterous crowd. "First things first, everybody. Let's thank the Parks Department for donating the space for today's blockbuster raft race to Variety Records and Garfield House. And let's give them a really big hand now. They are donating the proceeds from the parking area to our cause, as well."

Everyone cheered

"Next — I admit I'm partial here — but let's give the crew of the Kennedy Raft a big rip-roaring cheer. Talk about winning by a hair's breadth, I'd say they won by a splinter!"

The crowd went wild. Ted hung behind the rest of the crew as Greg led them onto the rickety stage. He tried to keep smiling, look proud, and keep his eyes off of Molly. She was standing right there, stage center, next to Peter, the shiny new medals looped over her arm. Her cheeks were rosy and her eyes shone, but her hands were shaking.

"And to do the honors, our judge from California, a white-water rafting guide as well as lifeguard by trade, Molly Ramirez!" Peter gestured toward Molly. She was wearing her red blouse and shorts, and every guy in the crowd started whistling and cheering. Peter gave Ted a curious look.

Molly flashed her warm smile at Greg, and stood on tiptoe to drape the medal over his head. Then she gave him a quick, shy kiss on the cheek.

Next came Monica, and Michael, and Kim, and Brad, and Henry —

Ted forced his feet to move across the stage. He knew he was smiling and he saw Molly smiling, too. For a second he forgot about the crowd, the cheers, Chris, everything. Then Molly was on tiptoe, the medal dangling from her hands. Her fingers trembled as they brushed the nape of his neck. Then she brushed his lips with hers, fleetingly. Ted forced himself not to kiss her back in front of all these people. In a little while, after he spoke to Chris, they'd be alone.

Somehow he found himself on the other side of the stage, following Henry down the rickety steps. He brushed by Brenda, and Tony Martinez. Peter was announcing something about the prize money check to Garfield House. Brenda met Ted's eyes and he quickly lowered his gaze. From the expression on her face he could tell she had seen that he was the only guy Molly had really kissed.

The next thing he knew he was face-to-face with Chris. She was standing near the steps, arms folded across her chest, a sailor's cap dangling from her hands. She was in the shadows so he couldn't see the expression on her face.

"We have to talk," Ted said solemnly.

Chris turned around. He saw her shoulders lift and settle in a deep sigh.

"We do have to talk," she repeated slowly.

She followed Ted a little way into the trees. The pines grew thick here, almost reaching down to the water's edge. The light was getting low, and beneath the trees it was nearly dark. Chris followed Ted until they were out of earshot of the crowd. She put her hand on his arm. In spite of the heat her hand was icy cold. "Here, let's talk right here."

She leaned back against a tree and scuffed at the carpet of pine needles with her feet.

"I know I've been pretty crummy lately," she began.

"*You!*" Ted said, shocked.

"Come off it, Ted." Chris's voice was trembling now. "I know you're jealous, and I don't blame you one bit. But of all the cheap, dirty tricks — kissing that girl like that, just because of Greg, right in front of everyone we know. I've never felt so humiliated in my life!" Chris burst into tears.

Ted shook his head. "Chris, what are you talking about? Greg who? Greg Montgomery?" Finally he began to piece the puzzle together out loud. "The guy on the raft today, the guy with the place on the Eastern Shore. You've been seeing Greg?"

Chris turned her face away for a second.

"I don't believe this," Ted said quietly. Then his voice rose. "I trusted you, Chris, I trusted you. I told you to go. You could have at least — "

"I could have at least what?" Chris was yelling now. "I could have called you from the shore and said, 'Ted, Greg wants to kiss me now, is it okay?' "

"Forget it, just forget it." Ted paced back and forth in front of Chris. His fists were clenched. She backed up against the trunk. She was beginning to get scared, but she was angry, too.

"Don't act so surprised. I mean, you've known all along, haven't you? Didn't you suspect something? Isn't that why you haven't called, didn't stop by once last week? Tell me the truth. You just bided your time until today, and then poof, you make a fool of me with that girl up there on the stage."

"The truth!" Ted growled. "The truth is I love that girl up on the stage. I love her more than I — "

"You love her?" Chris gasped. "You knew her before today? You mean you've been seeing someone else?" Chris's voice lowered to a horrified whisper. "Since Phoebe's party?" Chris suddenly understood. All the times Ted hadn't called, all the times he hadn't been home.

268

Chris suddenly felt like she wanted to throw up. She felt sick and scared and humiliated. "It's worse. It's worse than you kissing a girl you didn't know. And you didn't even tell me. After a whole year together, you could have told me." Tears were streaming down Chris's face now, and she wiped her sleeve across her face. Traces of makeup rubbed off on the new white cotton shirt. She didn't care. She didn't care if she ruined it. She had never felt so hurt and rejected in her life.

"You could have told me about Greg, too! You, with all your speeches about honesty and doing what's right. At least I *know* I make mistakes sometimes," Ted said sarcastically, then instantly bit his lip.

Chris couldn't respond. *Greg*. Just thinking his name suddenly brought her to her senses. She looked up at Ted, her eyes filled with tears.

"Ted, it's over between us, isn't it?" The anger had gone out of her voice. She sniffed a few times, but held his gaze.

Ted suddenly found it difficult to speak. "Yes, Chris, it has been for a long time. Even before Molly it was over." Ted held out his hand. "I think we both knew it was over but were afraid to admit it."

Chris placed her hand in his and took a deep breath. "Sorry for all that right now."

"Me, too," Ted said. "We had some stuff we both needed to get out into the open."

"Yes," Chris said. They were standing there holding hands. Ted drew his fingers through

Chris's hair and gently kissed her on the lips. Then she broke away. She gave one last look at Ted, and ran off through the trees.

Ted didn't look up right away. He didn't want to remember Chris crying. He sighed deeply and stared toward the parking lot. Then he heard the sound of a twig breaking.

He whirled around. "Molly!" he gasped. Molly was making her way toward him.

He rushed up to her. "Oh, Ted, I had to find you," she said. "I'm sorry to intrude on you like this. I've just never felt so sad about leaving anyone before."

"I love you so much, Molly Ramirez," Ted said. "I feel so lucky that I had the chance to meet you. Just think, we might never have met if that kid hadn't almost drowned." He drew her even closer into his arms and together they slid down the trunk of a tree until they were nestled in a bed of pine needles.

"I have to go now, Ted," Molly murmured, her eyes full of tears. "I don't think I could bear to spend more time with you tonight and then just say good-bye."

He knew she was right. They kissed, sweetly and gently, one last time. Ted felt tears forming behind his own eyes now, as Molly slipped out of his grasp and headed for the parking lot.

Chapter
24

"**O**h, Greg, there you are!" Chris cried out, throwing herself into his arms. He was standing behind the stage, helping some guys wind a spool of speaker wire. Peter was shouting orders from somewhere up above.

"Hey." Greg lifted her face toward his. He gently guided her into the shadows away from the curious faces of the stage crew. He didn't speak for a couple of minutes. He pulled a handkerchief out of his pocket and held it to Chris's nose. "It was that tough?" he asked quietly.

Chris bit her lip. "He — he's been seeing someone else, too, the girl who kissed him today on stage." Chris gave a shudder. She knew it was unreasonable, but she couldn't help but feel a twinge of jealousy.

Greg stifled a laugh.

"Are you laughing?" Chris gasped in horror.

271

"Seems to me you've been seeing someone, too." Greg crossed his arms in front of his chest and leaned back against a tree. His eyes were dancing with laughter, but he was trying to keep the smile off his face.

"But — it's unfair. I mean, he's been seeing her ever since Phoebe's — and I didn't even know it."

"I met you two days after Phoebe's party. We've been flirting ever since then, until *Attack of the Killer Tomatoes*, that is. Our anniversary will date from that moment in the car, okay?" Greg reached out both his hands toward Chris.

She looked down, trying to keep a smile off her lips. "I — I guess I'm embarrassed," she said, taking Greg's hands and letting him draw her toward him. She leaned her cheek against his chest. His heart was beating like crazy.

"You know, Montgomery, we have a lot in common," she said wickedly. "You're not as calm as you look, either."

Greg threw back his head and laughed. "I'm not calm at all, not with the most beautiful girl in the world in my arms." He tilted Chris's face up toward his. His voice grew very serious as he said, "I won't be calm again, unless I know she has no second thoughts, no regrets about all this."

"Oh, Greg," Chris said, "I have no regrets, none." Then her smooth forehead creased into a frown. "Well, to be honest, I have one. I'll miss Ted, as a friend. This has been a kind of messy way for our relationship to end."

Greg took her hand. He started leading her

back toward the clearing. All the crews had torn apart their rafts and were building an enormous bonfire. Greg shrugged. "I hope someday you will be friends again, because I like him, too. But I don't know much about these things," he added with a twinkle in his eyes. "I'm too young."

Chris playfully pummeled him on the chest. "Well, grow up, buster, or I'm really going to get arrested for robbing the cradle."

Greg silenced Chris's laughter with a kiss. She wrapped her arms around him, and murmured, "Now *that* was a very grown-up kiss."

"Shall we join the fun?" he whispered in her hair.

Chris's shoulder tightened. No one had seen them together as a couple yet, no matter what they might have guessed. Chris remembered Laurie was there, and everyone would be talking even before school opened. . . .

"Don't worry, Chris," Greg said, though she hadn't said a word out loud. "You'll love being the talk of the town! Ms. President is going to have to get used to it sooner or later!'

Phoebe kicked her way through the leaves in the willow grove, feeling what the future would be like without Michael. If she wanted to find him now she could. He'd be down by the river with everyone else, helping to build a big bonfire from the rafts and making music and a lot of noise.

But there was no point now. She had nothing to explain and there was nothing to talk about,

273

nothing to hope for. After the way he looked at her today from the raft, she was sure he knew where she had been all morning, and with whom, and he had made some kind of decision. Phoebe could tell that. It was written all over his face like a headline.

She headed toward the duck pond. The ducks were in the shadows now, and the sunset was almost gone from the sky, but it was a quiet place and she could be alone here. She looked around quickly. No one was in sight, but she thought she had seen something move. Or had it been a trick of light, the twinkling of the soft lights lining the paths of the park?

Phoebe backed away quietly. Maybe it wasn't such a good idea to sit down here in the near dark all by herself. Then a car pulled out of the parking lot, its headlights lighting up the grass. Phoebe gasped. "Ted? Is that you?"

Ted looked up quickly. He had been skimming stones across the pond. "Phoebe?"

He sounded so sad. "Ted, do you want me to go away?" Phoebe said carefully.

There was a long silence. "No, Pheeb."

She walked up and settled down on a rock at his side. It seemed natural to take his hand just then. "Ted? Do you want to talk about it, about Chris?"

"You know?"

Phoebe inhaled sharply. "We talked last Monday. She tried to call you, she really did." Phoebe felt awkward apologizing for Chris to Ted.

"That's okay, Phoebe, you're her friend. Besides, I was seeing someone, too." Ted's voice broke slightly as he said that. He sounded like he was about to start crying. He raked his hand through his hair, then sprang up and walked to the water. He stood staring at the water for a long time, his hands jammed in his pockets, his broad, strong shoulders all slumped and crooked.

He turned around and looked at her, his face full of pain. "Oh, Phoebe," he said hoarsely. "I really fell in love, and I might never see her again. Tomorrow she leaves. I don't even have her address." Then he told Phoebe all about Molly, about the first time they met, about how he had been feeling about Chris, about how free he felt with Molly. It all tumbled out. Then he ended, "I shouldn't tell you this. Chris is your friend." He paused. "But it felt like being in prison when I was with her. A very beautiful prison." He wrapped his arms around himself and looked up at the stars. From across the little path Phoebe could hear him sigh.

She sat very still and tightened her hold on the sides of the rock. Ted's story reminded her of her own nearly a year ago. She watched him scuff pebbles from the path into the pond. The ducks fluttered away into the dark.

"Ted, I think I know how you feel about Chris," she said finally. "I mean, it was something like that for me last year with Brad — and Griffin." Saying his name out loud suddenly sounded strange, as if she were talking about someone else's life.

Ted looked up quickly. He walked over toward Phoebe. She made room for him on the rock, then closed her eyes, folded her hands, and said, "My life, everything inside of me," Phoebe tapped her chest, "got all tight and funny with Brad. Then I met Griffin."

"He's so free, he's not afraid of anything, is he?" Ted said quickly. Then it dawned on him. "Molly's like that, too. Always trying new things, never dwelling on the past. . . ."

" 'If you don't take risks, you don't get anywhere,' Griffin once told me." Phoebe rubbed her eyes. They were tired and burning again. "He changed my life, Ted. He really did. And it sounds like Molly has changed yours." She took hold of Ted's arm. It was important to tell him this, to make him understand.

"Ted. Molly was a gift. A wonderful gift," she finally said.

Ted surprised her. His lopsided smile worked its way across his face like a light. "Like Griffin for you," he said.

Phoebe's heart seemed to catch in her throat. She sat very quiet, unable to find her voice for a long time. Finally she answered. "Yes, Ted, like Griffin for me."

Phoebe hugged Ted, then turned away. It seemed wrong to watch him cry, almost as wrong as to let him see her crying now. She walked quickly back into the shadows, hoping Ted hadn't seen her face.

Remembering Griffin's gift had made her cry,

276

then made her brave again. Loving Michael was worth every risk.

She ran through the dimly lit park toward the clearing. Flames from the bonfire licked at the starry sky. Woody was leading a jazzed up rendition of the Kennedy Fight Song. It was odd not hearing Ted's strong voice singing out, a little flat, but full of spirit, over all the others. Next to Woody, she spotted Greg dancing with Chris. They had their arms draped lightly over each other's shoulders, their foreheads touching as they swayed slightly out of time to the rhythm of the music.

Phoebe hurt inside for Ted just then. He belonged here in the center of things with a girl like Molly at his side. But she knew he would survive even if he never saw her again. Loving someone — someone like Molly, or Griffin — made you stronger in the long run, more alive, more prepared for life.

Phoebe saw everyone she knew crowded around the bonfire. Everyone except Michael. Then she noticed him off to the side talking to Jeremy. Monica walked up and handed each of them a soda. Phoebe heard Monica's laughter ring out across the lawn as she started walking toward them, very slowly. She felt as if she were crossing a creaky wooden bridge dangling high over a canyon. A bridge from here to there, she said to herself, from Griffin to Michael. It was a one-way bridge this time, no going back.

Michael must have spotted her then because

she saw him walking slowly toward her. Monica and Jeremy kept talking. They didn't seem to notice that Michael was gone. Phoebe waited for him under the trees. The firelight flickered across his face and she could see he wasn't smiling. Then she had an awful thought. What if he didn't want her anymore?

Suddenly they were standing face-to-face in silence. In the background Phoebe heard the singing die down as Charlie started playing the harmonica. The notes of a wild, beautiful song drifted down to her. It was happy and sad at the same time, and very familiar. Then she realized it was her song, the one Michael had written for her.

"Michael," she said, her hands dangling at her sides. At last she met his eyes, unable to read their expression. The light was flickering and Michael's face was all shadows, but even in the dark she could feel him looking right into her soul.

He stretched out both his hands for hers. They stood like that for a moment, studying each other, before he said, "You're back, Phoebe, really back."

She looked at him, not understanding at first. She caught her breath and closed her eyes. The music was back in his voice. He sounded relieved, relaxed. He had known all along about Griffin, and he hadn't said a word. She knew how much she must have hurt him and yet he had waited for her. He had known Griffin was something she had

278

to deal with alone. Phoebe suddenly loved him very much for that.

"Yes, I'm back, for good this time, Michael," Phoebe whispered as he folded her in his arms. The bonfire flamed up just before they kissed, and Phoebe knew the joyous smile on Michael's face matched her own.

Coming soon . . .
Couples #14
PICTURE PERFECT

Jeremy came toward the table, his thick brown hair bouncing a little with his quick movements. He wasn't terribly tall or muscular, but his stride radiated energy and when he smiled, his blue-gray eyes flashed with excitement. "What's going on?" he asked with a marked English accent.

"Gloria just brought her new neighbors over," Phoebe explained, then introduced Bart and Diana. "Jeremy is Monica Ford's cousin," she went on. "Monica and Peter work together at WKND, the school radio station. Peter is our resident DJ, in case you hadn't noted those resonant tones."

Peter stood up to take a bow. "And Jeremy is a secret agent sent over from England to find out what Americans are really like. You two should be warned to watch out at all times. He has more cameras than *People* magazine and he's always taking photographs of everything in sight."

"Blackmail material," Jeremy supplied, chuckling evilly. "The things I've seen through my viewfinder. . . ."

Diana looked up at Jeremy, suddenly remembering that he was the boy Sasha had said might be in some of her classes. The idea made her heartbeat quicken. He was cute and friendly and if they were both strangers to the school, it would give them something in common. She was suddenly acutely conscious of Jeremy Stone's intense gaze.

"I'd like to photograph you, Diana," he said, coming closer. "You have terrific bone structure and with those dark eyes and your blonde hair, you could be a model."

Diana felt red climbing up in her tanned cheeks and she became conscious of the tendrils of hair escaping from her hastily-tied ponytail and the way her sweater kept slipping off one shoulder. What a line, she thought to herself, but she couldn't explain the tingling sensation she felt when her eyes met his.

Diana smiled at the earnestness of his expression, captivated by the sparkle in his eyes and the honesty in his gaze. "I'll think about it, Jeremy," she promised, hoping that he wouldn't change his mind after school opened. There was something very exciting about Jeremy Stone — something that made Diana want to know him better.